THE VIGILANTE

JAMES PEIFER

ISBN: 979-8-9880646-2-6
Library of Congress Control Number: 2024901139
Cover Design by Beth Sanders and Janet Vautrin
Published by Peifer House Publishing
Napa, California 94558

DEDICATION

Dedicated to The New Yorkers
Mary, Frank, John, James, William, and Thomas

AUTHOR'S NOTE

"Sometimes good men have to do bad things."
~ Anonymous

The Vigilante is the first book of a trilogy. This is not history but a novel. It is peopled with men and women created out of the author's imagination. Many happenings did occur, but any resemblance to actual persons living or dead, events, or locales is entirely coincidental.

This adventure story is set in the small town of Los Gatos, California, located in the foothills of the Santa Cruz Mountains. It was the 1970s and a movement was formed to combat evil. It grew to become a powerful force in the United States. Events of unrest in America had been pointing towards a second Civil War. Little had been done to prevent the Nation from heading towards a collapse of the Republic.

This is a story, not as things really happened, but as I imagine they came to pass.

James Peifer

When America Despised the Irish: The 19th Century's Refugee Crisis

"Forced from their homeland because of famine and political upheaval, the Irish endured vehement discrimination before making their way into the American mainstream.

"The refugees seeking haven in America were poor and disease-ridden. They threatened to take jobs away from Americans and strain welfare budgets. They practiced an alien religion and pledged allegiance to a foreign leader. They were bringing with them crime. They were accused of being rapists.

"These undesirables were Irish."

~ Christopher Kein

The Ancient Arms of
Greaney

PROLOGUE

The Greaney Clan

The surname Greaney is of ancient Irish origin. It is derived from the Irish Gaelic woman's name "Grainne." It is unusual as it is one of only a few Irish surnames that are derived from the name of a mother or female.

Jacob Greaney was born in 1884 in Tralee, Ireland. It is the largest town in County Kerry, Ireland. Tralee is located on the northern side of the neck of the Dingle Peninsula. Anglo-Normans founded the town in the 13th century. Tralee is well known for the Rose of Tralee International Festival that is held annually in August. The festival is celebrated by Irish communities all over the world.

Jacob married Catherine Minor in 1910 and they had three children—Francis, Catherine, and William. Jacob had been a successful boxer and worked as a laborer for a concrete manufacturer. He had an obsession for keeping his hands clean and insisted on washing the dishes after every meal.

He was fond of visiting a local tavern after work. While drinking, he loved to sing sad Irish songs and recite poetry. He had a great memory for limericks and would recite them for the entertainment of his friends and bar patrons. One of his favorite poets was W. B. Yeats. Even though he was only 5'5" tall, locals knew never to cross Jacob. There had been times when strangers had paid a painful price mistaking him, because of his short stature, as someone they could push around. He always stayed in control of his drinking and his temper. He maintained a gentle and pleasant personality towards everyone that he met.

In 1919, Jacob emigrated to America with his wife and three children. They joined other Greaney relatives living in the Bronx, New York.

The Bronx is one of the five boroughs in New York City. It was named after Jonas Bronck (1600-1643), a Swedish-born immigrant who established the first settlement.

Members of the Greaney clan had been emigrating to the United States since the Potato Famine which had devasted the Irish population in the late 1840s.

Bootleggers and gangs dominated the Bronx during Prohibition (1920-1933). Irish, Italian, Jewish, and Polish gangs smuggled in most of the illegal whiskey. They set up illegal nightclubs, called Speakeasies, throughout New York City.

Jacob avoided the bootleggers and gangsters and found employment as a bridge-operator. His job was to open and close a bridge to allow ships to pass under it. He performed his job as a bridge-operator, until his retirement almost thirty years later.

The Irish Potato Famine, also known as the Great Hunger, began in 1845 when a mold caused a destructive plant disease to spread rapidly throughout Ireland. Over the next seven years, the infestation ruined about three-quarters of the potato crop. During the famine, approximately one million people died from starvation and a million more emigrated from Ireland—mostly to the United States. The British government had provided minimal relief to the starving Irish.

In March of 1930, Francis Joseph Greaney met Mary Agnes Peconne at a "rent party" in the Bronx. Rent parties were popular during that time due to the conditions of the Depression. A tenant would hire a musician to play music and then they would pass the hat to raise money to pay their rent. These parties were a means to eat, dance, and get away from everyday hardships.

Mary Peconne was a very pretty, but extremely shy woman. She was religious and loved to read and study. Three years out of high school, she became a registered nurse. Her father, George, was strict and intimidating. He did not allow Mary or her brother and sister to socialize outside the family. Her mother, Helen, was frail, weak, depressed, and prone to cry.

Mary was able to escape her home and attend a "rent party" by lying to her father. She said that she was going to visit her maternal grandparents for the weekend. At the party she met Francis Greaney, and was enthralled when he asked her to dance. They talked throughout the evening and she found him very charming. He was handsome and confident. She soon began sneaking out of the house to rendezvous with Francis. After six months of covert dating, they eloped and were married by a Justice of the Peace.

When Mary's father learned of her elopement, he disowned her and banned her from seeing her mother and siblings.

The newlywed couple moved into Francis' parents' home and she was welcomed by everyone in his family.

Francis and Mary married in 1934 and had six children—Mary Caroline, Francis Jr, John, James, William, and Thomas.

In 1956 Mary Caroline married a policeman who had been assigned to a Manhattan precinct. Francis Jr and John became policemen like their brother-in-law, and were assigned to precincts in the Bronx.

Francis' best friend and Godfather to James, Frank Bower, had moved from the Bronx to Sunnyvale, California and was now working as a foreman for a house painting contractor. Bower had notified Francis that he had a job waiting for him if he would relocate to California.

In July 1959, Francis Sr, moved with his wife and their three youngest sons to Los Gatos, California, leaving behind the three grown, older children. Los Gatos was a sleepy little town of less than six thousand residents. The Greaney family lived in a three-bedroom apartment on the first floor of a house on Wilder Avenue, across the street from St Mary's Catholic Church. They paid $75 a month for rent.

Francis was seeking a healthier environment for his family when they left New York and moved to California. He had grown up with members of the Irish Mob in New York. Francis attended school until the 8th grade. He was highly intelligent, but school was boring and he wanted to make money. He had been a successful amateur boxer, but lost out in the Olympic trials. He was good looking with blond hair that looked almost white. He was known to be arrogant and would sometimes walk down the center of the sidewalk forcing a passerby to step aside. At 5'7" tall, with a very muscular build, he was quick and agile. He also was known to have a temper—some referred to it as an Irish temper—that frequently got him into trouble.

While working as a cab driver in Manhattan, Francis had become acquainted with Hughie Mulligan, a New York mobster and bookmaker. Mulligan headed the "Irish Mob" and operated out of the Hell's Kitchen neighborhood in Manhattan. Francis did some work for Mulligan. His work was mostly minor errands like "running numbers," but sometimes Mulligan needed a strong arm to collect from his borrowers. With a reputation as a boxer, Francis accompanied Mulligan's collection man to ensure that loans were collected without any problems.

One evening Francis went to the local Catholic Church to pick up his youngest son Thomas who had stayed late for instructions to become an altar boy. As Francis entered the Church, he observed that the main seating area was empty. He heard talking coming from behind the sanctuary and walked quietly, looking for his son. As he came nearer to the talking, he recognized his son's voice. His son was yelling, "No, I want to get out of here." Francis moved quickly and opened a door to the private chambers and saw the priest with his pants down moving towards Thomas who was standing behind a chair.

Francis immediately recognized what he was witnessing and went into action—grabbing the priest and throwing him down on the floor. He began kicking him. He then stood the helpless priest up and began pummeling him with left and right punches to the head and body. When the priest fell to the floor again, Francis grabbed him by the hair and began bashing his head against the lower part of a desk. The priest's head was a mass of blood and his face was unrecognizable. Thomas yelled at his father to stop. His father did not stop until Thomas ran and threw his arms around him. The priest lay in a crumpled mess on the floor as Francis and his son left the Church.

The cops were called by an anonymous caller and an ambulance soon arrived at the Church to take the priest to a hospital. The priest had been badly beaten and the first medical team that examined him concluded that he did not have much chance of surviving.

The following day Francis went to see Hughie Mulligan. He told him what he had done to the priest and why. Mulligan told him that he had to leave New York City and asked him if he had any place to go. "A good friend of mine has a job waiting for me in California, painting houses," said Francis.

"Good. You've got to leave town immediately. I'll take care of this situation with the pervert priest. I'll talk with the bishop and give him a large donation. They won't even remember the priest's name in a couple of weeks. When you get settled, you can send for your wife," said Mulligan.

As Francis was leaving Mulligan's office, Mulligan gave him an envelope with $1,000. "Thanks Hughie. I really appreciate it."

1959 had been a very good time for Francis to relocate his family to California—distancing himself from his mobster friends.

Three months after Francis' departure from New York City, he received a call from his father, Jacob. Jacob said that the priest had lived, but "he won't be serving communion again for a very long time."

Hughie Mulligan died in 1973 and his successor was Mickey Spillane, a notorious Irish gangster. During the 1950s, Irish Mobs conducted a very dangerous practice of kidnapping Italian Mafia and holding them for ransom to raise money for their operations.

In the early 1960s the younger sons, James, William, and Thomas would graduate from High School in Los Gatos. The young President had called on their generation to be Patriotic and to make a commitment to serve the country. He had inspired many when he proclaimed in his inaugural speech:

"Ask not what your country can do for you—ask what you can do for your country."

Less than four years later the young President was dead—assassinated by a Communist sniper and his conspirators.

Unfortunately, in the years to follow, the American people would come to realize that the President's message of vision, idealism, and promise for the future, died with him in Dallas.

James and his two brothers responded to the young President's call for duty and service. He had been their hero, and they wanted to be like him. They were Patriots who would always be devoted to their country. They went on to graduate from college and join the military—serving in Vietnam. After their military service, they were business executives in the thriving Silicon Valley of California.

James, known to a very few, became one of the most powerful men in the business world. He founded a network of global corporations that were valued in the billions of dollars. He had become the "shadow" behind the "shadow governments."

He was The Vigilante.

Jacob Greaney passed away in 1970 and would never know that his grandson had become one of the most powerful men in the world.

BOOK ONE

"We all are like the Full Moon—we still have our darker side."
~*Khalil Gibran*

ONE
THE BEGINNING

It was a warm evening, with a full moon, in Los Gatos, California in July 1975.

High above the town of Los Gatos, in the Santa Cruz mountains overlooking the valley, Steve Satinborne, removed his jeans and briefs and placed them neatly on the right top corner of the blanket, next to his brown loafers.

This was going to be the third girl, in the last three months that he was going to enjoy. He was 5'10" tall, slender, and muscular, had slight scarring on his face from acne and blond curly hair that flowed to his collar.

Steve took a condom from his pack, and knowing that she was small and a virgin, pulled it on and applied Vaseline to it. He had placed a flashlight next to her head, shining it on her face. He wanted to watch her reaction. He straddled the unconscious, petite, frail, blond teenage girl as she lay naked on the blanket. He forced his entry into her. He began thrusting his hips against her, holding her down, with his hand on her chest. He climaxed quickly and withdrew turning her onto her stomach.

As she was being turned over, she uttered the word "Mommy," but seemed to be sleeping.

Preferring anal sex, he reached for a new condom and the Vaseline. He always recovered quickly from a climax and he kept his erection. He was soon ready for more.

As he was reaching forward to position the girl's hips, powerful hands grabbed him and dragged him away from the blanket. He was hit in the head and lost consciousness.

When he regained consciousness, he realized that his wrists were bound by plastic strips and his legs were taped together. The gag in his mouth was choking him. He could hardly breathe because of the tape sealing his mouth closed.

In the moonlight, he could barely see the two tall, large men moving nearby. They were dressed in dark clothes and wore masks.

One of the men knelt behind him and grabbed his neck. He forced Steve's head back as the other man grabbed his wrists, pulling his arms forward. Steve screamed when he felt a sharp pain in the thumb of his right hand. Little of his screaming could be heard because the gag in his mouth, muffled the sound.

The two men wrapped tape tightly around Steve's right hand and then they dragged him to his car. One of the men lowered the driver's side window. They bent Steve back and thrust his head through the opening, rolling the window up tightly under his chin. He was pinned and unable to move.

As Steve hung from his car door one of the men beat his

hands, arms, legs, and feet with a sap. His screaming was muffled by the gag in his mouth and he soon passed out from the pain.

A sap, filled with lead, is a very dangerous weapon and is capable of shattering bone. The man using the sap, carefully focused on generating great pain to Steve, while avoiding lethal injury.

As the two men left Steve hanging from his car window, they turned their attention to the young girl. One of the men placed the girl's blouse and skirt over her breasts and genitals. He then wrapped her in the blanket to keep her warm. She didn't move or make any noise. She appeared to be sound asleep.

Making sure that there were no clues left at the scene, the men moved away. They jogged slowly down the trail to the housing development below. As they came to the end of the trail, one of them threw the first joint of Steve's right thumb into the bushes. Both men removed their black shirts and masks to reveal colored t-shirts.

They checked each other's clothing and shoes to make sure that there were no signs of blood.

As they left the entrance to the trail, they walked slowly and began talking loudly about the 49er roster. They were discussing next seasons new players.

"I don't think Steve Spurrier is the answer," said one of the men loudly. "He doesn't have the accuracy that Brodie had." "I don't like Snead either," said the other man, "he is worn out. The niners need new blood and if they trade for Jim Plunket, will he be the answer? I think he has had the crap beat out of him with the Patriots. They never had an offensive line to protect him."

When they arrived at their car, they looked around for anyone who might have seen them. Satisfied that there was no one there, they placed their black clothes and masks in a plastic bag to be disposed of later.

They entered the car and drove away slowly towards downtown Los Gatos.

They stopped at a Shell gas station and while one of the men went to the pay phone, the other went in to talk with his friend who managed the station. He was just closing up for the night.

"Hey Virg," said James Greaney, "what's goin on?"

"Not much, it's been slow tonight and I'm closing up," responded Virgil.

"Virg, I've been arguing with Tom. Who do you think is going to be the next 49er quarterback?"

"I don't know. After Brodie they can't seem to find a good one," replied Virg.

❧

Virgil Dennis, had been one of James' teammates on the high school basketball team. He was tall and strong at 6'3" and 210lbs. Virgil had gone back to college. He had a semester of classes left to finish his undergraduate degree in management. After a three-year stint in the Army, he had returned to San Jose State and now worked at the gas station five nights a week to accommodate his class schedule.

The man at the pay phone was Thomas Greaney. He dialed a number and when the call was answered, he said,

"Mission accomplished, girl wrapped in a blanket, but we were too late to save her." He then hung up and joined his older brother, James. They continued to talk to Virgil about the 49ers' upcoming season.

The man receiving the "Mission Accomplished" message was William, another Greaney brother. He immediately called the Los Gatos Police Department and gave the call center the following message:

"A rape has been committed by Steve Satinborne. He and a young girl are at the new housing development, on Santa Rosa drive. Send an ambulance immediately!"

Thirty luxury homes were under construction on Santa Rosa drive. The average home was 4,600 sq. ft. and the lot sizes were around 45,000 sq. ft. The homes were located, running east to west, on the ridge that overlooked the Santa Clara Valley. They were situated high enough that the incoming airplanes, landing at the San Jose Airport, flew below them.

Young people frequented the area, as it was known to be a safe parking spot for drinking and making out.

The housing development was five miles from police head-quarters. The first responding police officer arrived less than eight minutes after the call. He was on his night-time cruise below Santa Rosa Drive on Kennedy Road. The ambulance arrived five minutes after the police officer.

The two EMTs, riding with the ambulance driver, began attending to the girl. They carried her to the ambulance. She was limp and still unconscious.

Two police officers removed Steve from the car window.

The officers cut the tape that was keeping the gag in Steve's mouth. They didn't touch the wrapping around his thumb but removed the tape wrapped around his wrists and ankles.

Steve was sobbing as they removed his gag and restraints. He said that two men had beaten him and raped the girl. As they attempted to get him up to walk, he slumped down. The officers grabbed him as he was collapsing and he began crying louder saying that the pain in his legs and arms were "killing him."

The police noticed a lot of blood on his legs and feet and on top of both hands. He was unable to put any pressure on his right leg. An officer called to the EMTs for a stretcher and asked for another ambulance. Steve and the girl were taken to the emergency room at the Los Gatos Hospital.

One policeman remarked to the others, "Someone sure beat the hell out of that kid. They really wanted to punish him and they also wanted him to be caught. Look how they left the girl wrapped up like that."

"That's enough officer. No more speculation on your part. Let's leave this up to the investigators," said the police captain.

When the police searched Steve's car they found a vial, half-filled, with a clear solution. They also found cocaine, marijuana, and some white tablets. The police forensic inspection team searched the surrounding area for footprints and other clues, but found nothing but a condom filled with semen.

The police inspector began questioning Steve, and he immediately blurted out that there had been two large men who had jumped him. They had been dressed in black and wearing masks.

The police report stated that Steve had been found tied up, naked from the waist down, gagged, and hanging from his car door window. He was bleeding from the blood-soaked bandage on his right thumb. There was also a lump on the right side of his head, with a minor cut in the skin. The victim was bleeding from wounds to his knees, ankles, and feet. The report detailed the drugs and white tablets found in his car.

The police sent everything that they had found in Steve's car, along with the used condom, to the lab in San Jose for analysis.

Late the following morning the attending doctor gave permission for Steve to be released from the hospital. Two Los Gatos police officers visited with him in his room just before noon. They arrested him for the rape of a minor and for illegal drug possession. Steve was released to the police and was driven to the Los Gatos jail.

The young girl had lapsed into a coma and was on life support. Her body had had an adverse reaction to the Rohypnol drug that Steve had dropped into her drink.

Steve Satinborne was the youngest son of Ira and Beverly. He was a very troubled young man. He was spoiled and had a child-like personality. He was 17-years-old. The teenage girls at his school found him to be good looking and many of them were hoping to meet him. He was a senior, 5'10" tall, 160lbs and had played football and baseball. He had been introduced to drugs by his older brother, Gregory, and his high school English teacher, Scott Donald.

Steve had an annoying habit of giggling during conversations and he did not seem to be serious about anything. He frequently whined to his parents for things he wanted and they always gave into him, to avoid listening to him. He was close to his mother and secretly hated his father after learning that his father had a mistress.

At school he was known to have a "big mouth," always bragging about his possessions and his parents' wealth. He had demolished two of his cars and his parents quickly replaced them. They found no fault with his behavior.

He was frequently a bully at school, but only picked on kids who were shy and easy to intimidate. When confronted by someone strong and equal in size, he always backed down and tried to laugh it off as if it was a joke.

When he was ten years old, Steve was discovered torturing the neighbors' cats in his backyard. He had the cats tied up and poured lighter fluid on them. He then set them on fire, watching them squirm and howl as they died. He watched passively as the cats burned to death. He liked the smell of the burning hair.

The woman living next door could see Steve from her upstairs window, but she couldn't see what he was burning. All she could see was smoke, and Steve, watching something very intently.

After she called the police to report her sighting, she approached the Satinborne home to speak with the parents. She rang the doorbell and getting no response, went to the sidewalk to wait for the police.

When the police officer, Daryl Walker, arrived at the Satinborne home, he met with the neighbor who was standing on the sidewalk. Together, they went to the front of the house and rang the doorbell.

No one came to the door, so Officer Walker and the neighbor went around the house to the backyard to see what had been burning. As they approached smoking objects on the ground, the neighbor suddenly recognized the remains of her cats and began screaming.

When Steve's mother returned home, she was confronted by Officer Walker. After questioning, he took Steve and her to the police station in his patrol car. The neighbor was very upset and filed charges against the Satinbornes for the loss of her cats. Beverly Satinborne called her husband Ira. She demanded that he come to the police station and help her with the police.

For the charges to be dropped, Steve's parents had agreed to pay the neighbor a significant amount of cash to compensate her for her loss. Officer Walker reported the crime, and the case was sent to Juvenile Court.

The Juvenile Court Judge required that Steve and his parents meet with a professional counselor of their choice. The Judge further ordered that the counselor was required to provide an official report to the Court on his findings.

Ira and Beverly chose to take Steve to Dr. Michael Ticktinsly, a psychologist who had an office in Los Gatos. They knew him and his wife socially.

Ticktinsly interviewed Steve five times, over a six-week period, in his office. He then met privately with Ira and Beverly to provide them with his observations.

He was very direct with Steve's parents and said that he normally didn't report to parents so candidly. However, since they were professionals, and acquaintances, he felt comfortable with them and thought it would be appropriate to let them know of his concerns. He said that even though Steve was only ten years old; he was demonstrating some very disturbing behavior. He said that in his interviews with Steve, that Steve was challenged to stay focused with the discussions.

He said that a child with an interest in watching animals suffer may, in the future, begin inflicting harm on humans. He was concerned with Steve's lack of empathy.

Ticktinsly read from a medical journal that explained:

"If a child frequently bullies or hurts others, but displays no noticeable emotion when their victims' expressed pain, they may have a glitch in the brain network connecting the orbitofrontal cortex and amygdala."

He went on to explain that this neurological trait had been noted in sociopaths and psychopaths. It might explain their inability to care about the harm they cause or the consequences of their actions. A lack of conscience and compassion are classic traits of a sociopath.

Ticktinsly went on to say that some children can outsmart adults. They employ charm, seduction, and glibness to make themselves more likeable, in a way that would allow them to manipulate others.

"What can we do? Is there a cure for this?" asked Beverly.

"No," said Ticktinsly. "Counseling sessions may be used as a training device for your son to mimic healthy behavior, but there is no medicine to instill empathy."

Ira asked, "How do you know that you're correct in your evaluation?"

Ticktinsly replied, "I'm not sure, because he is so young, but he is definitely displaying the behavior of a sociopath. We won't know for certain until he grows older. In a few years, we might have a chance to observe the type of young man he will become."

Ira and Beverly left the doctor's office stunned with what they had learned.

"I think that Jew doctor is full of shit," said Ira. "My kid is not crazy! He wants to counsel him for the rest of his life so he can bill us for a fortune."

"I don't know Ira," Beverly responded. "Stevie has been a lot of trouble for me. You're not around to see it. Sometimes I feel that I can't connect with him. He tells me he loves me, but if I won't let him have what he wants, he'll make my life miserable until I give in. I don't have the energy anymore to keep up with him and his demands.

Killing those cats, the way he did, scares me. You've got to spend more time with him, Ira. Is he going to grow up and kill us too?"

"You're talking crazy, Beverly. Steve is a normal kid who likes to explore. I know one thing for sure. We're not paying that Jew doctor to treat our kid. We've got to find someone else."

TWO
THE JUNTO

In the beginning there were twelve of them.

They had been friends since high school, in the small town of Los Gatos, California. It was the early 1960s and they had all played different sports together. They socialized by organizing poker games that were held at one of their homes. They played almost every two weeks. After graduating from high school, they went their separate ways. Many enrolled in colleges in different parts of the country. Others joined the military and a few of them went to war.

In 1975, after the Vietnam War ended, the members reunited in Los Gatos. They resumed their bi-monthly poker games. When not meeting for poker, they would frequently meet, for drinks and dinner, at the Bellows Restaurant in Saratoga, California. The restaurant was located just ten miles west of Los Gatos.

Six members had served in the military after college and four of them were combat veterans.

During the late 1970s, they formalized their meetings and referred to their group as the American Junto. Their Junto was styled after the Junto that had been created in the early 1770s by Benjamin Franklin.

❧

Junto: A small, usually secret, group united for a common interest.

❧

The founder of the American Junto, James Greaney, had read several biographies on Benjamin Franklin. He had learned about the Junto that had been formed by Franklin and his friends. James explained his findings to his friends, and they all agreed to have their meetings conducted in the same manner and spirit as Franklin's Junto.

❧

The morning after the assault on Steve Satinborne, James and Thomas Greaney attended Mass, with their families, at St. Mary's Catholic Church in Los Gatos. After Mass they went to James' home for brunch. It was a sprawling two-story, five-bedroom home, just under five thousand square feet.

After a brunch of bagels, cold salmon, and white wine, James and Thomas sat on the patio drinking coffee and smoking cigars.

James asked, "What was the girl's name?"

"I think her name is Rosemary Nelson," said Thomas. "I think she is a sophomore at Los Gatos High. I believe her family is from New Zealand."

"Dammit," said James. "We were too late to save her from being molested by that little prick. We've got to have better communication when we're pursuing a target."

"I agree, Jimmy, we should have realized that a Saturday night party would be an ideal time for that little creep to go after these young girls. Look, if he had done this to my child, he'd be dead by now. I don't care what our rules are about not killing."

"Tom, you can't get emotional. I agree, I'd kill him too if it had been my child, but we have no leeway for making mistakes. We must be in control of our actions. We must be right every time out. Keep in mind that this is just the beginning. Our planning must be done carefully. We'll get the others," said James.

"You're right," said Tom. "Can we take care of his old man, next?"

"No," replied James. "We need to take care of his brother before we go after old man, Satinborne."

James Greaney was 29-years-old and the founder and spiritual leader of the Junto. He was very fit. He worked out five times a week, jogging, weightlifting, and practicing karate.

James was Irish American and born in the Bronx, New York, to Francis and Mary Greaney. He was the fourth of six children. His sister Mary was the oldest and had married at eighteen years of age. She and his two older brothers, Frank and John, remained in New York, when their father had moved to California with his wife and three younger children. Francis had been contacted by James' Godfather, Frank Bower, who had left the Bronx, seven years before. Bower had offered Francis a job painting houses and an opportunity to move out of the Bronx. Mary Greaney was a nurse and soon found work in a hospital in Los Gatos, California, where she and Francis had purchased a home.

James had blond hair and piercing blue eyes, that missed nothing. He had a lean and muscular build. At 6'1" tall and 185lbs, he was known, among his friends, for mature judgement and wise decision-making. He was polite and competent. He remained in control of his emotions and was disciplined and confident.

Unless you knew him, a person would not realize that James was a very dangerous man. His military training, war experience, and daily workout regime had transformed him into a lethal fighting machine. He possessed exceptional skills in hand-to-hand combat and proficiency with many types of weapons. He had been trained in the military to conduct the planning and executing of combat missions. He dressed conservatively, wearing black or gray suits that tended to make him look intimidating.

James suffered from post-traumatic stress disorder, commonly referred to as PTSD. The VA doctors had diagnosed his disorder, but he didn't quite believe them. He did have bouts of depression and periodic feelings of emptiness. He also had flashbacks of the combat that he had experienced and his flashbacks would put him in a melancholy mood.

He felt a bitterness towards the lazy and incompetent military and civilian leadership that he had witnessed in the war. He would never forget the way veterans were disrespected and spat on by the liberal creeps when returning from the war.

He had lost his wife, Georgia, when she had been out

jogging and had suffered a brain aneurism. She had died almost instantly. They had been high school sweethearts, and they had had three children—Elizabeth, Georgia, and Vincent.

Georgia's sudden loss was devastating, and a stunning blow for James. He realized that he needed to be strong, and come out of his depressed funk, for the sake of his children. He increased the intensity of his daily workouts to fight his loneliness and sadness.

James was an up-and-coming executive in real estate. He kept his family shielded from his business activities. He considered himself to be a Patriot and was devoted to the Constitution of the United States. He had taken an oath to the Constitution when he had been sworn-in as an Officer in the Army. He continued to follow that oath in civilian life.

He was a devout Christian and attended Catholic Mass every Sunday with his children. He dedicated every Tuesday evening to spending time with them. He didn't allow TV watching or any other interruptions while spending time with his family.

He was disgusted with the Catholic Priests and fellow church members who condoned abortion by welcoming politicians who promoted the practice. He had been very disappointed with the passing of Roe vs. Wade in 1973.

He refused to donate money to the Church, because he believed it had become corrupt and hypocritical. Church leaders had protected priests when they had known they had abused thousands of children over the years. He would never consider leaving them money in the offering. He had let the hierarchy at his Church know that he would not support them.

His attendance at Mass was for the benefit of his children's education, and to take advantage of the discipline and quality of Catholic schools. He believed that public schools were a complete failure.

James was an elusive, talented leader, driven by a desire for justice and vengeance. He did not trust the government, and he believed that the system had failed to provide justice. He was convinced that the system had been rigged to favor those in power.

He only trusted his immediate family, his brothers, his sister, and a few friends that he had known since childhood.

James was a voracious reader and completed a book every week. He alternated his reading between fiction and non-fiction. His favorite books were biographies. When he was eight years old, his mother had bought him a box of books at a rummage sale. He had been reading books continually, since then.

James had founded a group, that he later named the American Junto. He formed the group with some of his former high school classmates. He was inspired after reading two biographies of Benjamin Franklin. He wanted to create the same environment with his friends as Franklin had accomplished several hundred years before, with his friends.

He wanted the new Junto, like Franklin's, to create a "Spirit of inquiry, improve the community, and to help others."

James learned that Franklin's Junto, also known as the Apron Leather Club, was a club for mutual improvement. It had been established in 1727, in morals, politics, and natural philosophy, and to exchange knowledge of business affairs. It was also a charitable organization that had created a subscription public library that had included books that they owned.

Franklin's group had twelve members drawn from diverse occupations and backgrounds. The original members shared a spirit of inquiry and a desire to improve themselves, their community, and to help others. Among the original members had been printers, surveyors, a cabinetmaker, a clerk, and a bartender. Although most of the members had been older than Franklin, he was recognized as their leader.

During high school, James, and some of his friends, would meet to play poker and socialize. They drank beer and smoked cigarettes.

Now, ten years later, after going to college, joining the business world, and with some serving in the military, they resumed their practice of scheduling bi-monthly poker games at members' homes.

James had convinced his friends to regard their group as a Junto. They would participate in discussions of mutual improvement. At first some were reluctant, but since all they had to do was talk, they went along with it. There were twelve original members, and at least eight of them would show up for poker on a regular basis.

In April 1975, the Junto members were looking forward to playing poker and the interesting discussions that they had during their meetings. At one of their meetings, John Dickson informed the group of the rape of a fellow member's niece. Dickson was very emotional when he announced that, "Pete

Stoeland's niece has been raped. That's why he's not at the meeting tonight."

THREE
LOS GATOS, CALIFORNIA

In 1959 Francis Greaney moved with his wife Mary and his three younger sons, James, William, and Thomas, from the Bronx, New York to Los Gatos, California. It was like he had moved them to a foreign country.

His three older children, Mary, Frank, and John had remained in New York. Frank and John had been hired as policemen in the Bronx. Mary had married a cop who had been assigned to a precinct in Manhattan.

The three younger boys had distinct New York accents and dressed differently than the local kids in Los Gatos.

Francis had been a boxer in his youth and had been a candidate for the Olympic team until he suffered a broken hand while in training.

His father had been a professional boxer, at the turn of the century, and had boxed in exhibitions in vaudeville shows with his twin brother.

Francis taught his five sons to box, beginning when they

were 5-years-old. It took a while for his three younger sons to adapt to their new surroundings in Los Gatos. Playing sports was the catalyst that helped them adjust and make friends. When they first moved to Los Gatos, the younger sons were challenged and threatened by local "tough" kids. The local bullies soon learned that it was a major mistake to pick on the Greaney boys. The Greaney's made "quick work" of the untrained, "tough" kids.

Los Gatos was a sleepy town of less than 6,000 residents when the Greaney's arrived in 1959. Located at the base of the green Santa Cruz Mountains, and surrounded by hills filled with redwood trees, it was the gateway to the beautiful scenery of the Santa Clara Valley.

The name Los Gatos is Spanish, meaning "The Cats." The name derived from the 1839 Alta California Land-grant that encompassed the area called La Rinconada de Los Gatos. "The Cats" refers to the cougars that are indigenous to the foothills located in Los Gatos.

The town's founding dates from the mid-1850s with the building of a flour operation named Forbes Mill. It was built by James Alexander Forbes along the Los Gatos Creek. The mill's two-story storage annex has been preserved as a museum. It is located just off Main Street.

Los Gatos has a Mediterranean climate and was incorporated in 1887. It remained an important town for the logging industry in the Santa Cruz Mountains through the end of the 19th Century.

In the early 20th Century, the Town became a thriving

agricultural area with orchards of apricots, grapes, and prunes. The area had become known as the "Valley of Hearts Delight," because of the fertility of the valley and the fabulous produce grown there. Eventually, the vineyards and fruit and nut trees gave way to housing in the post-World War II boom of high tech and then biotech. The name changed to Silicon Valley due to the manufacturing of semiconductors.

A short-lived oil boom took place between 1891 and 1929. About twenty oil wells were drilled in and around Los Gatos. Although commercial production was never established, small amounts of oil were produced for use as fuel, lubricant, and road tar by the residents.

Railway transportation was an early feature of Los Gatos. The South Pacific Coast Railroad had a popular narrow-gage line from Alameda to Santa Cruz. In the late 19th century, it stopped in Los Gatos.

By the 1920s, the Los Gatos area had a reputation as an art colony. It attracted painters, musicians, writers, actors, and their bohemian associates as residents.

The famous violinist Yehudi Menuhin lived there as a boy, and actresses Olivia De Haviland and Joan Fontaine (sisters), were graduates of Los Gatos High School. John Steinbeck wrote *The Grapes of Wrath* there (location is now Monte Sereno), and the Beat-Hero, Neal Cassidy, lived there in the 1950s.

Rosemary Nelson had been Steve Satinbornes' third rape victim. Three months before, Steve had raped and sodomized Susan Stoeland and another girl.

After being informed by John Dickson that his friend, Pete Stoeland's niece Susan, had been raped, James contacted Pete to see if he could be of any help.

They met in Pete's office. Pete confirmed that his niece, Susan, had been drugged and raped by a high school student named Steve Satinborne.

Pete said that he had spoken with his brother, Art, Susan's father, and Art also believed the rapist to be Steve Satinborne. Art owned a Ford Dealership in town. He said that Steve was a senior and his daughter, Susan, was a sophomore. He said he couldn't prove it as yet, because Susan had been drugged and had little memory of the event. She had been a virgin and when she had awakened felt pain in her genital and rectum areas. She had also noticed some bleeding.

She waited two days before informing her mother because she was ashamed and afraid of what her parents would say. Art's wife, Robin, was very upset, crying and yelling. She was demanding that Art do something about it.

Art and Robin sat with Susan and asked her to recount the story from the beginning. Susan remembered meeting with Steve at Maureen's party, as they had planned. Susan had a crush on Steve and was thrilled to have been noticed by a senior.

Steve and Susan had moved on from Maureen's party to Rudy Goosin's party. There were no chaperones and there were kids there from other schools. Rudy's parents were professional musicians and were out of town, performing in Las Vegas.

Steve brought her a drink from a punch bowl and they sat

together listening to the very loud music and talking to other kids. Susan said that she remembered going to Rudy's home and talking to her friends, Sharon and Sandy, but that was all that she could remember. The next thing she remembered was Steve dropping her off at the curb in front of her house. She felt very confused and tired.

Robin had been up most of the night, calling around asking for Susan. Some of Susan's friends said that they had seen her with Steve. When she left the house, Susan had told her mother that she and some friends were going to go to a couple of parties and that she promised to stay close to her girlfriends.

After her confession, Robin took Susan to their family doctor, Lew Newberg. Newberg had graduated from Los Gatos High School and Brown Medical School. He had returned to Los Gatos after his internship and joined his father's medical practice.

Newberg confirmed that Susan had had intercourse and that she also had been sodomized, resulting in the tearing of her rectum. He prescribed medication for her pain and said that he would perform additional testing. Art and Robin were convinced that Steve was responsible for their daughter's assault, but they didn't have any proof.

Art visited the Los Gatos Police Department and filed formal charges of rape against Steve Satinborne. Two police investigators assigned to the case met with Steve and his parents.

Art and Robin retained a lawyer, Alan Hagen, whose office was in Los Gatos. Hagen filed a lawsuit against Steve and his parents on behalf of Susan.

The police investigators were not able to find any information that would incriminate Steve.

FOUR
THE TRIAL

After learning about the rape of Pete Stoeland's niece, James was filled with anger. When visiting Pete in his office, James had asked him for details on the assault and anything else that he might know about the perpetrator.

Pete had heard from his brother Art, that his niece, Susan, was infatuated with an older boy named Steve. Steve frequently called the house. He was known to be an arrogant, rich kid who played sports.

Pete relayed to James the information that Art and his wife Robin had learned from their discussion with Susan.

Art had no evidence that Steve had done anything to Susan, but he knew his daughter and was confident that Steve was the one who had harmed her.

"Pete, I'm going to use my contacts to investigate this. Susan will have justice," said James.

As he was leaving Pete's office, James put in a call to his childhood friend, Victor Lewis. Victor was a lieutenant on the

San Jose Police force and a member of the Junto.

"Vic, I need your help. This is very serious. I can't talk about it on the phone. Please meet me at my house this evening at 7."

"Okay, Jim. I'll be there."

Ira Satinborne assigned a lawyer who worked in his firm, Josh Gordon, to defend Steve at his trial. Gordon was a graduate of Santa Clara University Law School. He was 32-years-old and had joined Ira's firm five years before. He was very bright, aggressive and a frequent cocaine user. He wore his hair tied behind his head in a manbun. He always tried to impress Ira in order to enhance his reputation and standing in the law firm. He assured Ira that he would do his best to clear Steve of the wrongful charges.

Josh was single and dating the daughter of a prominent Silicon Valley Venture Capitalist. He liked to generate publicity and was known to leak confidential information to the press when he thought it would enhance his reputation. He wanted to win at all costs and was willing to take risks—even if they were unethical. He believed that his aggressiveness was his key to success.

The trial took place in Santa Clara. The presiding judge was Patrick Browne. Josh Gordon requested a bench trial as soon as he saw that Browne had been assigned as the presiding judge.

Patrick Browne was single. He was fond of telling his family and friends that he had never met the right woman. He was 53-years-old and had been a judge for 9 years. He had graduated from Berkely Law School and had been a classmate of Ira Satinborne. He had low energy and enjoyed being a judge as he had little to do and a lot of time off.

Browne was a liberal Democrat. He was 6'2" tall, 240lbs, flabby and sedentary. He could not remember when he had last exercised. His hobby was fishing. He had maintained an infrequent social relationship with Ira and Beverly. It took him four days to rule Steve innocent of all charges.

During the trial Steve sat next to his attorney and had an arrogant smirk on his face. He made faces at his brother Gregory, who was sitting two rows back in the audience. Gregory had never been suspected of having any involvement in Susan's abuse.

Art and Robin were devastated by the judge's ruling. They contacted Pete to inform him of the trial results. Pete called James and asked him to come to his office.

When James arrived at Pete's office, they closed the door. After getting their coffee from the break room, Pete began speaking.

"I don't know what to do, Jim. My brother- and sister-in-law are very upset, and my niece has been brutalized. We need your help."

"No problem, Pete. I've reached out to some of my sources. We'll get those bastards. Please be patient and let me take care of this."

"What are you planning to do?"

"It's best that you don't know too much. I'll be back in touch with you soon, Pete."

James had an appointment with Gene Adams, a private investigator and former cop, who Victor Lewis had recommended. They met at Adam's office in San Jose.

James provided Adams with an overview of the rape case. It included a copy of the police report that Victor had given him, and the final ruling rendered at the trial.

He explained that Susan's family believed that Steve Satinborne was guilty of raping Susan, and they wanted justice.

Adams said that he was familiar with Judge Browne. He was not surprised to learn about the ruling and Browne's attitude towards the attorney representing Susan. The judge had been disrespectful to the attorney while he was stating his arguments before the bench.

"Judge Browne is a low IQ, lazy bastard who hates cops," said Adams. "When I was a cop, I arrested a couple of guilty dirtbags, and Browne let them back on the street in a matter of hours."

"I want a thorough investigation and a weekly update on your progress. Bill me and don't allow the costs to inhibit your investigation. I'm paying for all of it," said James.

Within two weeks, Adams had discovered details about the past and present relationships between Steve Satinborne's parents, Ira and Beverly, and Judge Browne.

His report shed light on why Steve's lawyer had requested a bench trial. The lawyer knew before the trial began that Browne would favor the Satanbornes. The Satinbornes and Judge Browne had been classmates in law school and had socialized in Los Gatos from time to time.

Adams' report included details of Steve and his brother Gregory's drug use. It stated that Susan's reputation was that of a sweet fifteen-year-old. She was an excellent student from a religious family and had many school friends. She had never had a boyfriend or gone on a date in high school.

FIVE
THE SATINBORNE'S

The patriarch of the Satinborne family was Ira Satinborne. He was an accomplished personal injury attorney born in San Jose, California. He was the majority partner in a large, prominent law firm located in downtown San Jose. In addition to his law practice, he had founded a bank, with other partners, that was a tenant in a building that he owned in San Jose. He had acquired many commercial buildings over the last ten years, and he leased them to high-tech start-ups.

At 5'9" tall and 190lbs, Ira was pudgy looking. He was 51-years old and a graduate of the University of California Berkeley School of Law. He dressed well, for his roly-poly stature, in expensive tailored suits and monogrammed shirts. He had an arrogant demeanor and was often very obnoxious when speaking with others. He was especially arrogant and short-tempered when addressing his employees.

He had been having a long-time affair with his office manager, Donna Pearce. She was divorced with two children.

Donna was in her mid-thirties, a slender brunette, with a round face, long neck and high forehead. She had an outgoing personality that made up for her unattractive looks. She was worried about her future and the possibility of not being able to find another man. Her ex-husband rarely provided money for the children's support, and she could not afford to lose her job. She, therefore, had succumbed to Ira's advances and demands.

Ira's wife Beverly was aware of his mistress and was happy that he had another place to go, to service his needs. They had maintained separate bedrooms for the last five years and neither of them had visited the other for romantic purposes. She was confident that he would not leave her because he wouldn't want to pay the very high price for a divorce. She had helped put him through law school, with her parents' financial support, and she was confident that she would receive far more than a fifty/fifty split of their common assets, if it came to a divorce.

Ira spoiled his two sons, Gregory, and Steven, but had never spent much time with them. He allowed them to have all the "toys" that they demanded—such as new cars and high-tech electronics. He had never disciplined them other than mild verbal counseling. He had always deferred to his wife to be the disciplinarian in the family.

Beverly Satinborne was the matriarch of the family. She was 49-years-old, 5'3" tall, stocky, and dumpy. A graduate of the University of California, at Berkely, Law School where she had met her husband, Ira. She had not practiced law but had spent the first years of the firm's existence as the administrative manager. She had hired the current office manager and then left the firm to focus on raising her sons. She played tennis with her girlfriend a few days a week. She also enjoyed being a member of a bridge club of women her age and affluent status. Beverly was very bright, mean, and selfish. Her sons could do no wrong in her eyes, and she believed that they were misunderstood by others.

Steve Satinborne had turned seventeen years old at the start of his senior year. He was a sociopath. He had no respect or compassion for others. He was charming and flirtatious with young girls. He was only concerned with getting what he wanted and would go to any length in doing so.

Steve was conflicted about his sexuality but had never talked to anyone about his feelings. He dated young girls, two to three years behind him in school. They were attracted to him because of his looks, family wealth, and his participation in sports. He did not date girls his own age, as he found it difficult and uncomfortable to relate to them.

He was aroused by some of the boys on his sport teams when they showered together after practice or games. He had not approached any of the boys but enjoyed watching them walking around naked in the locker room.

He liked to dominate the girls that he dated and could become rough with them when no one was around. His grades were average, but his test scores were high, indicating that if he had applied himself, he could have done well in school.

Steve's older brother Gregory was 20-years old, 6' tall, blonde hair, blue eyes and 180lbs. He had been a good athlete in high school but had not made any of the teams that he had tried out for in college. He was in his second year at Santa Clara University in Santa Clara, California, majoring in biology. He was a frequent drug user, and he had been introduced to all kinds of drugs by his cousins in Germany and his high school English teacher, Scott Donald.

Gregory was introduced to "roofies" on a family vacation to Germany to visit his cousins Fredrick, and Dieter. His older cousins used the drug that they had obtained from a source who had also been providing them with cocaine. They used the new drug on unsuspecting women when frequenting nightclubs. The cousins were very successful in using the roofies and they knew the correct dosage to use for each victim. They included Gregory in their conquests. He willingly participated in the sexual assaults on heavily drugged, innocent women.

The cousins took Gregory with them to several nightclubs where they selected women to be targeted. Dieter and Fredrick would initially engage them in casual conversation, buy them drinks, tell them funny stories, and dance with them while slipping roofie tablets into their drinks. They preferred to target older, outgoing women, who when drugged would be easier to have intercourse with—as opposed to young, inexperienced women.

After drugging their victim, they would walk them out of the club, explaining to others that the victim had had too much to drink and that they were taking them home. They would take the victim or victims to Dieter's apartment and keep them there for hours of sexual activity. When the victim began to sober up, they would return her to her home or back to the nightclub. None of their victims remembered much about the assaults, as the roofie drug caused memory loss that would last for hours. Some did notice pain or soreness in their genitals and rectum as the drug began to wear off.

Gregory had known that he was gay from the time that he was 13-years-old. He was afraid to share his true feelings with others, including his own family. He would not want to jeopardize his relationship with his friends who were "straight" by confessing to them that he was gay. He had enjoyed having anal sex and inflicting pain on the women in Germany. When he returned from his vacation, he introduced his younger brother, and his former English teacher to roofies.

SIX
THE PLANNING

After meeting with the private investigator, Gene Adams, and receiving his report, James contacted his two brothers, William, and Thomas. He also called his high school friend Victor Lewis. He told them that he wanted to meet them at his house at 8 pm that evening.

William and Thomas were the first to arrive at James' home. While the three were waiting for Victor to arrive, James discussed a conversation that he had had with their mother.

James began, "You know that Ma never strayed very far from her rosary beads. She knew more about the Bible than any Priest that I ever knew. When I first returned from Vietnam, I stayed with our parents for two weeks. I was trying to adjust to a new environment where I didn't have to be on the alert for an enemy trying to kill me. I spent a lot of time thinking about how I had been trained by the government to kill our enemies. Not to wound or capture them, but to kill them. And the killings were justified by God and Country. I even had been decorated for bravery in combat—killing the enemy. So, let me tell you about one of the conversations that I had with Ma.

When we were alone, I asked, "Ma, if I had been a civilian in Germany in 1933 and trained to kill, and I had had the opportunity to kill Hitler, would God have forgiven me? Or, if I had been in China when Mao came into power, and as a civilian, I killed him, would God have forgiven me? They were evil men responsible for the deaths and suffering of millions of innocent people. Would I have been justified in killing them, in the eyes of the Lord?"

Ma thought about my questions and said, "Jimmy, why do you ask me these questions? You have done this to me ever since you were a little child. I don't know what God would say, but I believe that he always forgives, if you ask for forgiveness. He'd probably make you pay a penance for a very long time, but I don't know," she said.

"That sounds like Ma. She was always ready to forgive," said William.

"Are you trying to understand or justify something that you have in mind to do?" asked Thomas.

"Maybe, but there's more. I met with Father Daughtery at St. Mary's and asked him the same questions. He wouldn't give me a straight answer on any of my questions and he basically dodged the whole subject. I decided to go with Ma's response since I believe she was closer to God than Father Daughtery. And yes, I want to think it through if we decide to kill some of these targets," said James.

Victor arrived as James was finishing his story. James

opened the meeting by sharing the findings of the private investigator, Gene Adams.

When the four men were seated and comfortable, James began, "We need to bring justice to these bastards. The Judge had no intention of providing justice for Susan, so we must make them pay a heavy price for their acts. This doesn't just go for the little punk kid. I want us to punish everyone involved including the brother, father, Judge and even the lawyer representing the dirtbag."

"Why don't we kill them? They are hurting innocent people including children like Susan," said William.

"No. At this time, I don't want to kill any of them. I want to punish them. We know that killing them would be the easier way, but let's save that option until it turns out that punishment is not enough," said James.

"Remember what Ma told you Jimmy. You can always ask for forgiveness," said William.

Thomas stood up with a beer in his hand and said, "I have a solution that you might want to consider, Jimmy. During the time I was stationed in Japan, I learned a lot about the Japanese mafia. They are called, the Yakuza. They are much smarter and far more dangerous than any of the Italian mafia families in the United States.

"Major companies in Japan, like Mitsubishi, have hired the Yakuza to intimidate and keep the peace at their stockholder meetings. They are referred to by the Japanese people as the 'Sokaiya.'"

In California, the Yakuza had made alliances with local

Vietnamese/American and Korean/American gangs, as well as with the Chinese Triads. The Vietnamese were the most common alliance for them. Vietnamese gangs were used as muscle, as they had the most potential to become extremely violent.

The Yakuza in New York City collect finder's fees from Russian, Irish and Italian mafiosos for guiding Japanese tourists to gambling establishments, both legal and illegal.

The Yakuza have a complex organizational structure. There is an overall boss of the syndicate and directly beneath him are senior advisors. The second in the chain of command governs several gangs in a region. The regional gangs are governed by a local boss.

The largest Yakuza family in Japan, is the Yamaguichi-gumi. They have approximately 55,000 members divided among 850 Clans. They are headquartered in Kobe, Japan. They have operations in other Asian countries and in the United States.

When a member of the Yakuza, "fucks-up," he will cut-off one of his fingers and present it to his boss, as a token of apology. At the same time, he asks for forgiveness.

⌒⌒

"I recommend that we cutoff the thumb of our target's writing hand. They'll never forget why they lost their thumb," said Thomas.

"Very spiritual idea, Tom. I would like to learn more about the Yakuza. Your idea is in line with my thinking. We want to give them a severe reminder, but we want to stop short of killing them," said James.

"Won't that be kind of bloody and hard to cover up, Tom?

You don't want to have blood all over you. That would be easy to trace," said William.

"How much of the thumb do you think we should take?" asked James.

"Only the thumbprint, to the first joint. We can keep the blood spatter to a minimum if we tape the thumb right after we do the cutting," said Tom.

"What about the beating that we'll give them? How are you going to do that while you're cutting off their thumb?" asked William.

"You first stun them with a sap. You just have to be careful not to hit them too hard," said Victor.

"What's a sap?" asked William.

"We used saps in the police department years ago. I still have a couple of them at home. A sap is a beaver-tailed leather weapon that is weighted with lead on one end. You can give a person one hell of a beating. You can knock someone unconscious with it. You can break bones. I can teach you how to use it," said Victor.

"I like that idea. We can practice with it and it will be easy to use in close quarters," said Thomas.

"I'm all in on this idea. Vic, you must go about your police work as if you know nothing about our activities. We need you to provide us with intelligence on our targets and to keep us informed about what the police department is doing," said James.

Bill, I'm assigning you to do surveillance on this little creep, Steve. You need to get us details on his habits and where he goes. You need to let us know when you think he might be ready to strike again.

Tom and I will develop an overall plan of attack. We'll purchase the equipment and we'll practice with the weapons," said James.

James and Thomas went to a local hardware store and purchased two hand pruning shears. Thomas had a sharpening machine in his garage and he sharpened the shears to a razor edge. He tested the shears on tree branches in his backyard and they cut through the branches like they were paper.

Victor gave them a couple of saps and they practiced using them. Just a flick of the wrist with a sap easily broke wooden boards. They had to practice being careful not to hit too hard. Victor also provided them with plastic handcuffs that had been recently introduced to the police department. The handcuffs were easier to use than the steel ones. They also would be easier to dispose of.

They purchased latex gloves to wear so that they would avoid leaving any fingerprints.

James and Thomas were soon ready, with their equipment, to carry out a mission.

SEVEN
THE VIGILANTES

James founded the "Vigilantes" when he was in the planning stages of going after Steve Satinborne for the rape of Pete's niece. The team consisted of his two brothers, William and Thomas, a childhood friend, Victor Lewis, and himself. He considered them to be a secret sub-set of the Junto. All four were members of the Junto.

William, Thomas, Victor, and James had extensive combat experience. James believed that the four of them would be the perfect team for the formation of the Vigilantes. Their political views were much more conservative than the other Junto members. The Vigilantes kept their formation secret from others.

James believed that the other members of the Junto would not agree, or support, the methods of the Vigilantes and it would be impossible to operate in secret. The other Junto members were not combat veterans, and they had not experienced the specialty training or the terror and excitement of combat. He knew they would not have the "stomach" for violence even if they were to agree with the end result.

With James' guidance and seed money, the Vigilantes set-up secret companies and bank accounts in the Cayman Islands, the Isle of Man, Hong Kong, and Singapore.

In California, the members of the Vigilantes lived modestly in nice neighborhoods and drove American-made cars.

Outside of California, and in some foreign countries, the Vigilantes lived very well. They avoided any behavior that could draw attention to themselves or their family members. They dressed well and paid cash, avoiding the tracing of credit card purchases. They kept large cash deposits in overseas banks.

James' business philosophy was supported by all of the Vigilantes. He believed that they should "own little, but control everything." He demanded that members be highly disciplined and maintain a low-profile to avoid inquiries.

Wives, family members, relatives, friends, and mistresses were to "know nothing about their activities."

On vacation in Hawaii, Mexico, France, Italy, or Singapore, the Vigilantes and their families would often stay in homes or condos owned by their corporate entities. Only the Vigilantes knew of the true ownership of the property.

James read about the works of Jung and was impressed with Jung's "stages of life" as quoted in the following:

The Athlete—It is characterized by being obsessed with our physical bodies and appearance.

The Warrior—All of a sudden, we can see objectives that we want to accomplish and the vanity of the athlete begins to fade.

The Statement—Your focuses shift from your personal achievements to accomplishing goals based on forwarding other people's lives.

The Spirit—We realize that we are divine beings in a journey of life that has no real beginning or end.

James vowed that the Vigilantes would punish criminals by branding them in a way that they would remember for the rest of their lives. The branding would mark them in a way that could not be changed. It would include the removal of the first joint on the thumb, followed by a severe beating. Every time one of their targets looked at their writing hand, they would be reminded of their wrongdoing.

The Vigilante's control of drug-flow and pushers, and the utilization of the underworld to include the Yakuza and Vietnamese and Latino gangs, allowed them to generate huge working capital. They took money from criminals, drug dealers, and drug wholesalers.

Through James' in-depth reading and research, he learned and eventually adopted the practice of "patience."

James was very philosophical. He believed that those with patience were the strong ones. To him, patience meant holding back one's inclination of the seven emotions—hate, adoration, joy, anxiety, anger, grief, and fear. If one did not give way to the seven emotions, they were patient and strong.

James had been taught to box at five years of age. He learned that losing one's temper contributed to losing power in one's punches. His father had explained to him that a professional fighter rarely lost his temper during a boxing match. That way they were able to avoid weakening their power punching ability. The successful fighters remained calm even when they were hurt.

William Andrew Greaney was one of James' younger brothers. He was 28-years-old, blonde, and 5'10" tall. He maintained a very rigorous conditioning regimen. He was handsome, flirtatious, and loved women. His playful personality allowed him to get away with comments that would have been troublesome for others. He also had a quick temper and was considered by many to be a "hot head." He was ready to fight at the slightest provocation and it did not matter the size of his opponent.

He was a Marine Corps Veteran of the Vietnam War. He served as an M60 machine gunner. His battalion fought in some of the bloodiest battles in Vietnam, and the province where they were located, lost more Marines than in any other province in Vietnam.

William was a conspiracy theorist and historian. He had always loved history. It was the only subject that he had enjoyed and excelled in during high school—except sports. He had been very curious as to why the United States had been involved in so many wars beginning with the Spanish American War, that had been fought at the turn of the twentieth century. He had become obsessed with researching and documenting factual data. He believed that he was different from most conspiracists as he had done extensive research on many historical events to support his conclusions. He developed an extensive library on government and social historical events that helped support his views on life. William had come to believe that the Council on Foreign Relations (CFR) was the root and source of a global "shadow government." He believed that the CFR was responsible for much of the harm and misery throughout the world.

The CFR was founded on July 21, 1921 in New York City, by Elihu Root, Edward House, Walter Lippmann and others. They supported a one-world government. Membership had included more than a dozen Secretary of States, CIA Directors, bankers, lawyers, professors, and senior media figures.

The CFR promoted globalization, free trade, reducing financial regulations on transitional corporations and economic consolidation into regional blocs such as NAFTA or The European Union. It developed policies that reflected those goals.

The CFR published the bi-monthly journal, Foreign Affairs. The CFR ran the David Rockefeller Studies Program, influencing foreign policy, by making recommendations to the presidential administration and diplomatic community. They testified before Congress, interacting with the media, and publishing studies on foreign policy issues.

The original members of the CFR were proponents of President Wilson's internationalism. They were particularly concerned about "the effort that war and the Treaty of Peace might have on postwar business." During the late 1930s the Ford Foundation and the Rockefeller Foundation created studies that were sent to government officials.

Confidential War and Peace Studies were funded by the

Rockefeller Foundation. Not all Council Members were aware of the War and Peace Studies existence. It was divided into functional topic groups: economic and financial security, armaments, territorial and political.

The CFR produced 682 memoranda for the U.S. State Department, marked classified and circulated among the appropriate government departments.

William believed that governments had been responsible for killing more people than wars in China, Germany, Cambodia, Bangladesh, and Russia.

Thomas Edward Greaney was 27-years-old and James' youngest brother. At 5'10" tall, he resembled his other brothers with his blonde hair and blue eyes. He became a Navy Seal at 19-years of age and served for five years. He was a martial arts expert and owned a martial arts studio that taught assault and defensive tactics. He was a quiet and very spiritual man. He served in the Navy, in Vietnam, and was later stationed in Japan. While stationed in Japan he became a student of Ninjutsu.

Ninjutsu is the traditional Japanese art of stealth, camouflage, and sabotage, developed in feudal times for espionage and now practiced as a martial art. A Ninja was a person skilled in ninjutsu.

Victor Clarence Lewis was 34-years-old and a close friend and neighbor of James and his brothers. He was 6 feet tall, with brooding, brown eyes, and a muscular physic. He was of Polish and Hispanic descent. He had served in the Air Force in

Vietnam and his specialty was as an Intelligence NCO. He was responsible for collecting data from external threats. He was an expert marksman in the military and later became an avid hunter and fisherman. After leaving the Air Force, he joined the San Jose Police Department. He was currently a lieutenant in the Department, responsible for drug enforcement. He was conservative and patriotic. He believed that the Federal, State and Local governments were corrupt, incompetent, and controlled by liberal politicians. As a Vietnam combat Veteran, he believed that the American Government betrayed the veterans that fought in the War.

EIGHT
SILICON VALLEY

Silicon Valley is a region in Northern California that serves as a global center for high technology, innovation, venture capital, and social media. It corresponds to the geographical Santa Clara Valley. San Jose is Silicon Valley's largest city. The other major cities in the valley include Sunnyvale, Santa Clara, Redwood City, Mountain View, Palo Alto and Los Gatos.

Pete Stoeland was an accountant and had obtained his CPA certification after four years at Stanford University. He was tall at 6'2", bald and gangly. Pete had married his high school sweetheart, Rosie, after graduation from college. She was soon pregnant with the first of their three children.

Pete and Rosie had met James when they joined the freshman class at Los Gatos High School in 1960. James' family had moved from New York. Rosie's family had emigrated from England and Pete's family had lived in Los Gatos since the 1940s.

Pete and Rosie were never close friends with James, but they had shared mutual friends throughout their high school years. Pete and James played on the same basketball team and ran track together for four years.

Pete was born with a heart valve problem and although he was very athletic and healthy, a military doctor determined that he was not eligible for military service. He was a good student and came from a conservative, religious family. He was attracted to accounting because he enjoyed working with numbers, was orderly, and preferred to work alone. James had a strong and aggressive personality and was popular with other kids. He once protected Pete who was being bullied by two brothers. They were known to pick on kids who were weak or timid. He liked James because he always treated him well and was a good friend to him.

Four years after James was discharged from the Army, he called Pete and asked for a meeting. At that time, Pete had a modest accounting business. He dealt with personal tax returns and small business accounting.

James asked Pete to take over the accounting for his new real estate business. During the meeting they discussed old times and James suggested that they try to resurrect their bi-monthly poker games with some of their old friends from high school. Pete was very pleased to receive James' business as he later learned that his operations and investments were growing rapidly.

James asked Pete to research tax havens—such as the ones he had heard of in the Cayman Islands, the Isle of Man, Singapore, and Hong Kong. He said that some of his business interests were going international and he wanted to know more about structuring his operations.

Pete said he knew very little about tax havens, but that he would do the research and educate himself. James said that he trusted Pete and that he would channel all of his business through him. Pete said that he would have to hire more help in order to keep his regular business going. James replied, "No problem, just let me know what you need. I trust you, Pete."

James' company purchased old commercial buildings and refurbished them to lease to startups and companies that were expanding. He also purchased underdeveloped land at the edge of the business development centers, anticipating future growth. He hired a construction company owned by a high school friend, Mike Fellows. Mike refurbished and built out buildings to be leased to high-tech companies. Whenever possible, James acquired options, or stock, in the companies that he leased through management negotiations.

Lessees were eager to explain why their companies were special. Startups, very often, would brag about their potential success due to their unique inventions or software development. James' questioning was not regarded as a threat to them. They enjoyed talking about their great ideas.

Pete learned that James had begun to partially fund a few high-tech startups that had agreed to lease his buildings. He had an ownership position in a well-established investment firm. The firm had recently taken on a new client's portfolio. It was valued at several million dollars.

James had acquired a minority ownership position with a new electronic distributorship owned by John Marshall and

Martin Bernee. He helped with some startup funding and in the purchasing of allocated electronic components from the broker market. He had no day-to-day involvement with the distributorship. The two owners provided him with investment information pertaining to the companies that they serviced and trends in the marketplace. He provided the leases for the distributorships' office building and warehouse.

Marshall and Bernee set up a sister company in Japan to work with their distributorship. The sister company, Nippon Global Distribution, owned and operated by a close friend of Marshall's, Yoshi Tanaguichi, distributed high tech components in Japan and exported them to Europe and China. Tanaguichi was also a front man for the Yakuza, which was Japan's version of the mafia. His Yakuza business belonged to a clan of the Yamaguichi-gumi family. The Yamaguichi-gumi was the largest Yakuza family in Japan. They controlled some 2,500 businesses. They were headquartered in Kobe and directed their activities throughout Japan.

The Yakuza, also known as Gokudo, translates as *the extreme path or gangster, are members of a transnational crime syndicate originating in Japan.* Yakuza, are regarded to be among the most sophisticated and wealthiest criminal organizations in the world.

The Yakuza had a complicated organizational structure. They had an overall boss of the syndicate, the Kumicho, and directly beneath him were Saiko Koman (senior advisor) and So-Konbucho known as the headquarters chief. The second in the chain of command was the Wakagashira. They governed several gangs in a region with the help of a Fuku-honbucho who was responsible for several gangs. The regional gangs were governed by their local boss, Shateigoshima. Each member's connection was ranked by the hierarchy of Sakazuki, sake sharing.

In California, the Yakuza had made alliances with local Vietnamese and Korean gangs as well as Chinese Triads. The Vietnamese were their most common alliance. They were recruited for muscle, as they had the potential to become extremely violent.

Tanaguichiu was given permission, by his superiors in the Yakuza, to work with his American contacts. He wanted to find channels to penetrate the U.S. high-tech companies with investment, as well as with real estate opportunities.

James and Marshall traveled to Tokyo on a business trip. Yoshi Tanaguichi introduced them to some of his associates in the Yakuza. They invited James to play golf at their club in Kobe. Japanese ladies wearing conical hats and scarfs, and carrying umbrellas, worked as caddies for the foursome. The ladies knew the intricacies of the course and they discouraged golfers who were using the wrong club. They would recommend the correct club, to the player, as they viewed the distance to the next flag. On some greens, large black crows would swoop down and pick up a ball and fly away.

There were escalators between some of the holes, to make it easier for a golfer to move to the next tee. After 9 holes, lunch was served and after 18 holes, the golfers would retreat to the clubhouse for a sauna and massage.

During dinner, Tanaguichi advised James not to ask any questions about the structure of the Yakuza—this included asking for the names of the leaders. He said that business would be conducted through him and that James would never know who the decision-makers were. James told Tanaguichi that domestic Japanese business was too confusing for him to spend time trying to figure it out. He welcomed working only through Tanaguichi.

NINE
THE EXECUTION

Art and Robin enrolled their daughter, Susan, at Saratoga High School, five miles from downtown Los Gatos. She had refused to return to Los Gatos High. She wanted to avoid the gossip about her rape. After the trial, Susan became deeply depressed and refused to eat. Eventually, her parents convinced her to go back to school, but she would only consider it—if it was a different school.

Steve Satinborne bragged to one of his close friends at school that he had had sex with Susan and that she wanted it "more and more." He said he gave in to her because she wouldn't leave him alone. After a while, the rumor of their sexual encounter spread. Steve told all his friends the details of the sex that he had had with Susan and how she was the one who had pursued him. Soon the story was repeated all over the school campus and it eventually came to the attention of Susan's family. Two of Susan's closest friends informed her mother. Robin contacted her brother-in-law Pete and told him about the hurtful story. Steve was spreading the false story all over the school.

Pete Stoeland called James and informed him of the false story that Steve was spreading at school.

James contacted William and asked him if he had heard anything about Steve's activities and if there was an opportunity to go after him. William said that there were a few parties coming up. He felt certain that Steve would be attending at least one of them.

"Okay. Get me the details." said James.

The following week, William asked James and Thomas to meet him at his house to discuss what he had learned about the upcoming parties.

William explained that two parties were planned for the following Saturday night. One at Rudy Goosen's and another at Beth Olson's home. William obtained both addresses and said that he would tail Steve's car to see if he was attending either party. "Chances are good that Steve will be there. Some of the kids that he hangs around with have said that they are going," said William.

"Great, Tom and I will have everything ready to go. You will have to let us know when Steve leaves the party and we will head up to Santa Rosa Drive. We'll get up there and be ready to get him," said James.

Steve went to Rudy's party. He was there for over an hour. The party wasn't as much fun because Rudy's parents were at home this time. They stayed in their bedroom, but came out occasionally to check on the party. Their being at home put a damper on the party and the music wasn't loud enough for the kids to enjoy themselves.

Steve soon hooked up with a very pretty redhead named Rosemary. She was fourteen years old and a freshman at Los Gatos High. When Steve went over to sit next to her, she was nervous and excited. She had been watching him from across the room and thought that he was very good looking. The kids around Steve were enamored with him and paid attention to his conversation. They all laughed at his comments.

Steve asked Rosemary if he could get her a drink. "Okay," said Rosemary, nervously. After Steve gave Rosemary her drink, he began dominating the conversation with the kids around him. He talked about his car, house, and family vacations. Rosemary was enthralled with him and was very happy that he focused on her and not the other girls at the party.

When Steve had picked up Rosemary's punch, he had dropped a white tablet into her drink. He purposely delayed a couple of minutes, before returning to her, talking with a friend—giving the tablet time to dissolve.

Half an hour later, Steve asked Rosemary if she would like to go to another party with him. She said, "Yes, but I have to be home before twelve." She was starting to feel sleepy.

He said, "No problem. This party is kind of slow, and I know that Beth Olson's parents aren't home. It should be more fun."

As Steve drove Rosemary to the next party, she became drowsy and could barely keep her eyes open. Steve parked on a side street near Beth's home and asked Rosemary if she wanted to go into the party. She said that she wanted to close her eyes for a little bit before going in.

Steve knew that the tablet had taken effect. He decided to go into the party and leave her in the car. As he was leaving the car, Rosemary slumped down in her seat and put her head on the armrest. Steve mumbled to himself, "She'll be ready when I want her."

William followed Steve's car, staying a good distance behind him. He saw Steve go into Beth's house alone. He thought that he had seen Steve leave Rudy's party with a girl, but was too far away to be sure. When following Steve's car, he could only see Steve's head. No one else appeared to be in the car.

Steve stayed at Beth's party for a couple of hours talking with many of the partygoers and drinking beer. He also went into a bathroom several times and snorted coke with a friend.

Eight kids left the party together, but William did not see Steve. Steve had left by the back door. He was well on his way to the Santa Rosa Drive parking spot with Rosemary, when William went to the front door asking for a kid whose name he had made up. He was allowed to go into the house and walk around to see if he could find who he was looking for. He did not see Steve.

William left the house and drove to the nearest telephone booth to call James. He told James that he had not seen Steve leave the house, but thought it would be a good idea for James and Thomas to check the parking spot.

James said he would leave immediately and pickup Thomas on the way. He said, "I can't believe you lost him Bill.

We'll take care of him if that's where he has gone."

James called Thomas and said, "I'm going to pick you up in ten minutes, so get your equipment and clothes together. We might catch the little prick at the parking spot."

James parked their car in a neighborhood near a park, that was situated below a hill on Santa Rosa Drive.

They walked and jogged up the trail to the top of the hill. They had done this many times as part of their workouts and to become familiar with the area. They had no trouble moving up the trail in the dark. As they reached the top of the hill, they spotted Steve's car.

As they moved toward Steve's car, they saw Steve kneeling naked, over Rosemary. He was turning her over, positioning her to be assaulted from behind.

James moved quickly, and silently, in the dark—towards Steve. As he closed in on him, he hit him on the side of the head with a sap and grabbed him around the neck. Steve went limp from the blow to his head. Thomas went for Steve's legs and began taping them together at the ankles.

Thomas put handcuffs on Steve, as James jammed a cloth gag in his mouth. He wrapped tape around his head to secure the cloth in his mouth. Steve's body remained limp as James pulled his head and shoulders back. Thomas grabbed Steve's right thumb and cut if off at the first knuckle, removing his thumb print.

As they were dragging Steve to his car, he regained consciousness and groaned as he felt pain in his head and hand.

He began to cry.

Thomas rolled the driver's side window down and pushed

Steve's head through the opening, rolling up the window. He closed it tightly around Steve's chin.

James beat Steve's legs and the top of his feet with a sap. He was hoping to break some bones. He moved on to his shins, targeting the shin bone of each leg. James then worked on Steve's hands, breaking the bones on top of each one. Steve passed out from the pain.

James and Thomas returned to the sleeping girl. They placed her clothes over her breasts and genitals and then wrapped her in the blanket. They checked to make sure that there was no sign of them being there. They double checked to make sure they had all their equipment—including their shears, and saps.

When they were satisfied that they had accounted for everything, they left the scene. They slowly jogged down the trail to the park and the housing area. As they moved along the trail, Thomas tossed the piece of Steve's severed thumb into the brush.

They entered the park and as they approached their car, they began talking about the 49ners. They removed their black sweatshirts to reveal colored t-shirts. They put their ski masks in the pocket of their sweat pants.

As they got into their car, they looked around to see if there was anyone in sight. James drove them slowly towards downtown Los Gatos and stopped at a gas station on Los Gatos-Saratoga Road operated by a friend of theirs.

"I'll go in and talk to Virg while you make the call," said James.

Thomas went to the telephone booth and called his

brother, William. He said, "Mission accomplished. The kid is hanging out of his car window and doesn't feel too well. We wrapped the girl in a blanket. She's unconscious and doesn't know that she's been raped by that dirtbag. We were too late to stop the assault on her."

After Thomas made his call, William called the Los Gatos Police Department and told the dispatcher that a rape had occurred at the new housing development on Santa Rosa Drive. "Steve Satinborne was the bastard who raped the girl. You'll need two ambulances," said William as he hung up.

The first cop to arrive at the scene of the rape was Bert Hanson. He had been two miles away, patrolling on Kennedy Road. Hanson walked around the scene and checked to see if the body stuck in the car window was alive. He then went to the girl wrapped in the blanket to determine her condition. Hanson called the police dispatcher and asked for two ambulances and back up.

While waiting for the ambulances to arrive he helped Steve out of the car window and laid him on the ground. The officer removed the gag from Steve's mouth and the tape from around his ankles, but not quite sure what to do next, left the handcuffs on. He could see that Steve was bleeding from both hands and feet and that his shins were damaged.

Steve began whimpering and talking about two men, but he was incoherent so Hanson decided to wait until his superior arrived to assess the crime scene.

Hanson walked over to the girl and could see that she was sleeping. He decided that she would be okay until the EMTs arrived. He knew not to touch the girl. He took another look at Steve who was obviously in a lot of pain.

This type of crime was very rare in Los Gatos. Almost every cop at headquarters arrived, followed by the police captain. The officers used yellow crime scene tape to surround the area. When the two ambulances arrived, they helped the EMTs attend to the victims, and helped them place them in the ambulances. Two of the officers collected the drugs and vials of liquid from Steve's car. One put the used condoms in a plastic bag and gave it to the officer gathering evidence. "It's amazing." said the police captain. "It doesn't look like anyone was here other than these kids."

The captain decided not to interview Steve until he had been stabilized. The officers knew from their training that it was better to wait before interviewing a victim of an assault. Victims may be in shock and not capable of revealing important details.

Steve and the girl were taken to Los Gatos Hospital. Their families were contacted by the police. They were placed in different hospital wards, as far away from each other as possible. The captain suspected that Steve was responsible for the rape. He directed the hospital personnel to keep them in separate wards.

The emergency room doctor, Robert Dickson, examined Rosemary and determined that she had been raped. He observed severe bruising and bleeding. Dr. Dickson, explained the results of his examination to her parents. He said that it also appeared that she had been drugged and told them that he had ordered a blood test. It would take some time to get the results. Rosemary's parents were deeply upset over the news and very angry.

TEN
THE RECKONING

Rohypnol is a central nervous system depressant. It creates a general slowing down of brain activity. Rosemary had been suffering from chronic asthma since she was ten years old. She had significant inflammation of the airway and a sleep disorder.

She suffered seizures from the ingestion of the Rohypnol and lapsed into a coma. She had to be revived after her heart stopped. She never came out of the coma.

While being treated for his wounds, Steve Satinborne, was arrested by two Los Gatos policemen. Since he was almost 18-years old, the district attorney charged him as an adult. He was charged with rape and possession of illegal substances.

Steve's father, Ira, a prominent attorney, used all his firm's influence and resources to try and keep Steve from going to prison. The evidence against Steve was too overwhelming for him to escape jail. The judge denied bail. The illegal drugs, including Rohypnol, described as the "date rape" drug, the condom filled with Steve's semen, and the doctors' report that Rosemary had been raped, convinced the jury that Steve was responsible. He was sentenced to prison for ten years for the rape of Rosemary, and the possession of illegal drugs.

One month after Steve had been sent to prison, his older brother, Gregory, was found bound and gagged in his dorm room at Santa Clara University. He had been restrained by plastic handcuffs and there was a gag in his mouth. An anonymous tip had been called into the Santa Clara County Sheriffs' office informing them that a student had been assaulted in a dorm room at the school. The anonymous caller gave them the dorm room number.

Gregory was unconscious and had a bloody swelling on the side of his head. His left hand was wrapped in tape and was seeping blood. His hands, feet, and legs had been so severely beaten that he could not stand up or walk. Gregory couldn't identify his assailants. He said one of them had spoken to him before he was knocked out, but he could not remember what he had said.

The masked man asked him where he was getting his drugs and a frightened Gregory gave him several sources. The man had threatened that if he told anyone about their conversation, he would come back and kill him. Scared for his life, he readily gave up his sources. He feared that he might be killed if he refused to answer his assailant's questions. It occurred to Gregory that the bastard might be a drug dealer checking on his competition.

Gregory did not reveal his conversation with his assailant

to the police, out of fear for his life. He told them that when he answered his door; he was overpowered by two guys wearing masks. He was knocked unconscious and could not remember anything until he awakened and found that he was tied up and gagged. His hands and feet hurt like hell. He discovered that the tip of his thumb was missing when the emergency room doctor removed the tape on his hand. Looking at his severed thumb, he became very scared. He realized that these bastards were vicious and capable of anything. He cried when he talked to the police and said that he had no idea why someone would do this to him.

Gregory was hospitalized and his parents were extremely worried when they learned that he had received the same punishment as his brother, from these anonymous people. The parents feared that they might be next. Beverly asked Ira if they should hire protection for themselves.

One of the men that Gregory had identified to his assailants was Richard Scott Donald, his main drug supplier. Donald taught English at Los Gatos High and dealt drugs to Gregory, Steve, and other students. Donald was a short man. He was 5'5" tall, 36-years-old, with a round pixy face. He considered himself a ladies' man and had participated in many community plays. He directed two plays a year at the high school. He married one of his students after she had graduated. He spent a lot of his weekends with some of the "cool" students at school and invited some of them to his home. Considering himself smarter than most, he believed that he could have made it in films if he had had the right breaks.

As he was growing up, and later as an adult, Donald had never been comfortable with people his own age. He had always looked young for his age and preferred to be around younger people. He loved to impress the young and naïve. He had had small roles in two "B-level" movies, always playing a juvenile. He made up stories about Hollywood stars that he was acquainted with. He also performed in local plays as far north as San Francisco, but had never had a leading role.

When he hosted high school students at his home, he told stories about getting "stoned" with Hollywood stars and studio musicians. He offered his students beer, wine, and sometimes a joint. For a few students, like Gregory and Steve, he introduced them to other drugs to enjoy and purchase from him.

Donald had sources for marijuana and cocaine and also for heroin. He continued to sell drugs to several of his past students. He found a local supply for a new drug, referred to as "roofies," that Gregory had told him about when he had returned from a vacation in Germany. Gregory had told Donald about a new drug that he had been introduced to by his cousins. The street name was "roofies" and it came in tablet form. Donald learned that roofies were already popular in Hollywood and with professional musicians.

While attending Los Gatos High School, Gregory had taken Steve with him on a weekend visit to Donald's home. Steve became a drug customer of Donalds. He thought Donald was a really "cool guy" and loved spending time with him.

Steve knew about roofies from Gregory and he purchased some tablets from Donald. With instructions from his brother, he planned to try the drug on a 15-year-old girl at school. He had been seeing a girl named Penny Sharpe without her parent's knowledge. They had had sex in her bedroom when her parents were away on a vacation. While Penny's parents were still away, he tried the roofies drug on her without her knowledge.

It was an exciting and scary experience watching her under the control of the drug. She fell into a deep sleep about 30 minutes after Steve had slipped the tablet into her drink. She was sluggish and unresponsive but he went ahead and had intercourse with her. He then rolled her over for anal sex. Several hours later, she was still asleep, and he became frightened.

Panicked, Steve called his brother and asked what he should do.

"I'll be right over, give me her address."

When Gregory arrived, and looked at the sleeping girl, he said, "I think she's okay. The women we drugged and fucked in Germany fell asleep, just like her. Let's stay here until she wakes up."

The brothers spent the rest of the afternoon and evening taking turns screwing the sleeping girl. She woke up at 9:30 pm, but was still very confused and groggy. As she became aware of her surroundings, she called out to Steve who was in the living room with Gregory. They were watching TV. Steve came into the bedroom and she asked, "Who else is here?" He said, "My brother Gregory is here and we're watching TV."

She asked Steve if he was going to stay the night. He said that he could not stay because he had to go to school early in the morning. She replied, "Why don't you come back to bed with me?" They had sex, off and on, for another hour. "I'm really sore and my butt hurts. Did you screw me while I was sleeping?" asked Penny.

"Yeah, a few times. You seemed to enjoy it." He didn't say anything about his brother also having sex with her. At 11:30 pm, the brothers left the house.

On the way home, Steve remarked, "That was great. She doesn't have a clue about what went on tonight."

"Next time you have to be careful about how many tablets you put in the drink. If the girl is small, only give her half a tablet," said Gregory.

ELEVEN
WHAT GOES AROUND COMES AROUND

Richard Donald's wife, Candy, left Friday morning for the weekend, to visit her parents in Los Altos. Donald always enjoyed his time while Candy was away. He couldn't stand her parents. They thought that they were worldly and had class since her father had been a distinguished corporate lawyer in Palo Alto. They informed their close friends that their daughter had married an English schoolteacher, many years older than she. They felt that she had married beneath her.

Richard loved it when Candy was gone. He could get wasted on pot and liquor and stay that way for a day or two. He was getting tired of her. Candy didn't have any ambition and couldn't hold a conversation unless it was about clothes or cosmetics. She spent all the money her parents sent to her on herself.

He was happy to party alone and had at least two days

ahead of him. It was late and Donald was "half-in the bag" after smoking pot, snorting lines of cocaine, and sipping bourbon from a bottle.

His TV was loud, and he did not hear the two tall, muscular men, dressed in black and wearing masks, enter his living room.

He sensed that something was wrong. Before he could make a move, one of the men hit him on the side of his head with a sap and knocked him unconscious.

When he awakened, he was sitting up in a hard, straight-backed chair. He was tied up and gagged. His hands hurt like hell and his legs and feet were throbbing with pain. He was bleeding through his pant legs and his right hand was taped. One of the men turned off the TV, and the other told him that he was going to remove the gag covering his mouth. The man said that if he screamed or yelled, they would knock him out again. One of the men placed a paper bag from the kitchen over Donald's head. He spoke softly, and it helped to calm Donald.

The man said that they knew that Donald was a drug dealer, and that there were drugs and money in the house. Donald started to complain that they were hurting him and the man hit him on the knee with a sap. He screamed in pain and the gag was shoved back into his mouth.

The tallest man said, "We have plenty of time and we'll beat you to a pulp if you don't give us what we want. We want the damn drugs and the money."

When Donald nodded, indicating that he would be quiet, the man removed his gag and resumed his demand for the drugs and money.

Donald's whole body was in pain. He said, "It's in my office." His office was a converted bedroom on the first floor. They dragged him there and shoved him into a chair.

Donald said, "It's all in a compartment under my desk." He had built the compartment using wood from the shop class at school.

When the masked man opened the compartment, he found a bag of marijuana and two envelopes of cocaine. "Okay, said the tall man, where is the money? We know you have a lot of it, because you have been selling to kids for a long time."

"All my money was used to pay for the drugs that I now have," said Donald. The man slapped him in the face and said, "Look at all these books in here. If we have to go through them, we'll beat the shit out of you and cut off your dick. Now, you have ten seconds to tell us where the money is."

Donald responded, "The moneys in the large books on the two top shelves." One of the men pulled down ten large books. They had been hollowed-out and when they opened them, they found $52,000 in 100-dollar bills.

"Now, we want to know all your sources for that poison that you deal," said the tallest man. You're our Bitch now. You can keep dealing to adults. But you deal to any kids and we'll take you out. Is that clear?"

"Yes, I understand," said Donald. "I have to keep moving product or my sources will think that I am dealing with someone else, and they'll kill me."

"The names you gave us better be the right ones, or we'll be back to take care of you," said the masked man.

"They're the right ones, I promise you—especially the Whistle," said Donald.

The two masked men left as quietly as they came.

When they got back to their car and were on the road, William said to James, "What an asshole! He's been dealing for a long time and keeps over $50,000 in cash in his office."

As they were driving away, William opened the envelopes of cocaine and allowed the powder to spill out onto the road. When they reached the highway and gained speed, he opened the bag of marijuana and let the contents fly away in the wind.

"There must be more money and drugs in that house," said James. "We'll get the rest when we visit him again. We've got to get to the big money and all his drug sources. When we get to them, we'll circle back and take care of that little dirt bag."

When the two men had left Donald, they had untied his ankles and removed his handcuffs. They warned him not to move or look out of the windows for twenty minutes. He was so frightened that he shook his head and said, "I won't." Donald was able to carefully remove the taping from around his throbbing righthand and discovered that the tip of his thumb had been cut off. He began to scream and cry. "Who are these bastards?"

It was pure luck that he still had well over $50,000 hidden. The men thought that they had gotten it all.

Donald drove himself with great difficulty to the hospital emergency room. When the nurse asked him how he had lost part of his thumb, he explained that he had been working with his table saw and slipped while cutting a piece of wood.

The nurse was suspicious because he had had difficulty walking into the emergency room and his hands were very bruised, swollen and possibly broken. A doctor cleaned and bandaged his thumb. He had to set the bones in his left hand, before bandaging it. Donald said that he was in great pain and the doctor prescribed a painkiller. After taking the painkiller, he drove home slowly and went to another one of his drug stashes for cocaine and a few joints. He wanted to get stoned as soon as possible.

Steve Satinborne was serving a ten-year sentence for the rape of Rosemary Nelson.

As he was returning from the cafeteria to his prison cell, he was grabbed by two heavily tattooed members of the White Brotherhood and dragged into their cell.

As one stood watch, the other punched Steve in the face breaking his nose, then continued to punch him in the head. He was barely conscious. The large man grabbed a fistful of Steve's hair and pushed Steve's head down to his crotch, while pulling out his penis.

Get to sucking this, Bitch, the man ordered. Steve began sucking the man's penis and when the man climaxed, he turned Steve around and pulled down his pants. The large man shoved his penis into Steve's ass and began humping him. The shorter man dropped his pants and demanded that Steve suck him, while the larger man was pumping Steve from behind.

Steve realized what was happening but was too weak to resist these powerful men. He remained submissive and complied with their demands. When the larger man was finished with Steve, the other took his place and continued to rape him.

The White Brotherhood told Steve that he belonged to them now. They said that he would be visited, by other members, whenever one of them wanted his ass.

At first, Steve was afraid, but since they didn't beat him anymore, he adapted to his new role as a favorite member of the Brotherhood. After a while, he was allowed to have sex with members of his choosing.

It was Tuesday night and Ira's mistress, Donna Pearce, had made dinner for him and her two children. Ira watched TV as Donna put the children to bed. After settling the children, she joined Ira. When the late-night news finished, they went to her bedroom and made love. Ira dozed for a while after having sex and when he awakened, said that he had to go home. She begged him to stay longer, but he refused, saying that he had a long day scheduled for tomorrow.

Ira left Donna's house at 12:45 am and walked to his car. Two masked men, dressed in black, came out of the shadows. One of them hit him on the head with a sap, knocking him unconscious. He woke up in the back seat of his Lincoln Town car, tied and gagged. His legs were bound and his hands were in cuffs and taped. He was in great pain. His feet were shoeless, very painful, and he could see that he was bleeding through his socks and pants.

"We're going to remove the taping on your legs so that you can walk," said one of the men. "Don't contact the police or we'll be back to finish you off."

Ira screamed, but the gag in his mouth prevented him from

being understood. One of the masked men said, "You are a corrupt bastard who allowed your kids to harm young girls. This is a reminder to you for the rest of your life. If you don't change, we'll change you—permanently."

When the masked men left, Ira struggled to get out of his car and limped slowly back to Donna's house.

When Donna opened the door, she was shocked by Ira's appearance. He was bleeding from his hands and legs. "What happened to you?" she asked.

"Two masked men knocked me out and beat me," he said. "My hand hurts bad. Take the tape off." When Donna unwound the tape, Ira moaned in pain. She saw that the tip of his right thumb was missing. "Why did they do that to you? Should I take you to the emergency room?" she asked. "No, not right now. Please help me look at my legs and feet. They're killing me."

She helped him out of his pants and saw that his legs were bruised and there was swelling around his right knee. Both of his feet were bloody and swollen. "Why would someone hurt you, Ira?" she asked. "Look, as an attorney, I make enemies all the time. These people might be involved with them. I can't take this pain. Take me to the hospital," he whined.

The emergency room doctor bandaged Ira's hands and feet and gave him an injection for pain. He also gave him pain pills to take home. He informed Ira that it was hospital policy to report Ira's beating to the police. "That's okay. Why don't you call them down here right now? I can tell them what happened," said Ira.

Two policemen showed up to meet with Ira in the ER. He

told the police that two masked men had accosted him while he was getting into his car. He explained that they had taken his money after tying him up and beating him.

"Why did they beat you? Mr. Satinborne," asked the policeman. "If they only wanted your money, they could easily have taken it from you."

"Well, at first, I refused to give them anything and then they began beating me," said Ira. "I was afraid they would kill me, so I gave them the money that I had in the trunk of my car."

When the policemen were in their car, one of them remarked, "I don't believe this guy."

"Why?" asked the other.

"This was more than a mugging for money. This was a punishment or warning beating. You don't stick around and beat someone if all you want is the money. You don't cut off his thumb just to rob him. This was a message beating and these guys are pros."

"I think you're right," said the other policeman. "Who cares? This guy is a fucking lawyer, and he probably screwed someone over who returned the favor. I'm not interested in following up on this one, are you?"

"No, I agree. Let's just fill out the paperwork, call it a mugging, and let it go."

The next day, Ira told his wife, Beverly, that he had been mugged and beaten. He told her they had cut off the tip of his right thumb as punishment for what their sons had done to the girls.

He said he believed that she was safe from harm as they were after him and not her.

"I'm still scared. This is a nightmare. I won't be able to sleep," said Beverly.

Judge Browne left Friday afternoon to go to his small, get-away house in Santa Cruz. His house was on the beach and he went there almost every weekend during the summer to get away from the San Jose area. He had inherited the two-bedroom house from his mother when she had passed away.

It had been owned by members of his family since the early 1950s and was used as a vacation home. He spent his time reading and walking on the beach. He frequented some of the bars on the beach and picked up young men, from time to time, to spend the night with him. It was a safe place for him and he avoided talking to his neighbors in order to maintain his privacy.

It was a little after 10 pm when he returned home alone, after a walk on the beach. He had had a fish platter dinner at his favorite seafood restaurant and had consumed an entire bottle of chardonnay with his meal. When he got home, he opened the door and as he closed it; he was grabbed from behind and hit on the head, knocking him unconscious.

When he came to, he realized that he was tied up with a gag in his mouth. Two masked men were sitting on the couch watching him. He felt a lot of pain in his hands and legs. He could see blood seeping through his pants.

A masked man told him that he was going to remove the

gag and warned him not to scream or call out. He nodded in agreement, and the man removed the gag. "Why did you do this to me?" he cried.

"You've been ruling in favor of criminals and dirt bags for too long, Judge. You ruled in favor of the Satinborne boy when you knew that he was guilty as hell. We know that you and Ira go back a long way and you ruled the way that he wanted you to," said the masked man.

"No, I didn't," said Browne in a weak voice.

"Don't bullshit me Judge. We both know you're lying. We know too much about you to believe anything that you say. You put your thumb on the scale of justice and now you've lost it. Next time we'll cut off your dick and you won't be able to play with the boys on the beach," said the masked man.

The Judge looked meekly at the masked men and moaned from the pain. He decided that complaining to these people would be fruitless.

"Call your friend Ira and tell him what happened to you. You and he can match stories about your missing thumbs. You two bastards can now reminisce about how you have harmed others. You won't hear from us again unless you fuck up and rule against another innocent person," said the masked man.

They removed the cuffs on his wrists and left him to remove the ties on his legs after they were gone.

Browne was in agony. When he was finally able to drive himself to the local emergency room, he told the attendants who he was, and that he had been mugged while walking on the beach.

The emergency room doctor and nurses cleaned his

wounds and bandaged them. The doctor gave him an injection and a prescription for painkillers. He told the doctor that he would see his own physician as soon as he was able to return to San Jose.

When he returned to his beach house, he poured himself a generous glass of scotch whiskey. The pain injection had not quite worn off when he made his call to Ira.

As he was about to tell Ira about his assault, Ira interrupted him to say that he had had the same punishment imposed on him. "Someone is getting revenge on us for the judgement you rendered for Steve," said Ira.

"I know. Who do you think they are?" asked Browne.

"Well, they must somehow be connected to the girls' families."

"Steve, Gregory, and both you and I are now missing the tips of our thumbs. What is that supposed to mean?" asked Browne.

"What did those bastards say to you?"

"Well, one of them said that I had put my thumb on the scale of justice and now I have lost it."

"Did they steal anything from you?"

"Nothing, nothing at all. They didn't disturb anything in the house. They didn't demand money. I don't know how they knew where I was staying," said Browne angrily.

"It would be easy for them to follow you to Santa Cruz, because you are there most weekends. They just ambushed you. They did the same thing to me when I was at Donna's house."

"These people are scary. I wonder how many of them

there are? They moved so quickly that I didn't have a chance. Do I have to worry about them every time I make a ruling in court?"

"I wouldn't put anything past these guys. They have it out for us. We need to keep a low profile and not mention any of this to the police. I don't think that the police would be able to protect us from them. You know that the police are not fond of judges and lawyers. They might even enjoy seeing us suffer," said Ira.

Two months later, Josh Gordon, attorney for Steve Satinborne, left Mountain Charles restaurant in Los Gatos. It was 11:35 pm, as he headed to his car.

Josh had been eating and drinking for a couple of hours and visiting with two of his former high school football teammates. His car was in a dark, far corner of the parking lot. He was feeling tipsy and was wobbling along when he was hit on the head and knocked unconscious.

He woke up in the back seat of his Mercedes sedan, bound and gagged. The headlights were on and both driver and front passenger doors were open. He was bleeding heavily through his pants. He felt a lot of pain in his hands and feet and could see that he was bleeding through the tape.

A man and woman, leaving Mountain Charles, spotted a car in the parking lot with the lights on and the doors open. They went to see what was going on.

They saw Gordon, gagged, and taped up, in the back seat moaning and trying to say something. Tape was wrapped around his head several times.

The man ran back to Mountain Charles' to tell the bartender to call the police.

A policeman, on patrol nearby, arrived and once he saw Gordon's condition called for backup and an ambulance. He unwound the tape and removed the gag and handcuffs. The officer told Gordon to be calm and that an ambulance was on the way.

When Gordon arrived at the emergency room, the nurses removed the remaining tape on his hands. It was then that he discovered that the thumb on his right hand had been cut off at the first joint.

His manbun had been cut-off.

His first response was, "What the hell is this? Why would they cut me and beat me like this?"

He began to moan and yell from the pain and fear. "I haven't done anything wrong. I haven't hurt anyone," he whimpered.

When he returned home from the hospital, he called Ira and filled him in on what had happened to him.

James contacted his two brothers, William, and Thomas. He called Victor too. "Let's meet at my house," said Victor. "My wife and daughter are out of town visiting my mother-in-law. Bring your own booze and I'll barbecue some steaks."

"Well, we have accomplished what we set out to do and now it's time to move forward to bigger challenges. We really became good at using the sap and cutting off thumbs," announced James.

"I'm really going to miss preparing and attacking those

bastards. It's been the most excitement I've had since my search and destroy missions in Nam," said William.

"It's been exciting for me too. I really got pumped up going out on those missions," said Thomas.

"Well, except for revisiting the schoolteacher, we're finished with these punishment missions. We can follow up on a couple of the drug suppliers. We've got $52,000 in cash that we took from Donald to invest in a new company. We can get more from him and maybe even more from his suppliers.

"I'd call this creative financing," remarked Thomas.

James continued, "I have an idea on how we can use this cash and more in a legitimate business. I know of component brokers who turn memory chips and microprocessors into large amounts of cash. I have a good contact we can use. The Yakuza is involved in moving memory chips and other components from the back doors of Japanese manufacturers, to their network of broker distributors in Japan. The broker market is very large in Japan and even greater in the United States, with the growth and demand of emerging high-tech companies."

As they were finishing their meeting, James told the group that he was going to meet with Pete and let him know what had been done to Steve and the others.

"I'll only provide him with the results of the 'mysterious people' who exacted vengeance on those dirtbags. No names and no details. He doesn't need to know that you guys were involved."

TWELVE
TIME TO COLLECT

James walked into Pete Stoeland's office and closed the door behind him. "Pete, I want to bring you up to date on what has been done regarding Susan's assault. Let your secretary know that we can't be interrupted."

Pete called his assistant and told her not to interrupt them for any reason, until further notice.

James began, "What I'm going to tell you is confidential. After today, I will not discuss it with you or anyone else."

"Okay Jim, this discussion never happened."

"Good."

James explained, "I made connections with some people to go after the monsters who hurt Susan, including those who gave support to them. Steve and his brother were given a severe beating and were marked for the rest of their lives by losing part of their thumbs. Others, including Steve's father, his attorney, and even the Judge who ruled against Susan, were punished in the same manner.

"We could have taken their lives, and they deserved it, but it would have drawn too much attention from the police and they would have had to pursue finding out who had done the killings."

"I understand. I know that you made the right decision. Wow, they all were punished like that, how were you able to do that? That's amazing."

"As I said from the beginning Pete, this is all that you are going to learn."

"Okay, okay, I understand. This discussion never happened, but thank you, thank you."

"How is Susan doing these days?" asked James.

"She's adjusting well. She's at her new school, but you know she will have those memories for the rest of her life."

"You're right. She will never forget what she went through. I hope she'll be able to cope with it and move on with her life."

"Thank you," said Pete as James got up to leave. "You did what I could never have done. You brought some justice for Susan, even though she will never know about it. I will never forget this, Jim."

"You're welcome and remember, this discussion never happened," said James as he left the office.

The following week, James contacted William, Thomas, and Victor and scheduled a meeting at his house for Thursday night.

James had lost his wife, Georgia, five years before. Georgia had been an avid runner and often participated in local 5k running events. She trained almost every day and was out on a run when she collapsed and died.

The autopsy reported that she had died of a brain aneurism. She had recently gone through a routine physical and her doctor had said that she was in excellent physical condition.

James' family doctor told him, "If it is any consolation Jim, Georgia died quickly and with little pain."

"I hope so. I wouldn't have wanted her to suffer," said James.

Georgia's death had left James with their three young children, Elizabeth, Vincent, and Georgia. He hired a live-in au pair, Mary Matlin from Ireland, to help care for the children. She kept the children occupied and away from James when he was meeting with visitors.

James met with his guests in the study. It had a bathroom, bar, two large lounge chairs, a small conference table, and a large oak desk.

Two large TVs hung together on a wall. There were bookcases on all the walls filled with books. The room had been built with reinforced sound-proofing so that James could work late and not disturb anyone in the house. He began the meeting by outlining the next challenge.

"We're going after that school teacher, Donald, again. I believe that he keeps a lot more money in his house then what he told us.

He's been dealing drugs to kids and others for many years. I'm sure that we only got a small amount of the cash that he's hiding in his house. I also want to learn more about how he receives the drugs and who his sources are.

After we deal with him, we'll pursue his suppliers."

Richard Donald's home was just off Los Gatos-Saratoga, road. There was a narrow driveway that opened to a clearing where the house was located. It was hidden from view by trees and foliage.

Richard and his pregnant wife, Candy, were returning from her doctor's appointment. They pulled up to the front of the house.

Just as Richard opened his door, a masked man appeared. Another masked man appeared on his wife's side of the car. Both men were holding handguns. The masked man closest to Richard ordered him out of the car and the other motioned to Richard's wife to follow him.

A third masked man came from the side of the house and joined the man escorting Richard.

The masked man guiding Candy took her to an upstairs bedroom and tied her wrists with plastic ties. He told her that if she was quiet that no harm would come to her. He said that they were going to talk to Richard and that they didn't intend to harm him. "I won't gag you, if you stay silent," he said. She nodded affirmatively and sat on the edge of the bed, frightened and quietly crying.

The two masked men escorted Richard into the living room, sat him down on a couch, and tied his wrists with plastic ties.

The tallest masked man began, "Okay, Richard. We are not here to hurt you, but we will if you don't cooperate. We want the rest of the money that you have stashed inside, or maybe outside, the house. We're only going to ask once, and if you don't comply, we'll hurt you far more than when we took your thumb. Is that clear?"

"You got all of my cash last time," said Donald.

The masked man punched Richard in the face, breaking his nose. Blood splattered all over the sofa.

"I told you we would only ask once, Richard. Do you want us to gag you and remove the rest of your fingers?" asked the masked man.

"No," cried Richard. He was sobbing from the pain, and in fear of more punishment. "I have a safe in my bedroom," he said.

"Let's go get it. We don't have much time."

When Donald opened his safe, one of the masked men removed bags of money and drugs. The small bags were filled with cocaine. The larger bags contained the money. He put the bags in separate backpacks.

The tallest man sat with Donald on the edge of the bed. He said, "We have one more thing that we want from you. Give us the names and locations of your drug suppliers. We'll keep the information confidential, but if you alert them, we'll return and kill you."

Donald gave them two names and their locations.

The two men bound and gagged Donald, tying him to the headboard of the bed.

"We'll let your wife know where you are and tell her that she can come and get you after we leave," said the masked man.

Donald nodded his head and began to cry.

The masked man, guarding Candy, told her to wait twenty minutes before leaving the room. He explained that her husband was fine, and that he was tied up in their bedroom.

Two of the men walked through the house, disabling all of the house phones. The three men calmly walked out the front door. Two of the men were wearing backpacks, and they walked into the forest behind the house. The men removed their masks as they walked through the trees. They were at their car within five minutes of leaving the house. They didn't speak until their car was traveling on a back road to downtown Los Gatos.

"Wow, there's a lot of cocaine in these bags," said William.

"As we ride along, open them up and dump them out the window," said James.

As the car traveled down the road, William held the open bags of cocaine out of his window, allowing the wind to blow the powder away.

"How much money is there?" asked Thomas.

"A lot, but we'll have to do an accurate count when we get back to the house. I know it's a lot more than what we got the first time," said William.

"Great," said James

When they returned to James' house, he put the cash in the gun-safe in his study.

"Tomorrow's Saturday. Let's meet here for lunch and we can count the money and determine our next step. I'll ask Victor to come over," said James. The other two nodded in agreement.

THIRTEEN
CONNECTED TO THE CARTELS

They met in James' study the next day and counted the money.

"Wow, we have two hundred and eighty-five thousand. With the fifty thousand from before, we have over three hundred thousand, tax free, to invest," said William.

"You're right, and we can get even more from his suppliers. Victor, one of the names Richard Donald gave me is Bruce Whistleman. They call him 'The Whistle.' Can you run a check on him?" asked James.

"Sure, give me the spelling of his name."

Bruce Whistleman, was a graduate of Los Gatos High School and had been one of Richard Donald's English students. He was an avid reader of mostly mystery novels. It was common for him to complete reading four novels a month.

Bruce had been a very quiet student and had not participated in any school activities. He had, with one exception, not dated any girls in school. He had been asked by a girl, in his senior year, to escort her to a Sadie Hawkins dance. The custom of the Sadie Hawkins dance was for a girl to ask a boy to be her date.

Bruce's father was a mail-carrier and his mother worked in the high school cafeteria. He was not close to his father who watched television every evening and played golf on Saturdays. His mother was not well educated and spent her evenings knitting and watching TV with his father. His parents enjoyed watching game shows and the Lawrence Welk Show.

In his sophomore year, Bruce experienced smoking marijuana and was soon hooked on the drug. It made him feel good. He got his drug supply from a senior at school and then began selling the drugs to kids in his own class. The senior student became his regular supplier.

After graduation, Bruce went to work at the Los Gatos Market grocery store. He worked as a butcher's helper and enrolled at San Jose State to study English and creative writing. Prior to his junior year in college, he was drafted. He did not bother to pursue a waiver for the draft, as his grades were not that good and he was bored with school.

Bruce was sent to Ft. Lewis, Washington for basic training and then to Fort Ord for advanced training. After training, he was assigned to a company at Ft. Ord as a supply clerk.

While stationed at Fort Ord, he was within driving distance to his parents' home in Los Gatos and was able to go home twice a month to visit with them. On one of his visits home, he met up with his former high school drug supplier who was enrolled at San Jose State. He was busy supplying college students with marijuana at a more advanced level than during his high school days.

Bruce and his supplier soon agreed to work together. It allowed Bruce to resume operating as a distributor for the supplier and to focus on selling drugs to the large population of troops at Ft. Ord.

Bruce became one of the largest marijuana dealers in northern California. He conducted his drug business out of his quarters at Ft. Ord. His customers were troops who were permanently stationed at Ft. Ord and the hundreds of troops that passed through on their way to Vietnam or other locations around the World.

He also had a large civilian customer base and made his drug suppliers and himself very wealthy. By the end of his military service, he was rich and had begun to add other popular drugs to his offerings. The new drugs brought him more profit than his marijuana sales.

Victor handed James a police report on Bruce Whistleman. It did not provide much detail. Victor explained that Whistleman was on their police watch list, but they had very little information on him or how he was connected to the drug world. He had never been arrested. However, a few small-time junkies had referred to him.

"He's kind of a legend in their world. He has a home in the Monte Sereno area and there is no way that he could afford to live there without a significant income," said Victor.

As Bruce finished watching his favorite TV program, Jeopardy, three men wearing masks and dark clothes walked into his living room. One of the men said, "Hello Bruce."

"I figured that you might get around to me. Look, I don't want to be tortured or beaten up—or lose a thumb. I'll give you what you came for, okay?" asked Bruce.

"How do you know about us Bruce?" asked one of the intruders. "Look, my customers always know what is happening, and I listen to their stories. You guys are getting to be well known."

"Well, you're right. We are here for your money and drugs. Let's make it quick and easy and we won't hurt you," said the tall masked man.

"I have a safe in my bedroom," said Bruce.

"Okay, let's take a look," said the tall man.

Bruce sat on a couch in his bedroom talking with one of the masked men as the other two went through his safe.

"You have just under two hundred thousand here, as well as these bags of cocaine," said one of the men counting the money. "Is this all of it?" he asked.

"Where is the real money stash Bruce? I'll only ask you once," said the masked man sitting nearest to him.

"I have another safe in my office. It's under the desk. You'll find another one hundred thousand there," said Bruce.

Bruce opened the floor-safe in his office and they pulled out a huge stash of money.

"Now you're talking Bruce. Where is the rest of it?" asked the tall man.

"That's it," said Bruce. "Please don't hurt me. I know I can start up again, but I swear, I'm getting out of town."

"What about this house?" asked one of the masked men.

"I lease it from a guy in Saratoga and I pay him in cash every month. He's making a killing with the monthly cash that he doesn't report. I prefer the arrangement, because all I generate is cash," explained Bruce.

"Okay Bruce, we are leaving now, but first we are going to tie you up. We know about your girlfriend, Emily, and we'll put you on the phone with her as we leave. She can come over and untie you," said the tall man.

Emily was a single mom and a daytime waitress at Sambo's restaurant in Los Gatos. Bruce frequented Sambos for breakfast and he and Emily began a friendship. He hired her to clean his house once a week. The relationship eventually became intimate and she would visit his home on Thursday nights to make dinner for him and have sex. He gave her two hundred dollars a week for cleaning, but he was only interested in the weekly sex. The two hundred dollars a week for sex was more than Emily brought home as a waitress.

"Thank you for not hurting me," said Bruce.

"By the way Bruce, it was Richard Donald who gave us your name and address, as well as others that supply him with drugs," said the masked man as he was leaving.

"That fucking little asshole. I knew he'd burn me. I should have cut ties with him long ago."

As they drove away from Bruce's house, James told William to dump the contents of the cocaine bags out of the car window.

When the three met Victor at James' house they went to the study to count the money.

"I can't believe it. Bruce was telling the truth. We have a

total of a little over three hundred thousand in this haul," said William.

"Jim, you know that you signed that schoolteachers' death warrant when you told Whistleman that Donald was the snitch," said Victor.

"Of course, let them do their own house-cleaning. Every one of the scumbags we're able to eliminate, saves children's lives somewhere," said James.

FOURTEEN
THE ASSASSINATION OF RICHARD DONALD

Richard Donald was taking his pregnant wife, Candy to her doctor's appointment on Main Street in Los Gatos. He stopped behind a car at the stoplight on North Santa Cruz Ave and Main.

A man on a Honda XL250 motorbike, dressed in a black shirt and pants, a black baseball cap, jacket, and sunglasses, pulled up next to the driver's side of Donald's car.

Donald's window was down. The bike rider pulled out a handgun with a silencer from his jacket and shot him twice in the head. He returned the gun to his jacket and took off through the stoplight, heading south towards the Highway 17 on-ramp. He soon disappeared down the highway.

Donald slumped down sideways in his seat, with his head landing on his wife's stomach. Her left arm and clothes were soon bathed in blood and particles from his brain were stuck to her face. Candy began screaming hysterically as she struggled to open her door. The car lurched forward, bumping into the car in front of it.

The bike rider rode his Honda south towards Santa Cruz. Sixteen miles out of Los Gatos, he took the Scott's Valley off-ramp. He pulled up next to a blue pickup truck that was parked behind a hardware store. He quickly pulled down a ramp from the bed of the pickup and pushed his motorcycle up and into the bed of the truck. He laid the bike down on its side and covered it with a tarp.

John Boothe stripped off his jacket, hat, and pants to reveal a t-shirt and shorts. He removed his boots and put on white tennis shoes with no socks. He drove his pickup to a nearby McDonald's and purchased a Big Mac, fries, and a coke. While eating his meal in the cab of his truck, he looked around to see if there were any cop cars. He saw none. He didn't hear police sirens either.

When he finished his meal, he went back into McDonalds to use the restroom. As he entered the restroom, he looked in the mirror. He silently mouthed the word "fourteenth," It was his fourteenth contract killing.

"Not bad at $10,000 a hit," he said to himself.

He kept his "hit money" in safety deposit boxes in different banks, in Long Beach. He did not spend any of it. He lived off his bartender salary and tips. His goal was to be a millionaire by the time he turned forty. He planned to up the price of his "killings" the next time an order came down for a hit.

John Wallis Boothe was 28-years-old, 5'9" tall, and 150lbs.

He had a lean, muscular build. He was very tan with long blonde hair and could easily have been mistaken for a surfer. He was very strong from racing motorbikes in competition over the past six years. He worked as a bartender in a nightclub in Long Beach five nights a week.

Boothe did not drink alcohol or use drugs. He kept himself in peak physical condition in order to be able to race competitively at a high level and win.

He was handsome and attracted young women at the race tracks. He preferred women from 18 to 22-years-old. The dumber they were the better, as long as they were good looking and liked to screw. He told women, early on, that he was not interested in getting married or having a committed relationship. If they were to get pregnant, they were on their own and he would be gone. Many women were drawn to him because he treated them roughly.

He despised the regular customers that frequented his bar. He listened to their crappy stories and complaints and nodded and smiled at them. He thought that the Harley riders who came to drink and bullshit were a joke. Most of them were fat and out of shape. They could never have ridden a bike as well as he did.

The bar customers were fond of Boothe and they knew of his racing prowess. They always tipped him generously. The bartending job was convenient for him. His hours were flexible, and he could continue his racing. He had freedom to perform his "execution" contracts.

Boothe was a Vietnam combat veteran. He had been recruited for his first hit job by a former regular customer of the bar, Paul Dorian. Dorian owned a machine shop and had recently been killed in an auto accident. Dorian had made a silencer in his shop to fit Boothe's pistol.

Most of Boothe's contract hits were in Los Angeles, but he had received his last job from an LA drug kingpin. The hit was a favor for a drug dealer in Northern California. He didn't care as long as the money was good. When he received the assignment, he purchased maps of Los Gatos and the surrounding area. It was part of his pre-planning discipline. He had to familiarize himself with the neighborhoods and possible escape routes, before he executed the job.

His reputation was legendary, and he was very respected in the underworld. He was an assassin who performed clean jobs that were not traceable to the customers ordering the killings.

Boothe called Bruce Whistleman, per the instructions he was given, from a pay phone near McDonalds. When Bruce answered his phone, Boothe said "It's done," and hung up.

He then proceeded to get into his truck. He dialed in his favorite country music station and drove carefully, within the speed limit. He had 315 miles ahead of him to get back to Long Beach.

FIFTEEN
ESCAPE AND A NEW IDENTITY

Bruce Whistleman knew that his time was limited. He had to get out of town as soon as possible. Scott Donald's naming him as a drug source put him in great danger with his drug suppliers and the cartels. He had maintained three cash stashes in his house. Two of them had been cleaned out by the robbers, but he had one more stash hidden behind wine racks in his wine cellar. It had close to two hundred thousand in cash. He thought it was enough money to make his escape to Mexico.

Over the last five years, Bruce had been creating a new identity for himself in Cabo San Lucas, Mexico. Cabo San Lucas is a popular vacation destination for foreign tourists. It has numerous resorts and hotel timeshares along the coast between Cabo San Lucas and San Jose Cabo.

Bruce adopted the name of his favorite high school teacher, Stephen Riddley. He had hired a local source to create new documents for his new identity. It had only cost him $2,000 to acquire a new identity with all the necessary documentation.

Riddley had been the only one of his schoolteachers who had shown a genuine interest in Bruce. Bruce had told him that he wanted to be a novelist and Riddley encouraged him to pursue his dream.

Under his new name he had purchased two fishing boats in Cabo and had hired a local American expatriate, John Summers, to manage his fishing business. They catered to avid fishermen from the U.S. and would take tourists out on fishing trips for up to two weeks at a time.

He purchased a newly built home in San Jose del Cabo, about 20 miles northeast of Cabo San Lucas. He hired a live-in, young Mexican woman, Lupita Cortez, to be his house-keeper. She soon became his mistress.

Lupita was nineteen and was working as a maid in a local hotel when she met Bruce. She was overjoyed to meet a kind American and was excited to have the opportunity to begin a relationship with him. He was sweet and generous to her. She had two brothers and four sisters. Her father had died when she was thirteen. Her mother owned a small jewelry shop in the town plaza and sold trinkets to tourists. Lupita only knew Bruce as Stephen Riddley. She liked to call him Stevie after they had become intimate. She couldn't pronounce his last name, Riddley.

Bruce made a clean get-away from Los Gatos, his family, and acquaintances. He arrived two days later at his home in San Jose Cabo as Stephen Riddley. It felt great to get away from his former life and he was ready to start a new life as a struggling novelist and legitimate businessman.

Steve loved sitting on his patio every evening as the sun set, listening to the ocean sounds, drinking margaritas, and smoking Cuban cigars. Lupita would be singing to herself in the kitchen as she made the evening meal that sent fantastic aromas throughout the house.

Three months after leaving Los Gatos, and establishing his new identity in San Jose del Cabo, Stephen Riddley and his mistress, Lupita, were found dead in their home by two women who had been hired to clean their house.

Riddley had been decapitated and his head had been placed on the coffee table, in the living room, with a $100 bill stuck in his mouth. The rest of his body was found in his bedroom. Lupita was found lying on the kitchen floor, shot three times in the head and chest.

Riddley's fishing business manager, John Summers, was found dead in his office on the wharf, by three customers from Arizona seeking to charter a fishing boat. He had deep cuts to his body, neck, and face. The Mexican police determined that he had been attacked by someone wielding a machete.

Arturo Hernandez, a high-ranking member of the Romero Drug Cartel, had ordered the killings on behalf of the Cartel. Hernandez managed cartel activities, and was responsible for the entire Baja Peninsula, from Mexicali, Baja, California in the north to Cabo San Lucas, Baja California Sur in the south.

Hernandez knew every move that Bruce had made in the last five years, including requesting the killing of Richard Scott Donald. He knew about Bruce's name change and the purchase of the new house in San Jose del Cabo.

When Bruce made his escape to San Jose del Cabo, and

abandoned his drug operation in Los Gatos, Hernandez was alerted. Bruce's escape was an embarrassment to Hernandez, and he feared that his own life was in jeopardy from his superiors in the Cartel. If he did not take immediate action against Bruce, the Cartel might think that he had been colluding with him.

Hernandez had remarked to his driver, "Those dumb fucking "wedos" don't understand. When you do business with us, it's forever. You can't quit us unless you die." Hernandez had his assistant take pictures of the dead bodies, including the decapitated head. He sent the pictures to his superiors in the Cartel. He also had pictures of the bodies and the severed head sent to local newspapers to be printed and circulated.

BOOK TWO

"If someone is coming to kill you,
rise against him and kill him first.
However, it should never be done
with glee."

~Hebrew Talmud

SIXTEEN
PARTNERING

Eddie Williams had a lucrative dental practice in Los Gatos. He was an Army veteran, but had not served in combat. James Greaney and Eddie had been friends since high school and Eddie was also a member of the American Junto.

James and many of his family members and friends were patients in Eddies' practice.

James was in the dental office to have a crown replaced. Eddie, always a friendly and talkative guy, had a habit of asking his patients' questions when they had dental equipment in their mouths. They were only able to grunt their responses to his questions.

Almost every time James had dental work done, Eddie reminded him of a particular basketball game that they had played in high school. During the game, James and an opponent were wrestling for the ball while they were lying on the floor. James managed to get control of the ball, but instead of passing it to a teammate, he attempted a shot while sitting on the floor—the ball, miraculously went into the basket.

Eddie liked to bring up the game, and James' lucky shot. On this occasion, Eddie asked James why he had not passed the ball to a teammate instead of shooting it himself.

James replied, "Ed, I never wanted to bring it up and hurt your feelings, but now you've asked. When I gained control of the ball, I saw you and McArthur extending your hands towards me, expecting me to throw you the ball. I quickly concluded the two of you were lousy shooters, so I took the shot from the floor. Fortunately, it went in."

"Jim, do you realize that I still have this drill in my hand, and I know that you hate pain—it does explain though, why you had the nickname, "Gunner.""

After Eddie finished the crown procedure and James was preparing to leave, James asked if Sal Cuffaro was a patient of his. James already knew that Cuffaro was a patient, but he wanted to hear it from Eddie.

Salvatore Cuffaro had attended Los Gatos High School at the same time as James and Eddie. James did not know him personally but was aware that Cuffaro's family was involved in organized crime. When they were freshmen in high school, Cuffaro's father had been featured in a magazine article. It stated that he was on the FBI's most wanted list and had ties to the Mafia in Italy and New York City.

"Yeah, he and some of his family members are clients of mine," said Eddie.

"Would you feel comfortable introducing us? I would like to meet with him to discuss real estate opportunities."

"Really? You wouldn't have any other interest in meeting

with him, would you? You know Jim, there are rumors out there about Sal inheriting his father's businesses, and they probably aren't legal operations."

"I know, I've heard those rumors. I'm just interested in real estate sales, and I believe that he has a lot of money to invest."

"Okay. I'll reach out to him for you. Sal and I always joke about Los Gatos and people that we knew in school. He's a friendly guy. I'll ask him if it would be okay for me to give you his contact information."

"Thanks Ed, I really appreciate it. Until next time—when you'll have another opportunity to torture me. Have a good day."

Two weeks later, James received a call from Eddie. "I talked to Sal, and he has agreed to a meeting. He said he wasn't interested in real estate property, at this time, but he remembers you from high school and he is willing to talk. Here's his personal number."

"Thanks Ed, I appreciate it. I'll keep you informed."

"If it's more than real estate business, I don't think I want to be informed," laughed Eddie as they hung up.

James' real purpose in meeting with Sal Cuffaro was to see if Cuffaro had an interest in partnering with him in the financing for purchases of huge quantities of allocated electronic components. These components were a critical part of a workstation or computer. No machines could ship without them. Many companies in Silicon Valley and other locations in the country were experiencing a work stoppage. Their assembly lines were down, because they lacked the critical components. The companies were experiencing huge losses, and some even had to lay off workers. James had a unique opportunity to buy memory and microprocessors, directly from Japan—by way of the Yakuza. The purchases would only be worthwhile if they could be made on a large scale, and therefore he needed a lot of cash to complete the transactions. He suspected that Salvatore Cuffaro had access to a lot of money that he might want to launder—in a legitimate business project.

The transactions would all be clean and legal, and an opportunity that Sal might want to take advantage of.

Sal and James met for lunch in Los Gatos. After discussing James' proposal, they decided to sign a Joint Venture Agreement to protect their partnership and investment.

James told Sal that he would send his attorney to Sal's office with the Joint Venture Agreement papers.

Don Ferreira showed up on time for his 1 pm appointment with Sal. The receptionist notified Sal that Don was waiting in the reception area. Don was just under 6' tall, had a burly build, and had been a successful baseball pitcher in college. He had a friendly face and was always smiling. He liked to tell jokes to break the ice, when meeting new people.

It was half an hour before the receptionist escorted Don into Sal's office.

Sal's office was dark with sparse lighting. Sal was sitting behind his desk smoking a cigar and drinking a glass of whiskey. The smoke from the cigar was so thick that Don had difficulty seeing Sal clearly.

Don sat in a chair across from Sal. To Don's right sat a menacing-looking man with large arms, who stared at Don with lizard-like eyes.

Don was immediately very uncomfortable and began to wonder why he had agreed to this meeting.

"Is this a good business deal?" asked Sal. "Am I going to make some money with you guys?"

"I don't know, sir," Don replied weakly. "I'm just an attorney. I don't know the business end."

"How long have you known, Greaney?"

"Since high school. I graduated with his brother Bill."

"Well, I'm trusting you guys that this is gonna be a successful deal. You know I don't like to lose, Mr. Don."

"It's Don Ferreira, sir," Don corrected.

"Ferreira? Are you Italian?"

"No sir, I'm Portuguese."

"Huh. Portegee, huh? You're one of our weak cousins. Well, you look like you eat like an Italian," laughed Sal.

An hour later, Don burst into James' office and said, "Whoa. I'm not going back there again."

"Did he sign the agreement?"

"Yea, he signed the agreement, but I was scared shitless during the entire meeting."

"What was the problem, Donny?"

"Don't Donny me. You're partnering with a couple of homicidal cretins. Tony, 'what's his name' sat to my right and stared at me. I swear he didn't blink during the entire meeting."

"Why didn't you loosen things up with one of your jokes,

Donny?" asked James—laughing.

"One of my jokes? I could tell by looking at their faces that they haven't cracked a smile in decades. I just wanted to get out of there."

"Did you learn about any of their businesses? I heard that they own some construction companies."

"Construction? I'll bet they're into making tombstones and cement shoes."

James and Sal worked together for the next eleven months, completing millions of dollars in sales transactions of memory and microprocessors. Sal was very pleased with the arrangement and was disappointed to learn from James, that most of the chip allocations had run out. The manufacturers had plenty of inventory to sell in the marketplace.

James and Sal met in Los Gatos, at a coffee shop, near the high school. "Well Sal, it was a great run while it lasted, wasn't it?"

"You're right. I've never made so much money with so little effort."

"It'll come around again. It usually happens about every 18 months, depending on the device. We'll have another opportunity, and we might make even more money than we made this time. We now have the supply chain under our control."

"Thanks again for the opportunity. It was great doing business with ya."

As he was getting ready to leave, Sal sat back down and said, "I do have a favor to ask ya."

"Sure, what is it?"

"I have a cousin, Ann, who will be needing a job. She and her husband are leaving the military and they want to settle here. Since you know Silicon Valley, I thought you'd be the perfect person to help her find a job."

"I'd be more than happy to accommodate her, especially since she is a veteran. Do you know anything about her military training?"

"All I know is that she and her husband were both Army officers. I think that she was in the military police. I have to tell you that she's not a normal woman. She was tough on me and my brothers when we were growing up. She used to kick our asses. My father and uncle wouldn't let us fight back and she made our lives miserable."

"Are you sure you want to help her?"

"Yeah, she was my fathers' favorite. He always said that if she had been a boy, she would've been Governor. When all is said and done, she's really a good person. Just don't cross her. She would help anybody, if they needed it tho. She might be a little crazy, and she's not afraid of anyone."

"Now I'm intrigued. I'd like to meet with her, and her husband. She might be a good candidate for my organization. I'm always looking for new talent who will carry on our business operations when I want to slow down. What about her husband? What do you know about him?"

"I don't know much. I only met him once. He stays in her shadow. I think that he tries to avoid all the drama that she generates."

"Send me their contact information and I'll give them a call. You can also take my business card and tell them that they're welcome to give me a call."

"Thank you, Jim. Until next time—when we'll make even more easy money together," said Sal as he was leaving.

William, Thomas, and Victor met in James' study to discuss how to handle the large amount of cash that they had taken from the drug dealers while avoiding scrutiny from law enforcement agencies.

James began by asking, "Do any of you need any of this money for personal needs?" They all said, no.

"Great, I believe that we can put this cash to work for us and create tremendous gain. We must keep this money and future money, confidential, from members of our families, including your wives. Do any of you have a problem with that?" asked James. They all shook their heads, no.

"I've been doing very well with my real estate investments. I have targeted homes to acquire near the growth areas of the Silicon Valley companies. I've founded a construction company that will be managed by Mike Fowler. We're going to be renovating old buildings for corporate expansion. We'll also be constructing new buildings and leasing them to companies that need additional space to accommodate their future growth," said James.

James continued, "I've also been involved in buying and selling computer chips that are on allocation. I'm selling them to start-up companies that aren't on the allocated list of the memory manufacturers. This is what they call, the broker market. It's extremely lucrative if you can obtain a quality supply of chips. I've been introduced to top-level members of the

Yakuza in Japan. They've been supplying me directly from the Japanese manufacturers. The Yakuza take their cut and then they provide me with a steady supply for the companies I'm selling to in the U.S. Many of them are the new tech start-ups. I've been able to leverage the sale of these chips for company stock options. My terms are cash only—and the cash flow is huge. The money is clean and I only report what I feel is necessary. I let my accountant have the final say on the reporting of the transactions.

"Amazing, how long have you been doing this?" asked William.

"Over two years now," said James.

"Can we get in on any of that action, using the new cash?" asked Victor.

"Not until the next shortage of components. Maybe in a year and a half from now. I've got some ideas as to how we can maximize the use of the new cash in different projects for significant returns. We need to set up a new company in Las Vegas. The ownership will include all of us. We'll invest the new cash from there," said James.

"Why Las Vegas?" asked Thomas.

"Favorable tax laws. It's the center of the gambling world and cash transactions. It's also the best location to put our millions into play without the scrutiny from the taxman," explained James.

"Okay, I'm in. Let's do it," said William.

"I'd like to know more about your relationship with the Yakuza. They are Japan's mafia and I hear that the Italian mafia are choirboys compared to them. Why would they want to do business with you, Jim?", asked Victor.

James responded, "The Yakuza are looking for a foothold in the U.S. Japanese companies are aggressively investing in the U.S. Many wealthy Japanese are buying up real estate and sending their children to universities here. I've been leasing homes to a few Japanese company executives in Palo Alto, Los Altos, and Cupertino. Some of the major companies buy the executive homes from me. The Yakuza are aware of my business dealings with the Japanese companies and the wealthy families. They want me to partner with them on investments in the U.S.

"You've got to be careful, Jim. How can you trust that they won't turn on you?" asked Victor.

"My relationship is with the very top members in Japan who have long-term plans for investment. They want to penetrate the U.S. real estate market and want our assistance to do so. They won't allow their underlings to mess with me," explained James.

James continued, "I want to discuss the other members of the Junto. There will never be a reason to let them know about our adventures with the drug dealers, and our involvement in meting out punishment. We can take advantage of some of their expertise in the business world without them knowing about our separate business. Steve and John are involved in my broker business. Pete's my accountant. Rudy, Steve, and Carolyn Speer are working with me in generating seed-money for start-ups."

"Who is Carolyn?" asked Victor.

"She graduated from high school with me and we dated a

few times. She's a very successful, smart stockbroker. She will be an excellent partner for us and she will only be involved in our stock investments," said James.

Carolyn Bailey Speer had been a high school classmate of James. They dated a few times and became very good friends. She was a tall, pretty blonde, and an excellent swimmer. She swam competitively in college.

After college she married Al Speer, a journeyman carpenter, and they had two daughters. Carolyn graduated from the University of Santa Barbara with a major in economics. She chose to apply for an entry-level job at a local brokerage firm.

Carolyn and James had met again at one of their high school reunions in Los Gatos. Carolyn was divorced by then and James was a widower.

James' businesses were growing and expanding and Carolyn had made significant inroads as a stockbroker. She was developing a large clientele, but as a woman, she was not doing as well as her male counterparts.

While she was in town for the reunion, she and James spent time together, catching up on their lives.

They soon became friends with benefits. After learning about her investment expertise, James asked Carolyn to manage his corporate accounts and investments. He told her that he wanted someone he could trust. He explained that he had no intention of remarrying and she responded that her divorce had been a painful and frustrating experience. She wasn't looking for marriage again either.

He introduced her to his chief accountant, Pete, and

instructed him to send her one hundred thousand dollars as a starting point for investing. Pete remembered Carolyn from high school, but had not known her.

After six months, the one hundred thousand that James had sent to Carolyn, had increased in value by almost 20%. Carolyn contacted James about an idea that she had for starting a hedge fund. They met at the Hacienda Hotel in Los Gatos to discuss her proposal.

Carolyn began by saying, "I'm never going to get a fair shot working at this brokerage firm. It's an all-men's club, and I have to fight for support for my clients. I'd like to make a proposal to you that you might think is out of the box, but I think you'll like it."

She went on to review the history of Hedge Funds. She went into detail about how they could start one together, avoiding failure, with a disciplined organization. She wanted to own part of it and also manage it. She suggested that James be a silent, majority partner and share the growth and profits with her. He wouldn't have to be involved on a daily basis and she would keep him informed about all transactions. She would contact him directly, but only about significant issues.

She went on to explain that the history of Hedge Funds began in the 1960s and 70s. She spoke in detail about the double-digit performance of Julian Robertson's Tiger Fund. Investors were flocking to an industry that now offered thousands of funds and an ever-increasing array of exotic strategies. They included currency trading and derivatives such as futures and options. Hedge Funds are typically private investment limited partnerships. They are open to a limited number of accredited investors. They are more expensive than conventional investment instruments since they have a 'Two and Twenty' Fee structure. They charge two percent for asset management and take 20% of overall profits as fees.

"I like it, Carolyn. We'll invest in the fund from Las Vegas. I have partners with money who will also be investing, but you will not need to know who they are. You'll work directly with me. I'm setting up the LLC in Las Vegas and we'll use it as one of the vehicles to invest in your program. You'll be able to make decisions on all transactions and can keep me updated on a monthly basis."

SEVENTEEN
AN EPIPHANY

James was meeting with his brothers William and Thomas, and his childhood friend Victor Lewis. He announced that he had reached a new perspective as to how they should punish drug traffickers, gang members, corrupt politicians and other criminals who were poisoning young Americans with illegal drugs and denying the poor, the weak, and the disadvantaged their liberty and freedom.

"We're going to follow some of the practices of the Viet Cong that I learned in Vietnam. As the leader of an advisor team to the Popular Forces in Vietnam, I had to figure out, in my area of responsibility, how to counteract the successes of the Viet Cong against the South Vietnamese military."

The Viet Cong was an armed Communist organization in South Vietnam, Laos, and Cambodia. It fought under the direction of North Vietnam. Its formal name was the National Liberation Front of Vietnam. American soldiers nicknamed them "Charlie."

James continued, "The Viet Cong operated as a "shadow government" in South Vietnam. Every hamlet and village in the south had two governments competing for the peoples' support. The South Vietnamese government elected official had a Communist counterpart who acted in secret at night or in the shadow hours of the day. The Communists would enter a village at night and provide the people with presents. They would lecture the people about the evils of capitalism and the Americans occupying their country. They would promise the people that they would redistribute the land to every villager when they came to power. The Communists would not steal from or harm the people. They would find out who were the government sympathizers in the village, and they would assassinate them. The Communists were able to take complete control of a village by only eliminating two or three village leaders. The Viet Cong were very successful in eliminating thousands of village and hamlet leaders. It allowed them to take over significant territories in each province. Their efforts exhausted the capabilities of the South Vietnamese military. Many South Vietnamese units were afraid to go into some provinces if they knew that they were controlled by the Viet Cong."

"Are you suggesting that we operate like the Viet Cong?" asked Thomas.

"Yes, I've decided that instead of injuring these scumbags that we've been pursuing, we should eliminate them. I know that's contrary to what I've been telling you, but everything has gotten out of hand. The police can't keep up with the criminals, and the court system is full of corrupt judges who won't support the police or enforce the law. Most politicians, today, are more interested in increasing their power and personal wealth than they are in the well-being of the people that they are supposed to be representing. If you take a good look at organizations in America today, you'll realize that every corporation, union, political district, and even street gang are controlled by less than five individuals. If we take out one or two of those individuals, we will cripple the organization and its purpose," said James.

"That's quite a different approach, Jim. Are you sure you want to commit to that? We're all going to have to be in agreement in order to go to that level," said Victor.

"You're quite right, Vic. At least when we served in Vietnam, we were killing enemy soldiers who were doing their best to kill us. They were also fighting for their own country and their way of life. Now these drug dealers along with corrupt politicians are killing the American people for personal profit. They couldn't care less about how many people they're destroying or whether their victims are babies or young children. On top of it all, those in political power are doing nothing about it. Whenever there is a one-party rule in a state, city or local government, over a long period of time—there will be political corruption at the expense of the people. In some cities, corrupt politicians have withdrawn their support for the police forces, and they've prevented them from protecting the people. Too many are doing drugs themselves, so how can you expect them to support law enforcement?"

"There are only four of us. What do you think we can do

about it? How effective do you think we can be, Jim?" asked William.

"Well, as a team, we can be very effective. You know from your own experience that well-trained soldiers, in small units, can defeat enemy forces many times their size. We belong to a special class of men, due to our war experiences. We are of the Warrior class. In my opinion, you can only be considered a Warrior if you have been in combat. All others have just served in the military. We have stayed in good physical condition. We can use our training and background to develop plans and operations to eliminate a lot of scumbags. It's clear to me that local governments are no longer up to enforcing the laws and protecting the public. In the future, we'll add others to our team who have similar backgrounds and share our beliefs," said James.

"I like the concept you're proposing. It's been difficult for me to adjust to civilian life, and I'm not adjusting any better working as a cop. The police have been inhibited by weak politicians and judges from pursuing criminals who are easily identified. It's extremely frustrating," said Victor.

"The cops are experiencing the same frustration that I experienced in Vietnam. My battalion would take over territory from the enemy and then, in a few hours, be ordered to retreat back to our starting position. A week later, we would be given the mission to take the same territory that we had given up. It was crazy and it happened many times. Commanding Officers at headquarters in the rear, and who never got their boots dirty, were making decisions about how we were supposed to fight the battles on the front lines. Even worse, corrupt and incompetent politicians like Lyndon Johnson chose bombing targets for our Air Force, in Vietnam, from his comfortable office chair in the White House. That whole Gulf of Tonkin fiasco was made up by him and his military sycophants in the Pentagon to justify escalating the war and calling for more troops. Johnson never had a real clue about what he was doing, and too many good men died, because of his incompetence. I hope that Johnson, McNamara, and many of their other cohorts' rot in hell," said James.

James continued his rant, "Warriors like us have been "used" by those in political positions for centuries, to fight wars that they started, but weren't willing to fight themselves. Do you know that during the time of the Civil War, wealthy people could pay someone to take their place in the military? After the politicians were finished 'using' us, we were disparaged by them and forgotten. Fellow officers in my unit would frequently recite our version of a Rudyard Kipling poem.

"God and the Soldier we adore, in times of danger, not before. The danger past and all things righted, God is forgotten, and the Soldier slighted."

"Jim, what do you have in mind? Are you saying that you're ready to consider killing these criminals instead of just branding them and beating them up? If so, how are you able to justify random killing to yourself—let alone anyone else?" asked Thomas.

"You know that I've done a lot of thinking about the subject of killing, Tom. Let me take some time to explain my thoughts to you guys. The following is the basis for my decision-making about the subject of killing.

First, the subjects of killing and murder are not found in the Constitution. There are only three crimes mentioned in the Constitution—Treason, Piracy and Counterfeiting.

"You may have heard the concept of a "license to kill." A license to kill was a license granted by a government or government agency, to a particular operative, to initiate the use of lethal force.

"The idea of a license to kill became popular because of the James Bond novels and films. It was signified by the 'OO' designation given to the agents in the series who were licensed to kill—Bond was OO7."

A former British MI6 agent stated that MI6 agents did not need a "license to kill." A spy's primary job is to violate the law in other countries, and if the agent is compromised, they are at the mercy of the authorities of that country.

During the Vietnam War, the CIAs' Phoenix Program was designed to identify and destroy the Viet Cong "shadow government" via infiltration, assassination, torture, capture, counterterrorism, and interrogation. The CIA described it as a set of programs that sought to attack and destroy political infrastructure.

Throughout the five-year program that began in 1967, the Phoenix Program "neutralized" over 81,000 people suspected of Viet Cong membership. The number killed was 26,369, and the rest surrendered or were captured.

"I'm proposing that we launch an operation in Santa Clara County that will eventually spread throughout the United

States. It will be like what was conducted against the Viet Cong under the name the Phoenix Program. We will attack those who are controlling the political infrastructure that has been harming the American people," said James.

"When I commanded an Advisory Team, advising a Vietnamese Army Battalion, and local Popular Forces, we coordinated with "death squads," engaged in assassinating members of the Viet Cong infrastructure. These killings were sanctioned as a "license to kill" by the Phoenix Program. They were conducted outside of conventional military units and the assassins did not wear military uniforms. I understood that there were thousands of assassinations that took place, throughout Vietnam. They were successful at suppressing the Viet Cong political and revolutionary activities," said James.

"You mean to say that you were working with government operatives who were involved in assassinations—that fell outside the rules of the Geneva Convention?" exclaimed Victor.

"You've got it. It was actually a formal program. It was sanctioned by the CIA and other government agencies. I'm sure that the President of the United States had to sign-off and give the go-ahead for the program. Of course, they probably had a procedure or methods to allow him to have some level of deniability. Politicians have always done a great job of covering their asses."

James continued, "The principle of an "Eye for an Eye" in the Old Testament was intended for judges and it was not meant to advocate personal vengeance.

"So, then I've gone to the Bible for enlightenment and researched the subject of killing. Actually, the Bible doesn't say, 'Thou Shall Not Kill.' It says, 'Thou Shall Not Murder.'

"A quote from Genesis 1:26–27, 9:4-6; "God hates murder because only humans are made in his image and likeness."

"Every life is important to God. Not all killing is wrong. Killing that is done during times of war and at the command of superiors is acceptable. There were quite a few instances in Scripture where God endorsed and allowed the taking of lives," said James.

"You have really explored this topic, in order to satisfy your own conscience haven't you, Jim?" asked Thomas.

"I can say that without question, Tom. When I shared with you guys my conversations with Mom and the Priest, I had been evaluating my own thinking and principles about the subjects of killing and death. My discussions with Mom convinced me that there could be room for salvation if you kill someone for the right reasons. The four of us were involved in killing the enemy in Vietnam. We were sponsored by our government. Those actions were permissible according to what I have read in the Bible," said James.

"Wow Jim, that's quite a turnaround in your thinking. I really don't have a big objection to eliminating these scumbags. I just need to prepare myself and have a clear mind, and know that it's an acceptable thing for me to do. It wasn't that long ago that you were telling us not to kill. Now your advocating killing. I can envision us spending a lot of time in therapy when this is all over," said William.

"Maybe not, Bill. I hope to maintain a clear conscience. We're declaring war on drug trafficking, drug traffickers, and political criminals who are promoting drug dealing that's poisoning Americans. We are seeking revenge, but we won't be acting in our own self-interest. We're not seeking personal gain. We're trying to save the country and our way of life."

"I like hearing your rationale, Jim. I think that I'll be able to live with that approach," said Thomas.

"We're declaring war on drugs and drug traffickers, because Federal, State and Local governments, have not seriously attempted to curb illegal drug trafficking—let alone gone to war on drugs.

"Drug traffickers are not just the Mexican cartels or low-level criminals who sell drugs on the streets. The traffickers today include leaders of nations, states, and local government officials.

"Today, bringing drug traffickers to justice is not justice anymore. Too many criminals are released before the police can finish processing their paperwork. Remember, everywhere there is drug trafficking, there are other crimes. Our efforts will also be addressing human trafficking, child abuse, murders, and political crimes," said James.

"Jim is right. I see it almost every day in our department. A cop spends an hour filling out paperwork on some scumbag that he has arrested, and the scumbag is back out on the street the next day. The morale in the department is at its lowest point ever," said Victor.

"I don't want you guys to decide right now on my recommendation. Let's all think about it for the next few days. How bout if we get together this Thursday at my place. Then we can decide if everyone is on board with my new strategy," said James.

They nodded in agreement. "So, Thursday is the set time. Thanks, Jim. We'll decide everything then," said Thomas as the three of them were leaving.

The following Thursday, the four men met. During the meeting they formally committed to the new policy. It would guide them in eliminating criminals.

"I'm glad that we're all on the same page. We'll carefully decide each target, before we move forward to sanction them," declared James.

"We're now going to be the new version of the Viet Cong. We're the new Shadow Government. Who would've thought," laughed William.

EIGHTEEN
FRIENDS FOR LIFE

Bui Quang Do was born in Hue, Vietnam on May 1, 1930. His family were wealthy, Catholic landowners. He and his two younger brothers were educated in a Catholic school and learned to speak French and English. Many of Do's relatives immigrated to the United States and France in the mid to late 1950s. They immigrated due to the discrimination against Catholics. Do was 5'5" tall, slim, with large ears. He had a round, pleasant face that did not betray his true demeanor. He was brilliant and was an advanced student in math, science, and language. When he was forced, by the Viet Minh, to do military training in China, he learned to speak Chinese and became fluent in four languages.

In the wake of the French defeat at the Battle of Dien Bien Phu in May 1954, the Geneva Accords decided the fate of French Indochina. After eight years of war between the French Union Forces and Ho Chi Minh's communist Viet Minh, Do and his family were able to take advantage of Operation

Passage to Freedom. It assisted in transporting 310,000 Vietnamese civilians, soldiers, and non-Vietnamese members of the French Army from communist North Vietnam to South Vietnam. This took place between the years 1954 and 1955. Eventually, upwards of one million people moved south. American naval vessels supplemented the French in evacuating northerners to Saigon.

Do's father had been jailed and tortured, by the Viet Minh, because of his politics and Catholicism. His family welcomed the opportunity to flee the north, although they were limited in what possessions they could take with them. It was at this time that Do came to hate communism, especially the Chinese Communists, who supported the Viet Minh.

Captain James Greaney met Bui Quang Do, in September 1969 when James commanded a Military Assistance Command Vietnam (MACV) Advisor Team. He was assigned to a South Vietnamese Army battalion commanded by Lt. Colonel Do. The two military officers developed a friendship and when off duty they would have long discussions about Vietnam and American history and culture. They shared the opinion that the South Vietnamese government and military were too corrupt to win against the North Vietnamese. They both were confident that as soon as the Americans left Vietnam, the South Vietnamese government would collapse.

Do's wife and children lived close to the battalion headquarters and Do introduced James to his family. Whenever James visited the family, he would bring gifts to Do's wife, Ha, and children, Minh, and Tran.

James and Do believed that the only effective way to lead troops was at the head of the battalion on sweeps and search and destroy missions. When the lead companies met with enemy resistance, Do would be upfront and prepared to direct his troops. Likewise, James would be nearby, prepared to call for artillery support, airstrikes, and even American infantry to support the Vietnamese troops during battle.

In early 1970, American and South Vietnamese military intelligence determined that there was significant enemy build-up of Communist People's Army of Vietnam (PAVN) and the Viet Cong (VC) in the eastern border regions of Cambodia.

The enemy troop level in that area was estimated at 40,000. Cambodian neutrality and military weakness made its territory a safe haven where PAVN/VC forces could establish bases for operations over the border into Vietnam.

With the Americans shifting toward a policy of Vietnamization and withdrawal, it sought to shore up the South Vietnamese government by eliminating the cross-border threat. President Nixon gave the go-ahead for the invasion of Cambodia.

Thirteen major operations were conducted by the Army of the Republic of Vietnam (ARVN) and U.S. forces between May 1st and June 30th, 1970.

On April 30, 1970, Do's battalion joined Operation Toan Thang 42, also labeled Operation Rock Crusher, the invasion of Cambodia.

They entered Cambodia in an area referred to as the Parrot's Beak, where the Cambodian border forms a prominent point into Vietnam, resembling the beak of a parrot.

The Vietnamese part of the offensive was under the command of Lieutenant General Do Cao Tri, the commander of III Corps. Tri had a reputation as one of the most aggressive and competent of the ARVN generals. Tri's part of the operation was to have begun on the 29th, but Tri would not move, claiming that his astrologer had told him, **"The heavens were not auspicious."** His decision to delay, due to listening to the advice of an astrologer, put into question his reputation as an aggressive and competent leader.

During their first two days in Cambodia, ARVN units had several encounters with the PAVN forces. They lost 16 soldiers, while killing 84 PAVN, and capturing 65 weapons.

Do's lead battalion lost ten soldiers while killing fifty-three of the enemy. James called for airstrikes to destroy the PAVN units in support of Do's battalion. American bombers and fighter Jets carrying payloads of napalm, responded to James' call from an Air Force Base located in Thailand.

As Do and James were returning to their jeep, Do, was shot in the upper chest and thigh by a sniper. James, immediately called for a Medivac helicopter and Do was airlifted to an American Field Hospital five miles away. After a few hours of treatment, Do was flown to an American military hospital in Saigon.

On May 3rd, the III Corps forces met up with units from IV Corps and searched the area for supply caches. They claimed 1,010 PAVN dead and 204 POWs with ARVN losses of 66 KIA.

On May 28th, Do's battalion, now commanded by Lt.

Colonel Cuong Tran, engaged the PAVN forces, killing 73 and losing 11 soldiers.

On June 3rd, the battalion was rotated out of the region to stand down for rest and refit. Results for the Parrot's Beak operation were 3,588 PAVN/VC killed or captured, and 1,891 individual and crew-served weapons captured.

When the battalion was rotated out of the battle region, James continued on to the Military Assistance Command Vietnam (MACV) headquarters in Saigon. He was informed that he must prepare for a debriefing in two days, on the Cambodian invasion, to Major General Mike Watson.

James went to the American hospital in Saigon and located Do's room. He found him, in bed, reading a magazine. "How ya doing, Do?" asked James.

"I'm fine Jim. I still have pain in my chest, but I can live with it. How did my men do in the last push?" asked Do.

"They did great. You should be proud of them. Colonel Tran led them well."

Do's expression became serious. "Jim, my family and I need your help."

"Sure, what can I do for you?"

"You know what we talked about many times. When the Americans leave Vietnam, the North is going to take over the South. They'll execute me if I'm still here. My wife and I are originally from the North. They'll rape my wife and hurt my children. They did that to many Catholics before our family came to Saigon in 1954. They'll know that I helped the Americans. Please help me get my family to the United States. I have money to pay people. My family members in San Jose, California will send money too."

Before the briefing on the Cambodian Campaign began, a member of General Watson's staff, Major Eric Larson, told James to go to the podium at the front of the room. General Watson was at the podium and he read from notes. He said that he had the privilege of awarding battle field commendations to Captain James Greaney.

The General read, out loud, to the audience, James' battle field heroism during two battles of the Cambodian campaign. He pinned Silver and Bronze Stars on James' chest.

After the award ceremony, James was one of the first officers to brief the General, his staff, and four U.S. State Department officials on the Parrot's Beak's area of the Cambodian invasion.

Two South Vietnamese generals and their staffs attended the briefing and sat quietly in the front row.

General Watson complimented James on his briefing and asked him to summarize his conclusions on the performance of the South Vietnamese Army.

James concluded by saying, "Sir, the Vietnamese soldiers, and their immediate commanders at battalion level and below, were brave and fought well. The Vietnamese command above battalion level had very poor communications and remained at the rear of their troops instead of leading them from the front. The top commanders seemed confused and unsure of what they were supposed to be doing. Their poor leadership created confusion among the fighting men at the front. They were not respected or trusted by the troops who were engaging with the enemy forces."

The two South Vietnamese generals in attendance, maintained stoic expressions, but their body language indicated that they were angry with James' comments. Their staff members were whispering to each other, and they looked to be very agitated.

After James completed his remarks, General Watson said, "Well, I asked for your opinion, Captain, and I certainly got it. Thank you."

James left the podium and went to stand against the wall in the back of the briefing room.

He spotted Major Larson and walked over to speak with him. "Sir, may I have your attention?"

"Yes, Captain. How may I help you?"

"It's personal Major. I request permission to meet with General Watson."

"What does it pertain to?"

"Again Sir, it's personal and I would like to speak with the General in private."

"Well, you're his hero of the day. I'll see what I can do, Captain. Wait until everyone clears out and I'll speak to him."

"Thank you, Major."

When the two South Vietnamese generals and their staffs had left, Major Larson approached the General and told him that James had requested an audience with him.

"Let's meet at my office in twenty minutes," said Watson.

Major Larson escorted James to General Watson's office and the general greeted them saying, "I understand that you want to speak with me Captain. How can I help you?"

"Well sir, It's not for me. I've a huge favor to ask of you

for a fellow combat soldier, sir."

"Okay, before we get started, would both of you gentlemen join me for a drink? After that meeting with the two ARVN generals I feel like a strong drink."

General Watson reached into the bottom drawer of his desk and pulled out a bottle of Kentucky bourbon.

"Yes sir," replied Major Larson. "Me too, sir," answered James.

"Good, I'm from Kentucky and that's where the best bourbon is made," said the General.

The three men toasted the United States of America, the Army and MACV in succession.

General Watson refilled their glasses and said, "Let's hear what you've got, Captain."

James spent the next ten minutes explaining the background of Bui Quang Do. He went into detail about the history of the persecution of Catholics in Vietnam and the migration of three million Catholics to South Vietnam after the fall of the French at Dien Bien Phu.

He touted Do's competence and bravery as a fighting commander in the Cambodian campaign. He explained that Do had many family members living in San Jose, California. They had been there since the late 1950s. He emphasized Do's fear for his family, and himself, and repeated that Do's family had been persecuted by the Communists because of their religion.

General Watson listened carefully and asked James many questions. "I'll see what I can do. This is to stay in this room, gentlemen. I share your friend's opinion, Captain, about what will happen when we eventually leave Vietnam.

The ARVN troops are good soldiers but due to the corruption in their upper ranks, their units will fold like an old tent when they're left to fight on their own. I think that the two little fat bastards in our meeting today probably bought their commissions or are political hacks in the Thieu government," said the General.

Three days later, Major Larson summoned James to MACV headquarters. "Good morning, Captain. I've got good news for you. General Watson has reached out to a number of people, and he has a solution to get your friend and his family safe passage to the United States."

"That's fantastic Major. What do we need to do to get them to the States?"

"Well, that's the tricky part. No one can be made aware that General Watson is pulling the strings. Your friend can never know who really helped him. Is that clear, Captain?"

"Yes sir, of course."

"As far as everyone is concerned, you Captain, made the arrangements. Is that clear?"

"Yes, sir."

Major Larson continued, "An individual from the U.S. State Department is going to visit your friend in the hospital and start the process to get his family to the U.S.

This individual's name is Warren Vandersyde. He's a high-ranking member in the State Department on assignment in Saigon. You need to contact him right away. You should be with him when he visits your friend. I recommend that you visit Vandersyde's office today and see if you can connect with him.

You don't have to sell him on anything. He has been well-briefed by the General."

"Thank you, Major, and please, thank the General for saving the lives of Do's family."

"Don't mention it, Captain. The General is fond of you and he's willing to help a combat soldier like your friend. If your friend was one of those desk-jockey soldiers in Saigon, he wouldn't have considered your request. Good day Captain, and good luck."

"Thank you again, Sir," said James, saluting as he left.

James went directly to Vandersyde's office. It was in a heavily guarded building next to the Continental Hotel in Saigon. He was directed to the second floor where he entered an office with no sign on the door. He asked the guard if could speak with Mr. Warren Vandersyde.

"Wait here. Your name is Captain Greaney?" asked the guard.

The guard was gone for what seemed like two minutes. A blonde man of average height and around 45 years of age came through the door ahead of the guard. He was dressed in a khaki shirt and pants.

"Captain Greaney, I'm Warren Vandersyde and I've heard a lot about ya. Yer some kinda hero, according to General Watson."

"Thank you, sir. I'm here for a friend."

"The General has filled me in. My job is to make it happen. I already have billets for your friend and his family to travel. I'll have to meet with them to get the proper paperwork completed."

"Let me know how I may help, sir. I'll do whatever you ask."

"No need, Captain. I'll have them on their way by next week. Let them know to be prepared to leave immediately and that they should not take too many personal belongings with them."

"Yes sir, I will. Thank you. This is outstanding sir. Goodbye sir."

James went directly to meet Do in the hospital. Do was going through his last examination, prior to being discharged from the hospital.

"Do, I've got great news. I met with a guy who is setting up your travel to the United States. You and your family will be allowed to go to the U.S. The guy's name is Warren Vandersyde, and he told me to relay to you that you and your family must be ready to leave immediately. It probably won't be until the middle of next week, but you must be ready to leave at a moment's notice."

"Oh, this is great news Jim. I don't know how to thank you."

"You can thank me by getting your ass on the plane to the U.S. I've got four months left on this tour and I want to see all of you in San Jose when I return."

"Goodbye Jim. I'll always be indebted to you for all that you've done. You've saved our lives."

"Don't worry about that, Do. I'll find some way to make you pay," laughed James, as he left the room.

NINETEEN
NGOC LAN

Bui Quang Do's sister-in-law, Ngoc Lan was the younger sister of Do's wife, Ha.

The name Lan, means Orchid, in the Vietnamese language.

Lan was fluent in English, and had been employed as a translator for government officials—meeting with Americans. She had been married to a South Vietnamese Army Officer, and they had had a four-year-old daughter named, Hoa. They were living in the City of Hue—known historically, as the Ancient Capital of Vietnam, when the Communist Northern Army (NVA) began advancing south. The NVA easily destroyed the South Vietnamese Army that was in its way.

Since the American military was preparing to withdraw from Vietnam, the corrupt and weak South Vietnamese Government was beginning to crumble—due to poor leadership, and with thousands of soldiers abandoning their military units.

Before the NVA entered Hue, they shelled the city with

artillery and mortar fire. Little Hoa, was playing with two children in her front yard when mortar shells rained down on their neighborhood—she and her playmates were killed by the shrapnel exploding from the mortar rounds.

When the NVA entered Hue, Lan's husband Khiem, disappeared. She never heard from him again, nor learned what had happened to him. She suspected that he had run away from the advancing NVA—he was always in fear for his life. He was worried about what the enemy would do to him if he was captured.

As the NVA began taking over districts in Hue, their troops began pillaging the homes and raping women. A squad of NVA soldiers burst into Lan's home and stole her possessions. Five of them stayed to ransack her home, rape, and beat her. They yelled at her in anger for being married to an Army officer, and for supporting the South Vietnamese Government—who had been nothing but lapdogs of the Americans.

Lan had been raped multiple times by the five soldiers, who had ransacked her home. Two of the soldiers had beaten her with their rifles and belts, so viciously, that she had suffered internal injuries. She began coughing up blood, and could not lift herself up from the floor. When the soldiers finally left, she was barely able to crawl to the entrance of her home and cry for help.

Lans' cousin, Tran Hung, and his family lived nearby. After the shelling stopped, Hung went to Lan's home to check on her. He found her lying in the entry way—unable to stand. He gave her water and a small amount of rice. He took her to get medical aid and told her that he and his family were leaving, right away, for Saigon. He said that she should go with them.

Lan was reluctant to leave Hue. She had just buried Hoa, and wanted more time to mourn her loss. Hung finally convinced her to leave with his family. He was very anxious to leave as soon as possible—he was very worried that more NVA troops might be coming through their neighborhood.

It was a long journey from Hue to Saigon—close to 600 miles. Along the way, the travelers witnessed the terrible destruction and burning of the villages and hamlets. They became emotionally upset when viewing the panic of thousands of Vietnamese families fleeing towards Saigon.

All discipline had left the South Vietnamese Army and many soldiers had discarded their uniforms and weapons. Many of them joined the caravans of people heading south—in fear of the advancing NVA troops.

When they reached the outskirts of Saigon, Lan asked her cousin to take her to the closest military headquarters. She knew that her brother-in-law, Bui Quang Do, was a Colonel in the South Vietnamese Army. She believed that if she could locate him, he would reunite her with her sister, Ha.

When Lan and Hung entered the headquarters of the South Vietnamese Military Police, they were greeted by a young police officer. They explained to him that they were trying to find Colonel Bui Quang Do—he was a family member.

It took three hours before the police were able to locate Do's battalion. When they reached his headquarters, they were able to speak directly with Do.

Do was surprised, but pleased, to learn that Lan was in Saigon. He immediately sent his jeep to pick her up and ordered his driver to take her to his home.

Tran Hung's wife had relatives in Saigon who would take them in. When Do's jeep arrived to pick up Lan, Hung and his family wished Lan an emotional goodbye—it had been an exhausting, dangerous, and frightening journey to freedom, from Hue to Saigon.

Lan was driven to Do's home and was greeted by her sister Ha and Ha's two children. They were excited to see her, and Lan brought them up to date on the events that had occurred in Hue and her long journey to Saigon. Ha and her children were saddened to learn about the death of Hoa. The sisters and children cried over her loss and the destruction of their country. They also feared the loss of their other relatives who might suffer under the advancing army.

Ha informed Lan, "Do has arranged for us to leave for America very soon—maybe by next week. We'll be flying to San Jose, California, and you know that we have many relatives living there. I'm going to ask him if he can get approval from the Americans, for you to travel with us. You must go with us. The Communists are going to kill us if we stay. If they learn that we helped the American military, they will have no mercy for us."

"I know what the Communists would do to us. They have already done many terrible things to me. I did not want to live until cousin Hung persuaded me to go with him and his family. I will tell you everything later when we are alone," said Lan.

After James Greaney's 14-month tour in Vietnam ended, he returned home to Los Gatos, California for a two-week leave. It was an opportunity to spend time with his parents and friends, whom he had not seen in two years. He was assigned to spend the remaining six months of his military career at Ft. Ord in Monterey, California.

During his leave time, he became reacquainted with a high school girlfriend, Georgia Conway. They soon began dating, seriously. He also looked up Bui Quang Do's family in the phone book and learned that Do's family owned a Vietnamese coffee shop on Senter Road in San Jose. James decided to visit the coffee shop unannounced, and surprise his friend, Do.

As James entered the coffee shop, all eyes turned toward him. He was the only Caucasian in the shop and easily taller than all the other customers. He looked for an empty table and as he was about to sit down, he heard a loud yell, "Jim!" Do came towards him yelling, "It's great to see you."

They came together in a hug. Do said to James, "I'm so glad you survived the last part of your tour." Do began introducing James to customers in the coffee shop. Most of them were former South Vietnamese soldiers. As Do walked James around to each of them, he explained how he and James had fought the Communists together and they were great friends.

The customers were excited to meet James. When Do introduced each of them to James, they attempted to tell their personal war stories in their broken English.

Finally, Do and James sat together at a table and ordered coffee. Do explained that his father was very frail, suffering from cancer. Since Do was the oldest child, he was expected to take over the family businesses.

Do's family owned three Vietnamese noodle houses, a

Vietnamese coffee shop, and three commercial buildings that were leased to electronic parts manufacturers in San Jose. Most of their businesses were growing rapidly and generating large, daily, cash flows. The family's plan was to use the significant cash flow to purchase unimproved land near the commercial buildings that they owned. They wanted to expand their real estate holdings by building family housing.

Do and James spent three hours reminiscing about the war, their friends and how they both hated Communism. As James was leaving, he promised Do that he would meet him at the coffee shop twice a month. Do told James that if he needed anything, including a job, he was welcome to come and work with him. Many of the customers stood and saluted as James left.

❧

James kept his promise and visited Do at the coffee shop around the first and fifteenth of each month. He had joined Georgia's father's real estate firm. Georgia and James had married after a year's engagement and settled down in a small house near the downtown area of Los Gatos.

When James made his bi-monthly visits to Do, their discussions centered around the War still raging in Vietnam. They discussed the refugee problem of the Vietnamese fleeing Vietnam, caused by the push by the North Vietnamese to drive south and destroy the South Vietnamese Army.

❧

When the South Vietnamese Government collapsed in 1975, as Do and James had predicted, it wasn't long before the South Vietnamese Army was pushed south to Saigon where they surrendered. The South held on until April 30, 1975 when the North's forces raised their flag over the Presidential Palace. The Northern forces immediately renamed Saigon, Ho Chi Minh City.

Do told James about the Vietnamese Boat People. He explained that thousands of Vietnamese had fled Vietnam, by sea, following the collapse of the government. They crowded into small vessels and fell prey to pirates from Cambodia and Thailand.

Many suffered from dehydration, starvation, and death by drowning. The pirates stole their belongings, raped women and children, and murdered many of the men. Do said that he had heard that the United Nations was reporting that as many as 400,000 Boat People were lost at sea.

"I hate those fucking Communists. I want to kill as many of them as possible," yelled Do.

James informed Do about the growing drug problem in the U.S. and that his friends in the Junto were very concerned about the mounting deaths due to drug addiction in local communities.

"Do, you know that the Communists from China and other countries are shipping drugs into Mexico for the U.S. market. Communists believe that they will defeat us by destroying our country from within. We are losing people who are dying from drugs every day."

"I know, many of my people say that their children are using drugs now and they don't know what to do. Their children are not listening to them anymore," said Do.

"I am leading a team of well-trained American war veterans who are going after the drug dealers to eliminate them. The police don't have the resources or leadership to go after them. I would like your help in working with us," said James.

"You know I will do anything I can to help you, Jim. My family owes you, our lives."

"No, you don't, but I appreciate your comments. What if we work together to go after these drug dealers, like we went after the enemy in Vietnam? Let's eliminate as many of them as we can."

"I'm with you, Jim. I have three friends who served with the Americans on the Phoenix Program. I helped them and their families get to the States and I gave them jobs. They'll work with me on any program that I ask them to. They were very well trained by the CIA and killed many Viet Cong (VC). They all speak English. I'll fund them in any activities that we agree to do together. You won't have to meet them. We can do this quietly."

Minh Le, Tran Thong, and Manh Dinh were the three friends that Do had mentioned. They were Veterans of the Phoenix Program, and they were now employed by Do in his business operations. They had been trained as assassins and had spent three years successfully pursuing, catching, and killing many VC. They were committed to Do. He had helped them and their families in getting to the U.S. He provided them with employment. They would eagerly conduct any missions that he requested.

The Phoenix Program was a program designed by the

United States Central Intelligence Agency (CIA) during the Vietnam War. The Program was to identify and destroy the Viet Cong (VC) by infiltration, torture, capture, counter-terrorism, interrogation, and assassination. The Program's effectiveness was measured by the number of VC members who were "neutralized,"—a euphemism meaning imprisoned, persuaded to defect, or killed.

U.S. government records indicate that the Program killed upwards of 41,000 VC.

❧

"That's great. There's no reason for you to meet officially with my team either. I do want to bring them to your coffee shop though, so you can meet them as fellow Veterans of the War."

"I'd like that Jim, and I will introduce them to my family and my customers."

❧

James invited his brothers and Victor Lewis to a barbecue at his home. He barbecued steak filets, to their liking, and served asparagus, bake potatoes and green salad. He purchased an apple pie for dessert from a Marie Calendar restaurant.

Prior to dinner, James fixed drinks for everyone and he and Victor enjoyed their favorite vodka martinis. While they were enjoying their drinks, he relayed stories about Bui Quang Do and their experiences while serving together in Vietnam.

He went on to explain how he had recently reconnected with Do and that they had agreed to work together to fight the drug problem in the community, as the police departments were overwhelmed.

"I'd like to introduce all of you to him and some of his fellow veterans. We could go together, some evening, and visit his coffee shop in San Jose."

"How can Do be of help to us and how can he work with us?" asked William.

"Do is very well respected in the Vietnamese community. They refer to him, respectfully, as Uncle Do. They go to him whenever they have a problem. He's famous with the Vietnamese people because of his war record. He's helped many in the community find work and establish their businesses. When we visit his coffee shop, you'll be introduced to many former ARVN soldiers. Some of them served with American units and some participated in the Phoenix Program. The Phoenix guys are trained killers, and they are very loyal to Do," said James.

"I'm ready for something new. Are we ramping up our operations to include eliminating some of these dirt bags?" asked Thomas.

"Yes, this is war. When we cut off thumbs and gave beatings for punishment that was revenge. We must create fear in the drug community. They must believe that if they are going to poison our children, they will pay with their lives. The police are poorly led and they're not supported by the courts. The courts are fucked up and corrupt," said James.

"How do you plan to do all of this?" asked Victor.

"You are a key player in our plans, Victor. You receive information on drug dealers and you're in charge of heading up the police anti-drug program. We need some basic information on each of these dealers, such as names, locations, and how they are selling drugs. As long as you verify that we have the right individual, we'll take it from there. I'll provide Do with the information and his team will execute the mission. Do's people won't know the source of the information. Do also wants me to be shielded from his people. You'll be kept totally anonymous," said James.

"I like it. If you can keep me anonymous, I can provide detailed information on the dealers without alerting anyone in the police department. I hope Do's people are professional and not sloppy," said Victor.

"You can count on it," said James.

While they were eating their dessert, James said, "You know, I watched an old movie called "The Thomas Crown Affair" last night. I rented it. It was made in the late sixties. Steve McQueen has always been one of my favorite actors."

"I remember that movie," said William.

"I do too. McQueen was always Mr. Cool. I think that Faye Dunaway was in it too," said Thomas.

"Yes. Remember how he pulled off the robbery with those guys? They never knew who he was and they didn't know each other either. That's what I want us to do," said James.

"I didn't see the movie. What was it about?' asked Victor.

"McQueen plays this rich guy who has everything. He comes up with this scheme to hire guys that are small time crooks. They each have some expertise or skill. They steal over $2 million from a bank in Boston. McQueen gets away with the money and deposits it in his bank in Switzerland. He doesn't need the money, but he does it because he's bored and loves to take risks," said James.

"He sounds like you, Jim. You don't need the money and you get-off by taking the risk," said Victor.

"Our new project doesn't involve taking money, but we can do a great service to the community if we get rid of these fucking drug dealers. It could be fun too. Don't you think so, Victor?" asked James.

"I guess so. We'd better be careful and very good at what we do though. And Do better be as good as you say he is."

TWENTY
SPEEDBALLS

On May 13, 1982, the Junto members were having their quarterly meeting. It was a Thursday night, and they were meeting at the Bellows restaurant in Saratoga, California. Since some of them had left the bay area and were living in different states, only eight members continued to attend regular meetings.

Sometimes as few as five members would show up. They had agreed to meet quarterly instead of bi-monthly.

James Greaney and Victor Lewis attended all the meetings. There were eight members in attendance on May 13th and they met in a private room where they could also order dinner and drinks.

It was their practice to designate a member in advance, to speak on a topic of his choosing, prior to the start of the meeting. After the speech, the discussions would cover many other topics.

It was Victors' turn to give a speech. He chose to speak

about the actor and comedian, John Belushi.

Victor was a childhood friend of James. He was a lieutenant in the San Jose Police Department, in charge of the Criminal Drug Division.

Victor began his speech, "I want to comment about the drug epidemic raging today in our communities. Most of you probably know who John Belushi was. He died in March of this year, due to a drug overdose. He was a very funny, fat guy, on Saturday Night Live and he starred in a couple of movies.

Belushi was a funny guy, but he had a big personal problem that wasn't funny. He was a drug addict who had the financial resources to purchase unlimited drugs. Even his own business manager hid money from him, because he was aware that Belushi was out of control with his addiction.

Our department received some details about his death, and I'll share what I can with you. It's important for everyone to know about these addictions. There are many drug-related deaths occurring with the youth in our communities and it's getting worse.

Belushi was staying at a bungalow at the Chateau Marmont Hotel on Sunset Boulevard in West Hollywood. The Marmont was a short and long-term residence for celebrities.

He left his hotel and visited his manager to ask for money. At first, his manager refused, because of his concerns with Belushi's addiction. Extensive efforts were being made, by family members and friends, to keep Belushi from buying drugs.

Belushi repeatedly asked his manager, Bernie Brillstein, for money. Brillstein finally relented and gave him some cash.

On the morning of his death, Belushi had been visited,

separately, by Robin Williams, Robert De Niro, and a woman named Catherine Evelyn Smith.

Belushi was found dead at 12 pm on March 5th, by his bodyguard, Bill Wallace. They determined the cause of death was due to drug intoxication involving the combination of cocaine and heroin.

The drug community had referred to this combination as a "Speedball." Under interrogation, Catherine Smith had admitted to furnishing the cocaine and heroin, and to giving Belushi the fatal injection," said Victor.

"Are 'speedballs' popular in Santa Clara County?" asked Pete.

"Yes, we have already seen some overdoses and deaths in the local communities. It's really a very toxic mixture and part of the new drug culture. We predict that there will be many more deaths due to this drug cocktail. The users can't control the mixture, like in Belushi's case, and therefore they are playing Russian Roulette every time they inject the mixture into their bodies," explained Victor.

"What are you guys doing to try and stop the proliferation of speedballs?" asked Steve.

"There's nothing special that we can do. We're going after the drug dealers and users, but we can't stop drug addicts, or first-time users, from injecting these poisons into their bodies. The typical speedball user is an addict who is far along in his addiction. When he needs his fix, he couldn't care less about the danger to himself. The users don't think twice about the risk," said Victor.

"It sounds like the only solution would be to stop the flow

of cocaine and heroin at the border," said James.

Victor responded, "You're exactly right. It's crazy to think that we can stop the drug flow at the local police level. We're not given the resources to fight the drug problem. You have to fight the drug war at the federal level, country to country. We're in the midst of a drug crisis. Cocaine in powder form is expensive, but now they're selling a cocaine derivative called "crack." Drug dealers are able to move more cocaine by converting the powder into a solid 'smokeable' form of the drug. It's sold in smaller quantities to more people. It's cheap, simple to produce, ready to use, and highly profitable for dealers.

We know that the Mexican Cartels are also involved in methamphetamine distribution. They're increasing production in Southern California, as well as increasing large-scale meth production operations."

❧

The following evening, James, Victor, William, and Thomas met at the bar in the Los Gatos Lodge. They took a table in the rear corner of the room.

"Victor, please explain to Bill and Tom the comments you made to the Junto group last night since they weren't there."

After Victor summarized his speech from the previous evening, William remarked, "Wow, I didn't realize these bastards are destroying our society like this. We've got to find a way to eliminate these fuckers."

"You know what we can do." said Thomas. "We can get hold of these animals and give them a Belushi. If we do away with enough of them, in that way, we can scare the hell out of the big dealers. They're all cowards anyway."

"I like that idea, Victor. You can get us the names of the assholes who are pushing drugs, and we can, as Tom said, give them a Belushi. It would be easier than trying to cut off thumbs to send a message. Remember, that for the foreseeable future, we're going to limit our coverage to Santa Clara County. Once we're confident that the County is in good shape, we'll move on to other territories," said James.

Victor responded, "I kinda like that idea too. We would be ridding the public of these scumbags, and no one is going to miss them. The cops aren't going to waste their time chasing the perpetrators. They're not going to care about the deaths of drug dealers."

"How do we get the drugs and syringes?" asked William.

"No problem with that. I can get you the syringes and you can get the drugs from the drug dealers' own supply," said Victor.

"How do we know how much to put in the syringes?" asked Thomas.

"We're not going to worry about that either. We'll load the syringes with enough to take down an elephant. We want them dead," said James.

"This will be our first mission, employing our new strategy, to kill these fuckers, Jim," said William.

"You're right. This is not revenge. This is war," said James.

"I can also get us a list of drug dealers and offenders," said Victor.

"Our territory is the entire Santa Clara County. Get us a list of those dealers pushing drugs on kids. They'll be our first targets," said James.

Over the next six months, two known drug dealers, living in Los Gatos, overdosed on speedballs. Three drug dealers and one heavy drug user in Saratoga, were found dead from speedball overdoses. Five drug users died from overdoses in San Jose. Two of them were known to hang out near San Jose High School. All died from overdoses, due to injecting speedballs.

Police Captains from San Jose, Los Gatos, Saratoga, and Mt. View met for lunch. They met in a private meeting room at Original Joe's in downtown San Jose. Their purpose was to discuss the drug crisis in Santa Clara County, and specifically, the spike in deaths of drug users injecting speedballs.

Since they were meeting in the city, Captain John Flannery, of the San Jose Police Department, took the podium and opened the discussion. "It's amazing how these drug users are taking themselves out with these overdoses. I'm not upset about losing them, but I'm concerned that our youth might start upgrading their drug usage to injecting speedballs."

Flannery had invited Lt. Victor Lewis to the meeting, and they had traveled together, in Flannery's car. He felt that it was important for Lewis to be there since he was head of the San Jose Police drug unit. Victor remained silent during the meeting and took notes on the conversations.

TWENTY-ONE
JUST SAY NO

In 1982, Nancy Reagan was visiting Longfellow Elementary School in Oakland, California. When asked by a school girl what to do if she was offered drugs by her peers, the First Lady responded, "Just Say No."

James Greaney explained the meaning of Nancy Reagan's slogan to Bui Quang Do. Do liked the slogan and had his assistant make up 3x5 cards with the wording, "Just Say No."

James had created a network that relayed information from Victor Lewis to him and then on to Do. Victor would review the information on the police computer and print intelligence data on the illegal drug community. He would then meet with James. They would review the data and agree on the targets. The targets had to be drug users or dealers that had been preying on children and young adults. James would visit Do at his coffee shop and hand him a detailed summary of the information on each target. Do would use the data to plan, with his execution team, the assaults on the chosen targets.

Ron Gonzales was found dead, at 8:15 pm, in his police car on the East Side of San Jose, California. Ron was average height, 44-years-old and a nineteen-year veteran of the police force. He had a square body, was obese, and his belly protruded over his gun belt. He had a large head and his face had pockmarks due to a history with acne. He had never been married and his friends could not remember if they had ever seen him with a woman. He had not responded to calls from the police dispatch and officers, already out on patrol, were sent to find him.

Two San Jose police officers, scouting the area in their patrol cars, spotted his parked car. They got out of their cars and found Gonzales in the drivers' seat. He was leaning back in his seat—dead—with a syringe stuck in his arm. The fly on his pants was open, exposing his penis. There was a 3x5 card lying on his chest with the typed words, "Just Say No."

When police investigators visited Gonzales' apartment after his death, they were shocked to see framed pictures of young boys, in different suggestive poses, on the walls. They found videotapes of young children having sex with adults and a pamphlet on the coffee table, from an organization called Nambla. A closet drawer in his bedroom revealed small bags of cocaine and marijuana, along with drug paraphernalia.

Gonzales was a "dirty cop." He preyed on young men and boys. He would give them money, gifts, and drugs in exchange for them performing sexual favors on him. He targeted boys near San Jose High School and two nearby middle schools. The autopsy revealed that he had probably been unconscious when a lethal dose of heroin and cocaine had been injected into his blood stream.

Gonzales had been parked in a shopping mall where he frequently took his break. He had beckoned a young, feminine-looking Asian male over to his car. The male had been standing under a streetlight. As the young man approached his car, Gonzales unzipped his fly revealing his penis.

The young man entered the front passenger side of the car. As he was about to speak, Gonzales was hit on the head through his opened window, by someone who had approached his car from the drivers' side. The assailant was wielding a sap when he struck Gonzales on his left temple. Gonzales was rendered unconscious. The young male in the front seat, pulled out a syringe from his jacket and injected it into Gonzales' arm. The syringe contained a powerful speedball of heroin and cocaine. The young male stayed with Gonzales for a few minutes and watched his body twitch as the speedball's liquid raced through his bloodstream to his heart. He then placed a 3x5 card, with the words, "Just Say No," on Ron's chest and left the car. Ron's heart stopped beating soon after the young male left.

After a thorough police investigation had been conducted, that exposed Gonzales' pedophilia, the elaborate plans for a cop funeral were cancelled. His family received his remains, and they had a private ceremony. It was attended by a few people at the cemetery.

Frank Just, a San Jose State College professor, was found dead in his office with a syringe dangling from his left bicep.

There was a 3x5 card with the words, "Just Say No," stuck between the middle and ring finger of his left hand. He had a bruise on his forehead. Just was 48-years-old, divorced, 6'2" tall and 180 lbs. He had a lean build, pale complexion, and a Van Dyke beard. His beard and moustache were dyed brown. Just avoided any type of exercise and his physical condition had been deteriorating. His health was getting worse due to prolonged drug abuse, poor eating habits, and lack of exercise.

Just regarded himself as handsome and suave. He failed to recognize that his declining health and drug abuse had been changing his appearance. He taught English classes and his favorite subject was Shakespeare. He could easily quote passages from Shakespeare's sonnets and plays. He enjoyed the response from young female students who were enthralled with him while listening to him recite.

Just was a major drug dealer on campus. He had begun selling marijuana to students on campus when he had first arrived ten years ago. He became very wealthy from his drug sales. When he elevated his drug dealing to include hard drugs, like cocaine and heroin, his income skyrocketed. He recruited some of his former students as members of his sales force.

Their potential customer base for drug sales were the 30,000 students at the college and nearby high schools and middle schools. His plan was to retire, in two years, at the age of 50 and never work again. He wanted to spend the rest of his life, traveling the world, enjoying tropical islands, and doing drugs.

Just's death posed a problem for his two major drug suppliers as he had never divulged the names of the members of his salesforce. He was careful to protect his sources and his distribution network. The drug suppliers were set back by his death as his weekly volume was significant. The autopsy determined that he had received a "hotshot" of cocaine and heroin. The quantity of drugs that were injected into his bloodstream, could have put a large animal to sleep. Just's funeral was attended by his mother, older sister, and an ex-wife. A few women students from his Shakespeare classes also attended.

❧

Janice Brucestar, was found dead in her apartment in Mountain View, California. She was found naked in her bathtub, which was half-full of water. She had been 37-years-old.

It was determined that she had been dead for three days and the apartment was starting to smell rancid. The police found a syringe at the bottom of the tub and there was a small red mark in the crook of her left arm. They also found a 3x5 card with the words "Just Say No" next to the sink on her bathroom counter. She had a bruise and a cut on the left-side of her head.

Brucestar had graduated from Santa Clara University, where she had played volleyball. She had returned to the school as an assistant coach for the volleyball team. When she played for the school, she was a pretty, brunette. She was 5'7" tall, had a lean and muscular body, and was able to jump and spike the ball against her opponents.

In the second year of her coaching, she had begun to put on weight. The weight went to her lower body. Her buttocks and thighs were now very large. The head coach asked her why she had put on so much weight and said it was not a good example for the student athletes. She told him that she just had to find time to work-out and eat a healthier diet.

Brucestar had a severe alcohol and drug addiction. Almost every Friday evening, she and her girlfriend would drink beer and snort cocaine. They would not stop until late Sunday night. Her female lover, Sandra, provided the drugs and alcohol and they would binge drink and eat large quantities of junk food throughout the weekend.

Soon, her drug and alcohol purchases were consuming her paycheck and depleting her savings. She was late paying her bills. She decided to sell drugs in order to catch up on her obligations. She began selling drugs to customers at a local bar.

She met a middle-aged woman at the bar named Shirley. She was a schoolteacher at a local middle school. They soon became lovers and Shirley helped Janice sell drugs to other adults and a few of her students at the Kurtner Middle School.

An 11-year-old student at Kurtner overdosed on cocaine during recess. The child was a Vietnamese American boy who was taken, by ambulance, to San Jose Hospital. He had a very rapid heartbeat. His life was saved by two quick thinking emergency room nurses.

While the student was recovering in the hospital, he was visited by two San Jose police officers. The officers asked the parents of the boy to join them in the questioning of their son. The child explained that he had purchased some cocaine from friends at school who had bragged about having their own drug supply.

The story of the young boy's overdose spread quickly throughout the close-knit Vietnamese community. The parents were outraged, and they complained to the Vietnamese Elders in their community. The Elders were led by Bui Quang Do. After meeting with the young boy, the Elders had traced the drug supplier to a woman named Janice Brucestar. Her name had also been on the San Jose Police Department's Drug Unit watch list.

Jerry Stafflinger was a successful sales rep for a major electronic distributor in Silicon Valley. He was 5'8" tall and 125 lbs. His skin was pale, and he had sunken cheeks. Due to prolonged snorting of cocaine, he had a hole in the septum of his nose. It made his speech hoarse, and he always sounded like he had a cold.

He wasn't a salesman who was knowledgeable about the products that he represented. After a couple of years in the sales business, he realized that his talent was in his ability to ingratiate himself with certain purchasing managers who were using drugs.

He gained favor with the managers as he was a reliable source for drugs. He would typically meet the managers in their offices and discuss their purchasing needs. As he was leaving their offices, he would hand them envelopes containing cocaine. The managers would provide Stafflinger with significant purchase orders for electronic components. He was not required to spend time with the manufacturing engineers to explain the benefits of the components he represented, like his competitors had to do. Stafflinger only had to inform the purchasing managers of the components that he had for sale. The managers did his job for him.

When critical components became scarce and on allocation, Stafflinger would source electronic component brokers who had large stocks of "black market" product. The purchasing managers would provide him with significant orders for the stolen parts, and he was able to enjoy even larger profits.

The management at the distributorship, where Stafflinger was employed, knew that he was working outside of normal channels, but they looked the other way—they didn't care. He was their top producer, and he was generating more profit for the firm than the rest of the sales force. The profit that he generated from his sales, during product allocation time, kept the Distributorship operating in the black.

Like many drug dealers, Stafflinger had made the critical mistake of becoming hooked on his own drug supply. He had also recently been added to the "drug suspect" list of the Los Gatos and San Jose Police Departments.

Instead of driving directly home after work, Stafflinger would stop at Mountain Charles' restaurant and bar. It was his favorite bar in Los Gatos. He liked to make this stop before making the long drive over the hill, on Highway 17, to his home in Scotts Valley.

He had his own favorite booth in the rear of the bar. The booth was shielded from most of the other patrons. He would order a whisky and after the waitress left his drink, he would take a pinch of cocaine from an envelope that he held below the table. He would snort a line of cocaine when he was sure no one was looking.

After a few hours, Stafflinger would be fully loaded. His mood would swing from a high on cocaine, where he became loud and obnoxious, to a depressed state when the drugs were wearing off. He then would become melancholy and sometimes cry.

The steep and winding road from Los Gatos to his home in Scotts Valley was very dangerous. It was a challenge for sober drivers, even in daylight. Typically, when Stafflinger left Mountain Charles' he would stagger to his car, sit behind the wheel for a few seconds, and then lean back and go to sleep. After a long night's sleep in his car, he would drive home to clean up and prepare to return to work.

This morning Stafflinger did not wake up. He was found dead in his car at 11 am, by a Los Gatos police officer, cruising the parking lot. When the officer approached the driver's side of Stafflinger's car, he could see that there was a syringe stuck in the right arm of the dead man.

He also noticed a 3x5 card with the words, "Just Say No," on the dashboard of the car.

The officer alerted the police dispatcher and recorded his findings. He put out crime scene tape and stayed away from the car while waiting for help to come.

⌒

Peter Tran was the leader of a Vietnamese criminal gang in San Jose called the Lords of Saigon. He was thirty-five, very handsome, and he looked much younger than his age. He led a gang of fifteen members. His gang members ranged in age from 16 to 40-years-old. The gang members were violent and had recently been involved in a shoot-out at a Vietnamese restaurant with another local Vietnamese gang.

Vietnamese gangs plagued the Vietnamese community in San Jose and were involved in assault, extortion, narcotics, book-making, and illegal gambling. They controlled massage parlors and financed many of the Vietnamese nail shops. Most of the businesses that they controlled operated with cash only. There were very few credit card transactions. Their members were typically older, and they were known to be more brutal than the Mexican gangs.

Bui Quang Do and two other Vietnamese community leaders invited Peter Tran and the leaders of two other gangs, Alex Cheung of the Dragons, and Andrew Nguyen of the Kings to meet them at Do's coffee shop after closing.

Do was highly respected and feared in the Vietnamese community. He was regarded as the unelected mayor of "Little Saigon," in South San Jose. Many in the community referred to him as "Uncle Do."

San Jose had more Vietnamese residents than any other city, outside of Vietnam. Little Saigon was an area of rapid development in businesses and housing, populated by Vietnamese immigrants. The boundaries of Little Saigon began on Story Road and expanded along Senter Road to McLaughlin Avenue.

The business area was so successful that it generated the highest tax revenue for the city—more than any other location in San Jose.

Do quickly took the lead in the meeting and spoke in Vietnamese.

He stared at the three gang leaders and said, "I want to make it clear; we don't care about your businesses or who you do business with. Drugs are killing our children. We didn't fight the Communists and lose many of our people, who tried to escape by boats, to have our children die from the drugs that you are selling."

He went on to inform the gang leaders that selling drugs to children would not be tolerated. This included any sales to college students or anyone under the age of twenty-one.

He continued, "When I talk about drugs, I mean marijuana or even prescription drugs. Anyone selling cocaine or heroin will receive the death penalty from us. I'm not interested in your opinions. You will obey our orders, is that clear?" asked Do.

Tran, Cheung, and Nguyen nodded their heads in the affirmative.

"You may leave now," said Do.

When the three were in the parking lot, Tran spoke to the other two in English.

"I'm not taking orders from these old men. No one is going to tell me how to do my business."

"I wouldn't fuck with these old men if I were you," said Cheung.

"I agree with Cheung, I'm not going to take any chances with them," said Nguyen.

"You two are pussies," said Tran, as he got into his car.

One month later, late in the evening, Peter Tran and his girlfriend, Linh, were leaving Hue City, a Vietnamese restaurant. As Linh and Tran were heading to their car, Tran stepped back and said, "I'll be there in a minute. I've got to piss." "Go back into the restaurant. Don't do it out here," said Linh.

He walked into the shadows next to the building. As he was finishing and pulling up his zipper, a man stepped out of the shadows and fired four shots into Tran's chest.

The gun shots were muted by a silencer and Linh did not hear a sound, but saw Tran lying on the ground and a man wearing a black hoody standing over him. When the man left, she ran to Tran. She stood over his body and said nothing. She did not yell out or cry. Tran's eyes were open with a blank stare. Blood was seeping out of his mouth and drenching his shirt.

Two of Trans's gang members, leaving the restaurant, saw Linh standing over Tran's body. They asked her what had happened. She was in shock and could not speak. She began to cry hysterically.

One week after Tran was shot, Do summoned Alex Cheung and Andrew Nguyen to his coffee shop at 7pm. When they arrived, Do led them to a booth in the back.

When they were seated and had ordered coffee, Do asked, "Are you still selling drugs to children?"

"No," they both exclaimed at once. "We don't do drugs with kids," said Cheung.

"That's good," said Do. "Tran didn't hear our message. After we met with you, we learned that his members were selling drugs at two high schools.

I'm ordering the two of you to contact Tran's members and tell them that if they want to live, they will stop selling drugs. If they continue, we will hold them responsible, along with the two of you."

"We can't control Tran's people, Uncle Do," said Nguyen.

"You'll find a way or you will die with them. Now leave me," said Do.

When they left the coffee shop, Cheung and Nguyen were trembling and their eyes were wide open in fear.

"I know they'll kill us if Tran's people continue to sell drugs," said Nguyen.

"How are we going to control them? We've got to meet with them and explain the situation," said Cheung.

"We've got to make them understand that those old guys will have us all killed if they continue to sell drugs to kids. We've got to fix this," said Nguyen.

Alex Cheung and Andrew Nguyen met with the two top lieutenants in Peter Tran's gang, Duc Vu and Manh Dinh.

Cheung explained the order from Do. They must cease selling drugs to anyone under the age of twenty-one. They must stay away from schools. If they don't, they'll receive death sentences.

"I'm not afraid of those old fuckers. Their time has passed. We'll do our business our way. They better not mess with us or they'll die," said Duc Vu.

"I don't agree with Vu," said Manh Dinh. My people will stay away from schools. You have my word. If Vu wants to go his own way, that's his business. I'm not involved with him. Most of Tran's people are with me. I respect Do and the old soldiers. My father told me about them when I was growing up. He said that they're combat guys and they killed a lot of people in the war. They know many ways to kill. They won't hesitate to kill us if we defy them."

"One more time Vu. Are you going to obey Uncle Do's order?" asked Cheung.

"No fucking way. Fuck Uncle Do. Tell Do and those old fuckers to stay out of my business, or I'll come back at them. I'm not afraid of them," said Vu.

When the meeting was over and Cheung and Nguyen were in their car, Cheung said, "It's clear to me that we've got to stop Duc Vu. He's not going to obey and he'll put us at risk with Do."

"I agree, we'll take care of this together. We can explain it to Do, after it's done," said Nguyen.

Two weeks after the meeting with Cheung and Nguyen, Duc Vu was in bed asleep with his girlfriend. At 5:30 am, three men crept into Duc Vu's apartment and burst into the master bedroom. The assailants opened-up with hand guns on the sleeping couple. The autopsies revealed that Duc Vu had been hit nine times in the head and chest and his girlfriend suffered six wounds to her head and stomach.

Cheung and Nguyen visited with Do at the coffee shop the morning following the killings. Cheung explained that they had met with Paul Tran's lieutenants and that one agreed to follow Do's order but the other did not.

They reported that they took it upon themselves to take care of Vu, because he wouldn't agree to cooperate.

"You must keep everyone away from the schools. I still hold you responsible if anyone sells drugs to the children. Is that clear?" said Do.

"Yes, Uncle Do. We understand," said Cheung.

"We understand," echoed Nguyen.

Bui Quang Do and his wife, Ha, were devout Catholics and they rarely missed the 10:00 am Sunday Mass at St. Joseph's Cathedral in San Jose. After Mass, Do and Ha were walking to their car when they were approached by two middle-aged Vietnamese women who asked to speak with him.

Do agreed to speak with them and suggested that they return to St. Joseph's. The four returned to the cathedral and sat down in pews at the rear of the church. The women were very apologetic for taking up Do's time, but he brushed aside their apologies and asked, "What is your problem?"

The women explained to Do that they each owned two nail shops in San Jose. They said that they were threatened and pressured by a Vietnamese gang to pay protection money, or their businesses would be destroyed.

They said that it was the Dragon Gang that was threatening and demanding money. They said that they were also threatening other Vietnamese business owners who were afraid to say anything.

Do listened to their stories and was able to get the name of the gang member who was threatening the women. It was Alex Cheung, and he had threatened to demolish their shops if they didn't pay up.

The women had paid for two months but couldn't continue the payments. It was too much money and put a strain on their businesses.

Do told the women that he would investigate, and that they

should not make any further payments.

Do and Ha were in their car, driving home, when he angrily hit the steering wheel with his fist and yelled, "How can these young bastards prey upon our people? They have no respect! Our people have suffered too much."

"You can't allow them to hurt our people," said Ha.

"I won't. I'll stop them immediately," said Do.

Do had also received complaints from owners of three Vietnamese noodle houses. They reported that members of the Kings Gang were demanding that they pay "protection money." He did not tell his wife about the demands on the noodle houses, because he knew that she would become upset and angry. He would take care of the Kings gang very soon.

Do summoned Cheung and Nguyen to his coffee shop on Thursday evening. When they arrived, he questioned them about their gang activities. He said that he had heard that some Vietnamese businesses were being pressured and threatened by Vietnamese thugs for protection money. They have been threatening to break up the owners' shops.

"Do you know anything about this?" Do asked the two men.

"No, Uncle Do. We wouldn't do that to Vietnamese people," said Cheung.

"Who is threatening the owners?" asked Do.

"We don't know, but we'll find out for you, Uncle Do," said Nguyen.

"Do that. Report back to me immediately."

As they were walking to their cars, Cheung said, "We've got to take care of Do before he finds out that it's us."

"You're right. If we don't stop him, he will be up our asses over everything we do. It's time we get rid of him," said Nguyen.

Alex Cheung left Do's coffee shop and drove to his girlfriend's house. As he was getting out of his car, he was ambushed by a man coming out of the shadows. The man fired four shots from a handgun with a silencer. He was hit in the head, neck, and twice in the stomach. He was dead before he fell to the ground.

Andrew Nguyen left Do's coffee shop to drive home. He was two blocks from his house and stopped at a red light. A car pulled alongside him and a gunman in the front passenger seat opened fire using a handgun with a silencer.

Nguyen was hit in the head by three shots and slumped forward in his seat. His car lurched into the intersection and stopped. A female driver stopped behind him and began screaming. She had seen the gunman reach out of his car window with a handgun, but she did not hear the shots. She saw the gunman's hand jerk three times as he fired the gun.

⌒〜⌒

Do met with his hired killers, Minh Le, Tran Thong, and Manh Phan Dinh at the coffee shop late that night. The shop was closed and Do brought out a bottle of whiskey and poured drinks for the four of them.

"You've done well, my friends," he said as he passed each of them an envelope filled with $2,000 in cash. He could have paid much less, but he wanted to insure clean and professional work with no mistakes. He only hired the best.

"I don't understand these young bastards. They have no

pride and they have been corrupted by drugs and the easy life in America," said Do.

"They're scum to me," said Minh Le.

"I didn't feel anything when I shot them. I respected the VC that we killed. They believed in something, even though it was Communism," said Tran Thong.

"It was easy work for me. I only made $500 a month killing the VC. Let me know when you have more work for me, Uncle Do," said Manh Phan Dinh.

"It will be a while before I'll need you for another mission. Go back to your regular jobs, and I'll contact you," said Do.

The three men bowed to Do as they left his coffee shop.

TWENTY-TWO
CHARMED

James visited Do's coffee shop to discuss their campaign against drug dealers and corrupt politicians in Santa Clara County.

While waiting for Do to join him, he noticed a beautiful Vietnamese woman working behind the cashier's counter. She was stunning—with long dark hair that fell to her waist. She had high cheekbones, and he guessed she might be part Chinese. She was 5'6" tall with a slender build. She seemed to be very shy.

When Do joined James at his table, James asked Do about her. "Her name is Lan. She's, my sister-in-law. She came to America with my family. She's been here for a long time, but has worked mainly in our office at the rear of the shop. You're responsible for her coming to America, Jim."

"I forgot about that."

"Yes, I had asked Vandersyde if I could include another person on our trip to America. He told me that I could take one more person. She was that last person."

"Lan had just arrived in Saigon, from Hue, when we were about to leave for America. Ha begged me to get permission for her to join us.

"She's beautiful. How old is she? Is she single?"

"I believe that she's 33. I think that she's two years younger than Ha."

"That's surprising. She looks like she's much younger. How well does she speak English?"

"Excellent—she worked as an English language interpreter for the Hue City government. She was also an interpreter for Americans and Australians who were trying to do business with the South Vietnamese government."

"I'm very interested in hiring her to care for my children. My au pair, Mary, plans to return to Ireland soon. She has been corresponding with an old boyfriend. I think they're talking seriously about marriage. I need to find a suitable replacement for Mary. Do I have your permission to speak with Lan?"

"Of course—but I think that you should first discuss things with Ha. There's a lot of Lan's history that you should know. She has had serious health issues, due to the torturing she received from the Communists. Lan's little daughter was killed, and her husband ran away. I hope the bastard is dead. If he's not, and I can catch him—I'll kill him myself.

Lan is getting better with the help of Ha and our children, but she has a long way to go. You should hear more details from Ha; then you may decide if you are still interested in her."

"That's fair. I'll ask Ha if she'll meet with me. Thank you, Do."

When Do arrived home that evening, he informed Ha that James would be calling her, and that he was interested in hiring Lan to care for his children. The following day, James contacted Ha and asked to meet with her at a location away from the coffee shop.

Ha, like her sister, was a beautiful woman. She also had black hair that fell to her waist. At 5'4" tall, she was shorter than Lan. She had the same high cheekbones. Small wrinkles around her eyes reflected the extreme anxiety and fear that she had experienced over the safety of her husband and children while they were living in war-torn Vietnam. Ha was strong-willed, and it did not take her long to adapt to her new country. She was grateful to have been allowed to come to America with her family. She was excited to be free and to live in this beautiful country.

When Do had informed Ha about James' interest in Lan, her first concern was whether or not Lan was ready to be away from family members.

Lan seemed to be adjusting well living in America and she did not have the nightmares that had haunted her when she had first arrived in the United States.

Ha was very fond of James and was grateful to him for saving her family. He had always been kind and respectful to her and her children.

James and Ha agreed to meet in the lobby of the Hyatt Hotel, near the San Jose airport. When they arrived, they looked for a quiet place at the rear of the lobby where there were comfortable lounge chairs. After they were seated, Ha ordered an orange drink and James requested coffee from the waiter.

"Thanks for meeting with me, Ha. As Do might have told you, I'm interested in hiring Lan to care for my children. She might also be able to help me with managing my household expenses. I understand that she handles your accounting at the Coffee Shop. My children's Nanny is returning to Ireland soon, and I must find a replacement for her."

"Dai Uy. We are grateful that you saved our family from the Communists. We owe you our lives and we'll never forget what you've done for us."

"Dai Uy" means Captain, in Vietnamese. The English pronunciation is "Die We."

"Your family doesn't owe me anything, Ha. Do was a great commander, and he risked everything serving with the Americans. If he had stayed in Vietnam, the Communists would have executed him. I'm very happy that your family is living in the United States, and that they will now be free to live a safe life. Ha, please call me Jim."

"Yes, Dai Uy, I mean, Jim. I must tell you about Lan. You should know what she has been through. She's just now recovering from her ordeal at the hands of the Communists. She lives with terrible memories every day. She's getting better, but she still has a long way to go."

"Yes, please tell me everything. I'd like to understand her circumstances. I know how the Communists treated the Vietnamese people when they took over the south. I also know how they mistreated the American POWs."

Ha began, "Let me start from the beginning when Lan and I were born in Hue City. She's two years younger than I am. She was an excellent student and excelled in languages. That's why she speaks English so well. My parents arranged the marriage between Lan and her husband Khiem.

Lan didn't want to be married—she didn't even know Khiem. Our father insisted, so Lan went along with his demand. She would never defy our father.

"Khiem's family was very distinguished and wealthy. My father was a good friend of Khiem's father. Our mother didn't like Khiem. She thought that he was a weak man and a playboy. She didn't believe that he was serious enough to take on the responsibility of a family, but my father's decision was final—Lan would marry Khiem.

"Khiem joined the military. He didn't want to be drafted, so his father paid for him to be commissioned as an officer in the Army. His father also paid for him to be assigned to a post in Hue City, not far from his parent's home. He had little training as a soldier. He was irresponsible and didn't take his role as an Army Officer seriously. He drank alcohol every day and frequented the nightclubs where there were prostitutes. There were times when he came home drunk and abused Lan. On two occasions, he beat her with his fists. The NVA was very powerful and when they launched their attack on the South Vietnamese Army, they easily destroyed them. As the NVA entered Hue City and began killing our defense forces, Khiem and some of his fellow soldiers disappeared. They left the city and we don't know where they went. Do says that he will kill

Khiem if he ever sees him. He says Khiem is a coward and that he should be shot."

Ha continued, "The NVA went house to house raping and killing women and children. Lan was captured by some soldiers. They spent three days raping and beating her. They beat her body with their belts and punched her in the stomach and ribs many times. She had internal bleeding and almost bled to death. They left her to die. She was lucky to survive. If our cousin hadn't visited her home when he did, she would have died. You know that her daughter was killed by the artillery shelling."

"What's her state of mind now? How well has she recovered?" asked James.

"She has been progressing. She still has the memories of the ordeal though. Working at the Coffee Shop and meeting former South Vietnamese soldiers has been good for her. The soldiers treat her with much respect. They know that she's Do's sister-in-law and they'll always protect her."

"My au pair is returning to Ireland in a few months. She has an old boyfriend, and they have been corresponding—they might be considering marriage. I have three young children to raise. Do you think Lan is ready for a responsibility like that?"

"She might be ready now. I'm not sure. I'll have to speak with her. This could be a good opportunity for her, and a way for her to heal."

"Taking care of three children won't be easy, but the kids could help her focus on other things and take her mind away from the terrible memories of the war. They've been raised to be respectful, and she would have my total support for any disciplinary issues. My au pair would help her get acquainted with the children. Mary will still be here for a few months. We could have a smooth transition if Lan were to accept the job."

"How would she be able to get to your house every day?"

"I'd like to have her live in my guest house. It has two bedrooms. She would live with my au pair—until Mary leaves. It's very comfortable, and it has all the amenities—even a nice fireplace. Transportation would not be a problem for her. My driver is also my bodyguard. He would keep her safe when she leaves home. He takes the children to school when I'm away on business trips. He would also take her shopping or wherever she wanted to go. He would also take her to your home, Ha, whenever she wanted to visit with you."

"I'm excited for her. I'll speak with her today Dai Uy—I mean Jim. Thank you for considering her."

"I look forward to hearing from you. Hopefully she'll say yes," said James as he stood to leave.

After Ha had explained James' proposal, Lan immediately agreed to accept the offer. She told Ha that she was a little afraid of being responsible for James' children, but she would love to have that type of job. She loved the idea of spending time with children.

"If that's your decision, you should call Dai Uy yourself. He probably would prefer to hear from you, instead of me. Oh, he wants us to call him Jim—not Dai Uy."

Lan was very nervous when she called James to accept his proposal. He was very pleased to hear her decision. He told her that he would send a car to pick her up so that she could come to his home to meet with the children and him. Lan was surprised and excited to ride in a limousine. For the first time in her life, she felt privileged. Hopefully, this will be a new beginning for me—she whispered to herself.

Lan's introduction to James, his children, and Mary went very well.

Lan spoke with each child, and it was clear from their initial discussions that they were beginning to like her. After the introductions and brief discussions, the children gave Lan a tour of their bedrooms.

Mary was helpful in helping Lan understand what her duties would be. It was obvious that Mary loved the children, and that they loved her. Mary became very emotional when she spoke about leaving and said that it was going to be very difficult to leave the children. She explained to Lan that she and her old boyfriend had become reacquainted, and that he had asked her to marry him. She said that she was going to be 31-years-old soon, and it was time to settle down and have a family of her own.

Three months later, it was time for Mary to return to Ireland. She was sad and began to cry as she said goodbye to the children. The children began to cry too. James was very emotional as well. He told her to contact him, at any time, if she needed help. He handed her a sealed envelope with $5,000 in 100-dollar bills. He told her not to open it until she was on the airplane. It was his wedding gift to her.

When Lan assumed full responsibility for the children, she

would eat her meals with them and James—unless he was at work or away on a business trip.

James observed and listened to Lan while she was playing and reading to the children. He did his best to stay hidden from them, so that he would not interrupt their fun. He was pleased to see that Lan made the children laugh. She read books to them and had different voices for all the characters. The children responded well to her demands, and they obeyed her instructions when it was bedtime.

James was impressed with Lan's knowledge when they discussed various topics of the day. He enjoyed speaking with someone who was well-versed in many subjects. It became obvious to him that she was well educated. He was surprised that she could comprehend his explanations of some of the business transactions that he was negotiating.

As the weeks passed, James found himself wanting to stay close to home, and to be around Lan. He had begun to regret leaving for his office every morning—or traveling on a business trip that would take him away from home.

James began to question himself. Why was he so attracted to Lan? Was it because she was so beautiful? Was it the way she took care of the children? Was it because he felt so comfortable talking with her? Was it because he was so lonely? Was he falling in love with her?

He knew that he must be very careful. Lan and her family felt obligated to him, for helping them escape Vietnam. They held him in the highest regard. He would never want to hurt or embarrass them. They had suffered so much during the war.

"I've got to think this through. I've never been so unsure

of myself—and I don't like it. This is just not like me. I think I've fallen in love with her," James finally admitted to himself.

James took the children and Lan to church with him every Sunday. He considered himself a devout Christian, but not a practicing Catholic. Too much had happened in the Catholic Church, with abusive priests, for him to stay a practicing Catholic. He wanted his children to attend church and Catholic schools for their well-being. Public schools were a disaster. Lan was Catholic, so it was natural for her to attend Mass with the children and him.

The first Mass that the family had attended together, after Mary returned to Ireland, was eventful. As James and Lan entered the church with the children, many members of the congregation stared, whispered and a few of them pointed. James and Lan seemed to be oblivious to those paying attention to them.

James' brother Thomas, his wife Joan, and their two daughters, Erica, and Valerie, sat across the aisle from James. As James entered his pew, he smiled and nodded to Thomas and Joan.

Joan whispered to Thomas, "Wow, they sure look like a power couple. You didn't tell me that she was so beautiful. She could be a model. Is there something go'in on between them, Tom? The tongues will really be wagging in the congregation."

Thomas was annoyed. "Look, the tongues are already wagging. I thought gossip was a sin, Joan."

TWENTY-THREE
THE PROMISE

James maintained a family program of busy weekends, dedicated to his children. Almost every weekend the family participated in a special event. Lan always accompanied them, as a member of the family, to enjoy the fun. They visited the Boardwalk in Santa Cruz, Great America in Santa Clara, the zoo in Sacramento, and small public parks in Los Gatos. They watched movies that were produced specifically for children.

One evening, James walked by his daughter, Elizabeth's, room. He stopped to listen to Lan, who was reading a book to the children. The book was Vincent's. Although much older, his sisters enjoyed listening to Lan read the story to them. The story was Snow White and the Seven Dwarfs. Lan was acting out each character as she read. The children were laughing, hysterically, as she changed the sound of her voice while mimicking each character in the story.

When she finished reading, she told the children that it was time for them to go to their rooms—it was their bedtime. James quickly walked away so that he would not be discovered. He went to his study to review some business papers. He was pleased to see that his children were fond of Lan, and that she enjoyed being with them.

Two days later, late in the evening, James went to the guest house to visit Lan. When she answered the door, she was wearing a silk nightgown. She had just stepped out of the shower and her hair was wrapped in a towel. She had removed her makeup. He asked her if he could come in. She welcomed him in, and with a quiet voice asked him, "How may I help you Dai Uy?"

"I just want to thank you for being so loving and kind to my children. I can see that they really care for you."

She asked him to sit down on the couch in the living room.

"I'm happy that you've given me the opportunity to be with them. They have helped me cope with my depression over the loss of my daughter, Hoa. I wish that she could have had the opportunity to grow up like them."

"I know that you've been through some terrible times, Lan. Now you're in a safe place."

"I'll always be grateful to you, Dai Uy. You saved us all."

James moved towards her on the couch and gently cupped her face in his hands. He said, "Lan, I've fallen in love with you. I want you to be more than a Nanny to my children. I want you to be their mother and my wife."

When he lowered his hands to his sides she responded, "Dai Uy, you don't know what they did to me. You wouldn't want me for your wife—if you knew." she cried.

"Lan, you're wrong. I know what they did to you and it

doesn't matter. I want you, Lan. I've talked with Ha and Do. They've told me everything. It's okay. I want to take care of you and protect you. I won't allow anyone to hurt you ever again."

"Oh, Dai Uy. I've been in love with you since I first saw you at the Coffee Shop. That's when Ha explained to me that you were the one who saved our family. I remember when one of the waitresses, Quin, hid behind a screen near the customer tables to get a good look at you. I joined her. I was curious about you too. The other waitress, Tran, took drinks to you and Uncle Do. When Tran came over to us, she whispered, 'When I took him his drink, he smiled at me and said, "cam on co" (thank you). He's so handsome. I want to have his baby.' We laughed loudly about that, but you and Do didn't look our way. You were having a serious conversation. As you were leaving, I saw how the Vietnamese soldiers showed you so much respect—as they stood and saluted you. I saw you smile and salute them. It made me cry."

James put his hands on her shoulders and kissed her forehead. When he stood and picked her up in his arms, she put her arms around his neck and kissed his cheek. He carried her into the bedroom and placed her gently on the bed.

"Dai Uy, please don't leave the light on. I don't want you to see the scars on my body. It's what they did to me. Please— I don't want you to see them. I'm sorry," she said as she began to cry.

"Don't worry sweetheart, they couldn't take away the beauty that's in your heart. I have scars too. Some are on my body, but most are in my mind. We'll heal together, my love."

James removed her nightgown, and she slipped under the covers. He then removed his clothes and joined her. As they lay together and embraced, Lan began to tremble.

"Lan, please relax. I'm only going to kiss you and hold you in my arms. I want you to calm down. You're safe with me."

"I know Dai Uy. The memories of what the soldiers did to me are always with me. I'm afraid of the pain," she replied.

"We're just going to hold each other until we fall asleep."

The following night James visited Lan again, late in the evening. They kissed and held each other until early morning, when James left to go to the main house and dress for work.

On the third night, while lying in bed, Lan turned to James and said, "Please love me, Dai Uy." While they made love, he kissed the scars on her back and legs. Lan began to cry. He gently rolled her over onto her back. He then moved down below her waist and proceeded to pleasure her with his tongue in a manner that she had never known. She began to moan. Her moaning became louder and louder until she gave out a sound that was almost a scream. It was her first time to feel the pleasure.

After their lovemaking he pulled her towards him. He wrapped his strong arms around her with her back to his chest. As they began to fall asleep, "Lan murmured, "I love you Dai Uy. I'm so happy."

He replied, "I love you too, my little one."

At 4 am, James awakened and began kissing her face and stroking the tuft of hair between her legs. She was quickly aroused and beckoned him to mount her. He pleasured her with his tongue again—then helped her to reach the ultimate pleasure. James left the guest house at 5 am to prepare for his workday.

Late in the afternoon, James' assistant informed him that Lan was on the line. His first thought was that something must be wrong. When he picked up the phone he asked, "Lan, is something wrong?"

"No Dai Uy—I'm sorry for calling you, but I've missed you all day. I haven't been able to think of anything but our love-making last night."

James was relieved and began to laugh. "I've missed you too little one. I've been busy with visitors and phone calls. When there has been a break in the action here, I've been daydreaming about you. Last night was great."

"It was amazing, please come home as soon as possible. I'm sorry that I interrupted you," she said.

"Never be concerned or hesitate to call me. I'm available to you and the children at any time. My employees have been instructed to put through any calls from you. You, and the children are my world," he said.

"Thank you Dai Uy. I love you—see you soon," replied Lan as she hung up.

Lan and James made love almost every night when the children had gone to bed. They made love in the middle of the night and early in the morning before he left for work. He taught her many sexual positions and they would come together, spontaneously, in different rooms of the guest house. He even approached her while she was preparing food in the kitchen. They made love in the swimming pool and under the trees on the lawn. Their physical desire for each other was insatiable.

As they lay in bed, Lan asked James, "Dai Uy, how do you know so much about lovemaking?"

"That's a long story. Are you sure that you want to hear it?"

"Yes, I want to know everything about you, my love."

"It began when I was fifteen. I was a junior in high school and was looking for a job. I played basketball and at the same time, I was taking Karate lessons. I had to pay for my lessons, so I had to find a job. I answered an ad for a part-time gardener, and I interviewed with an older woman who was a widow. She was from France and spoke with a strong accent. She was also a college professor."

"What subjects did she teach?"

"She had a PHD, and taught psychology at Stanford University. She also taught Yoga classes to adults in the evening at the Los Gatos Community Center. I had been working for her for about three months when one day she put her arms around me and kissed me."

"She approached you—and kissed you?"

"Yes, she kissed me, and I was shocked. From there we ended up in her bedroom. We were constant lovers for about two years until I went off to college. I met with her during school breaks, and we continued our relationship. She taught me everything that I know about lovemaking. She also taught me many of the sexual positions of the Kamasutra."

"What's Kamasutra?"

"It's an ancient Indian text on sexuality, eroticism, and emotional fulfillment. It contains graphic pictures of sexual positions. So far, I've only taught you a few of them."

"You must teach me more. I want to experience all of them with you."

"Okay, I promise I'll teach you everything that I know."

"What happened to her?"

"One day when I visited her during a break from college, she told me that we couldn't be intimate any longer. She had been diagnosed with cancer ten years before I had met her. She was told, at that time, that it was in remission. The cancer came back, and it was very aggressive. She had to undergo treatments that weakened her. She passed away just before I had to leave for Vietnam. She left me an inheritance."

"She must have been in love with you, Dai Uy."

"Yes, I know she loved me. I loved her. She was a remarkable woman."

TWENTY-FOUR
SENSEI

Sensei—in the world of martial arts means "teacher."

Doctor Irene Curie Lantz was 49-years-old when she met 15-year-old James Greaney. James had answered her ad in the Los Gatos newspaper looking for a part-time gardener and maintenance worker.

Irene was a professor of psychology at Stanford University. She was born in Paris, France. She was mildly attractive and always had a serious expression on her face. She was short in stature, with a trim figure. Irene was an only child, of parents who had emigrated to America with her when she was 19-years-old. Her husband had also been a Stanford professor. He had died two years before James had met Irene. He had been a heavy smoker and died from a heart attack while undergoing treatments for lung cancer.

Irene had been born with one leg an inch and a half shorter than the other. Her father had had shoes specially made for her to compensate for the difference in the length of her legs.

As a young girl, she had to work hard to stay physically fit. She was able to participate in sports with other girls and very few paid any attention to her deformity. In her later years, she continued to maintain a conditioned body and had the appearance of a much younger woman. She taught Yoga twice a week in the evening, to adults at the Community Center.

Irene was impressed with James' pleasant and respectful demeanor. When they first met, he was polite, referring to her as ma'am. He looked into her eyes when they were talking and wore a T-shirt and shorts. He was tall, tan, and good-looking. He had ridden his bicycle to her home. She explained, in detail, her gardening requirements, and wanted James to maintain her gardens and grounds, keeping them well-groomed and in immaculate condition.

Irene hired him and said that he could begin work the following Saturday morning. She informed him that he would also be working a few hours every Wednesday afternoon when he finished school.

James worked very diligently and kept the gardens and grounds in pristine condition. He was always on time for work and was thorough in completing his tasks. During the hottest days he would remove his T-shirt and add to his tan while he worked. He did not wear a hat and the hot sun bleached his blonde hair to a silver shade. The color had the effect of making his blue eyes look bluer in color and more penetrating. He had a muscular build, and his abdominal muscles were prominent and well-defined. At noon on Saturdays, Irene's cook/housekeeper, Virginia Crawford, would have lunch waiting for James and Irene. During their lunch, they would discuss local topics of the day and world events. James asked many questions and Irene enjoyed their discussions about philosophy, history, and numerous other topics. They both laughed often during their discussions. After lunch, James would return to his gardening duties. At 2 pm, he would put his tools away and leave for home.

After he had been working for Irene for several months, James noticed that she was watching him. He would often catch her peeking from behind the window curtains in her bedroom. At first, he thought she might be checking up on him to make sure that he was working. He was not concerned, because he had been very attentive to his work. Later, he learned that she had other things on her mind.

On a hot Saturday, late in the morning, Irene called him to lunch. James started towards the house and then stopped. He yelled, "I have to get my shirt." She replied, "Don't bother with that, come as you are, lunch is ready. Don't let your soup get cold."

They sat down for their lunch and began talking about psychology and its meaning. James asked her to explain schizophrenia, and the difference between a psychopath and a sociopath.

Irene was pleased with his questioning. She went into detail discussing the different maladies in medical terms, while avoiding technical language that would be too confusing for him.

After lunch James stood up to leave. Irene rose and said, "Jim, please wait."

She walked towards him and placed her arms around his waist while laying her head on his chest. He put his arms around her and caressed her back. They did not move or say anything but stood holding each other. Finally, she said, "Please forgive me but I couldn't help myself."

He replied, "I'm glad that you came to me. I've been thinking about you for a long time."

She squeezed him tighter and then ran her hands over his back. He moved his hands gently down her back and began massaging her bottom.

She raised her head and kissed him on the neck. She whispered, "Please come with me," as she took his hand and began leading him towards her bedroom.

When they reached her bed, they began kissing and groping each other. She unbuttoned his shorts as he removed her blouse and bra.

They finished undressing and lay together on the bed. He moved to mount her, and she whispered to him to go slowly. "We have plenty of time. Let's enjoy each other."

She guided him slowly into her. He began thrusting his hips and climaxed quickly with a loud groan. For a moment, he lay still and then rolled slowly onto his back. She moved on top of him and began licking and kissing his neck. She continued moving down his chest. She was aroused by the touch of his hard body and the taste of the salt on his skin from working in the hot sun. She continued moving down his chest to his groin. He lay with his eyes closed and did not know what to do other than to just enjoy her movements. She proceeded to kiss and lick him as she took his member into her mouth and began gently sucking. He was startled, but pleased and he began to get an erection again. As his erection enlarged, she mounted him and began moving her hips rhythmically—while looking down at him with her hands on his chest. He moved his hips in timing with her rhythm. As she began to move faster, she pressed her body down until she had reached a height of pleasure—and emitted a quiet moan. She then fell forward kissing his face and neck. He continued thrusting his hips until climaxing. They rested—holding each other in a warm embrace.

While they lay together, she said, "I hope that I haven't disappointed you. I've been longing for you for weeks. I couldn't help myself any longer."

"I've wanted you too. I was afraid to approach you. I thought that if I did, you'd reject me."

"No, my dear. I've been obsessed with you. I'm embarrassed to admit it."

"Please don't be. I want you—like this. This is what I've been dreaming about."

"We must be discreet. No one can know about us—they would never understand. What about your family?"

"My family will never know. I don't share my personal life with my brothers or with my parents. This is between us. I hope you'll want it that way."

"Yes dear, I'd like to teach you about many things."

"You'll be my 'Sensei' and teach me how to make love."

"What's a Sensei?" asked Irene.

"I'm taking Karate lessons. In class, we refer to our instructor as, Sensei."

"Okay, then I'll be your Sensei—for lovemaking."

For over two years, on most Saturdays, and after they had

finished their lunch, Irene and James would spend the remain-
der of the afternoon in her bedroom. She would have the
turntable on her record player loaded with records of French
singers, including her favorite, Edith Piaf. She taught him lovemaking while the music played softly. She taught him that it was
best not to rush. She taught him that moving slowly and
carefully was the most enjoyable way. He must be careful to
ensure that his partner is satisfied. She followed the graphic
illustrations contained in the Kamasutra text, as a guide to
teaching him the enjoyment of sex in countless sexual positions.

James began to lose interest in girls his own age as he
became consumed with Irene's teachings. He knew that the
girls would not make love like Irene. Many girls were afraid of
sex and others were too silly. Irene was much safer for him,
and with her, there was never any fear of pregnancy.

Irene and James would often take pictures of each other,
naked, with her polaroid camera. They would lie in bed and
admire the pictures. She kept them in her bedroom dresser
drawer.

After he had gone off to college, they would schedule times
to be together, for a few hours, when he had returned home
on break.

One Saturday he arrived at her home for a scheduled
appointment, and she had sad news for him.

"As they sat in her living room, she said, "Mon Cher, we
won't be able to be intimate any longer. I've become very sick
again. Several years ago, I was diagnosed with cancer. Later,
they told me that my cancer had gone into remission. Now, it

has returned, and it's even more aggressive than before. I'll begin treatments next week. I feel very weak now."

Listening to her, James became very emotional, and tears welled up in his eyes. He asked that they lay down and hold each other while they talked. They talked for two hours about their relationship and the future. He told her that after graduation, he would be entering the Army.

"I've finished ROTC training and I'll be sworn-in to the Regular Army as an officer. I'm sure that everything will go well. You know that I've always been a lucky guy. I found you, didn't I?"

"I hate to think that your precious life could be wasted in that foolish war."

When James had completed advanced training at Ft. Ord, he received orders for Vietnam. His mother had written to him that he had received a large envelope. It was waiting for him. It was from Virginia Crawford. He returned to his parents' home for a ten day leave before reporting to Travis Air Force Base for the long flight to Vietnam.

Sitting alone in his old bedroom, he opened the envelope. Inside were three small envelopes. One was from a law firm. Another was from Virginia Crawford, and a third had lettering on the outside that read, "Please open when you are alone."

He opened the letter from Virginia first. In it she had explained that Irene had suffered a stroke after a cancer treatment and had died in her sleep. She said that Irene had left him a large amount of money that would be explained in the letter from the law firm. She wrote that Irene had written instructions for her ashes to be spread over her garden. She wanted Jim to spread her ashes when he was available.

He opened the letter from the law firm. The letter informed him that Irene had left him half the value of her estate—$100,000. A check for that amount was enclosed in the envelope for him.

When he opened the third envelope, he found that it contained the naked pictures that they had taken of each other. A simple note read, "My dearest love—please remember me."

He laughed when he read her note and said out loud, "What an extraordinary woman you were. We will meet again—I loved you."

He then noticed that he had not seen a few of the pictures. They had to have been taken by a third person.

When James met with Virginia to spread Irene's ashes he asked, "Virginia, you must have been the one taking pictures of Irene and me. How did that happen? I had no idea that you had been watching us."

"I wasn't being a voyeur, Jim. Irene asked me to take pictures of the two of you while you were making love. I must admit that I did enjoy taking them. She was obsessed with you. Towards the end of her life, and when she was bedridden, she would ask me to bring her the pictures. She would look at them for hours and then she would give them back to me to place in her dresser. They were a comfort to her. She truly loved you, Jim. She told me many times that you were the love of her life."

"I'm glad that you took them Virginia. I've burned the pictures and I have the ashes in this envelope. I don't need pictures to remember her. I'll always remember her. Let's add these ashes to her ashes and then Irene will have them with her for all eternity."

"Thank you, Jim. I know that she would love that. It's a beautiful idea."

TWENTY-FIVE
GREAT NEWS

James visited Lan at the guest house around 10 pm. Earlier in the evening they had put the children to bed, after Lan had read them one of Vincent's books. Lan seemed unusually quiet and James thought that she might not be feeling well. After the children were in bed, James went to his study for a few hours to review documents on his latest commercial real estate purchase, and Lan went to the guest house.

When Lan opened the door, James could see that her eyes were red and her face was swollen from crying. "What's wrong little one? Why are you so sad?"

"Oh, Dai Uy, I've got some bad news," she said and began crying.

"Well, let's sit down and you can tell me all about it."

"Dai Uy, you know that I told you that because of my internal injuries, a doctor in Vietnam explained to me that I would never be able to have any more children."

"Yes, I remember you telling me that. It's okay, Lan. It's not a problem for me as long as I have you—you know that," he replied.

"For several weeks, I've been feeling sick in the morning. I'm nauseous and I'm having headaches. I thought that I might have had a virus. I told Ha, and she took me to her doctor. When the doctor examined me, he said I was three months pregnant. I was shocked. I'm sorry Dai Uy. I didn't mean to deceive you. If you are upset, I'll leave and go to live with my sister," Lan cried in anguish.

James began laughing. "You're something else, little one. I'm extremely happy—I'm not upset! This is great news! We must celebrate. This is fantastic—we're going to have a baby!"

"You're not mad at me? I thought that you'd be angry, and so did Ha. We were afraid of what you would do. I've been upset all day waiting for you to come home. It took all the energy that I had to get through dinner—and to put the children to bed, Dai Uy."

"Lan, I've got a surprise for you. For weeks now, I've been planning to ask you to marry me. I was going to propose to you on your birthday. Last week I went to a jewelry store, and I bought a ring for you. I have it in my bedroom. I've been waiting to give it to you. We're going to have a baby! Will you marry me, Lan?"

"Yes, of course, my love—I can't believe it! I've been so miserable all day. Now I'm the happiest woman in the world!" she yelled.

"I'll give you the ring tomorrow. It's late, and I want you to go to bed now and get some rest."

"I can't go to sleep now. I must call, Ha. She's been worrying about me all day."

"Are you sure it's not too late to call?"

"Oh no, not for wonderful news like this. She'll be very excited to hear that we're to be married."

"Lan, you should stop calling me Dai Uy. I don't know if I want my wife calling me Captain," he joked.

"I love to call you, Dai Uy—you are my brave Captain who saved me and my family from the Communists. But I'll call you, Jim, if it will make you happy," she replied.

"On second thought—you can call me whatever you like," he laughed.

"Thank you, Dai Uy," she laughed as she put her arms around his neck and kissed him.

Lan was extremely excited when she called her sister, Ha. Lan spoke in Vietnamese.

"Sister, did I wake you? Ha, I've great news. Dai Uy is happy that I'm pregnant. He asked me to marry him!—he said that he had planned to ask me on my birthday—but he asked me after I told him about our baby. Of course, I said yes. I can't believe that we were so afraid about what he was going to do. I'm so happy, Ha—I love life again. I'll call you tomorrow."

"Is Ha happy that we're going to be married?"

"She was surprised and excited to hear that you're happy about the baby, and that we're getting married. She said, "Dai Uy is joining our family—I must tell Do, right away.""

The following day, James called Bui Quang Do. "Do, I'm

sure that you've heard by now that Lan and I are getting married."

"Yes, I heard about everything last night. Ha woke me and kept me awake for two hours. She's so happy you'd think that she was the one getting married. We're happy for both of you."

"Thank you, Do. I'd like you to be my best man."

"I would be honored—have you set a date for the wedding?"

"Not yet, but it will be soon. As you probably know—we're having a baby. I'd also like Ha and you to help me with the arrangements—I want to have a Vietnamese Catholic wedding—will you help me? The cost is of no concern—I want it to be a spectacular event for Lan."

"Of course, we'll help you. Ha knows far more about weddings than I do. I know that she'll be happy to jump in and plan everything for you."

<hr>

After Mass on Sunday, the family returned home to a brunch that had been prepared by their cook, Margarita Hernandez. Lan sat next to James at the table. He asked the children for their attention. "Kids, I've got some great news. I've asked Lan to marry me, and she's said yes. She'll be the new Mom around here."

"That's great Dad!" exclaimed Elizabeth and Georgia, together.

"When are you going to be married?" asked Elizabeth.

"Can I be in the wedding?" asked Georgia.

"We haven't set a date, but it'll be soon, and yes, you'll have a part in the wedding," James responded.

The girls went to Lan and threw their arms around her.

"We love you, Lan," said Elizabeth.

"Yes, we love you," said Georgia.

"I love all of you," said Lan as she began to cry.

"Are you still going to read my books to me?" asked Vincent.

"Yes, every night."

"Dad, I knew something was going to happen. I saw how you looked at Lan in Church—and how she looked at you. I'm so happy for you. I know that you've been lonely," declared Elizabeth.

"Thank you, Liz. I love you," said James as he hugged her and kissed her forehead.

James called a special meeting of the Vigilantes. When William, Thomas, and Victor arrived, he led them into his study. There were four glasses on a table and a bottle of Macallan Single Malt Scotch Whiskey.

"Wow, what's the occasion? That's probably a five-hundred-dollar bottle of whiskey," declared William.

"Close, this is a special day for me. I'm getting married, and I wanted to drink a toast with you guys," said James.

"Joan guessed it. I know who it is. It's the Vietnamese woman that you bring to Mass, isn't it Jim?" asked Thomas.

"You guessed right, Tom—her name is Lan. I've asked her to marry me."

"Joan saw that there was something special with the two of you. Lan's a very beautiful woman—you guys. She's a knockout. Congratulations Jim," exclaimed Thomas.

"Well, let's get to drinking a few toasts to the happy couple. This is the best whiskey one can buy," said William.

"You've got to tell us all about Lan, Jim. This is quite a surprise," said Victor.

"When are you getting married?" asked William.

"We haven't set a date, but it'll be soon. I'm going to be a father again."

"We'll have to drink a few more toasts to that good news. Another little Jimmy is coming into the world. I don't know if the world is ready," joked Thomas.

"Here's to you, big brother, and Lan. I hope this marriage brings nothing but happiness to both of you—you both deserve it," toasted William.

The activities at the Greaney home continued as usual. James and Lan decided that she would live in the guest house until their wedding day. They also decided that they were not going to tell the children about Lan's pregnancy for a few more weeks.

James helped Lan sign up for yoga classes three times a week. The classes were in downtown Los Gatos. Margarita gave Lan cooking lessons and helped her prepare some of the foods that James and the children liked.

James' driver, Brandon Foster, drove Lan and Margarita on their errands and observed them from a distance, for security purposes.

TWENTY-SIX
FLEETING

Gangs in Santa Clara County, California had been fighting over turf, and the control of illegal drug distribution. Violence between Vietnamese gangs had been escalating. The Vietnamese gangs were also battling Mexican gangs who were controlled and directed by gang leaders doing time in prison. Mexican gang leaders, incarcerated in San Quentin, were encouraging the Mexican gangs in San Jose to fight the Vietnamese. Their purpose was to regain control of the drug territories that had been lost to the violent Vietnamese gangs. The drug territories had become increasingly lucrative.

Employees at high-tech companies in Santa Clara County were becoming the premium targets for drug dealers. They were being paid large salaries as incentives to join the start-up companies who were spin offs of the larger corporate entities. Some were becoming very rich, and a few were already millionaires in their twenties, due to stock windfalls. Flush with cash, the employees could easily afford to pay whatever the drug supplier asked—especially after the employee had become addicted. Cocaine had become the drug of choice for some purchasing managers, design engineers, office workers, and upper management. It was a popular compliment to take with wine, beer, or hard liquor. It was used as an incentive to have sex—or to secure a corporate contract.

The Vigilantes were content to watch the gangs destroy each other. It did not change their plan to pursue the elimination of drug dealers and corrupt politicians.

❧

Bui Quang Do's wife Ha, had organized a luncheon, at the Hoang My restaurant on Tully Road in San Jose. She had invited five of her closest women friends, to celebrate her sister Lan's upcoming wedding. Lan would be discussing the detailed plans of the wedding. They were discussing the number of attendees, the dresses for the attendants to the bride, and the decorations needed for the reception hall.

Lan was excited as she was getting dressed for the luncheon. She kept looking at her engagement ring as she applied her make-up. There were times, while daydreaming, that she could not believe that this was happening to her. Lan chose to wear a soft pastel blue ao dai—Vietnam's national dress, and one of the country's most striking symbols of beauty. When she looked at herself in the mirror, she knew that she was beautiful, with her long, black hair reaching her waist. She also knew that beauty was only temporary—but her love would last forever. Dai Uy said that she was beautiful, and that was all that she needed to hear. He said that he loved her—and no one else's opinion mattered to her. "I'm fortunate that my scars are hidden by this ao dai," she whispered to herself.

⌒

Brandon Foster was James Greaney's driver and body-guard. He was African American, and a Vietnam Veteran. He had been assigned as a sniper in an infantry company that was located near Cu Chi, Vietnam. He had been wounded by a rifle bullet to the shoulder. He suffered from PTSD, and was having difficulty finding employment. He was contacted by an employee of the Santa Clara County Veterans Group (SCCVG). The Group helped returning veterans find employment and also apply for their VA health benefits—Brandon had signed up with them.

James Greaney had been looking to hire a new driver. He contacted SCCVG's office and told them that he wanted to hire a veteran to be his personal driver.

When James and Brandon met, they immediately liked each other. Early in their discussion, James knew that Brandon was a legitimate combat veteran. There were a lot of phony people claiming to be combat veterans. James believed that only a combat veteran could determine another combat veteran's legitimacy. They discussed their war experiences for over an hour. James hired him on the spot. James had learned, from their discussions, that Brandon was an expert marksman with a rifle. Brandon also claimed that he was very proficient with a pistol.

"I'm hiring you as a driver/bodyguard. Your pay will be based on both jobs. I'll help you obtain the necessary licenses for your weapons," said James.

⌒

James Greaney was in Dallas on a business trip. It had been arranged by a good friend and local Congressman for him to meet with Jim Bob Chandler, the chief of staff of the Texas Governor's office. The State of Texas had been aggressively promoting incentives for companies to relocate their businesses. Chandler and his staff enthusiastically greeted James as he entered their offices.

James' business investments were thriving in California, but he was beginning to see some alarming signs of decline. State government regulations were handicapping economic growth and the tax rates for corporations had continued to rise.

James was pleased with his meetings, and considered them to be successful. He liked the people that he had met, especially Jim Bob. On his next trip, he planned to meet community leaders and to survey the home market, as well as look for small ranch locations. He had been gone three days on this trip and he was anxious to be going home. He said his goodbyes to Jim Bob and his staff and was driven to his hotel in a limousine. He finished packing his luggage and then called Lan. She was elated to hear his voice.

"I'm coming home tomorrow, sweetheart."

"Oh, I'm so excited, Dai Uy. I've missed you so much."

"I haven't slept well in this hotel. I wasn't able to hold you and fall asleep like we always do. From now on I'm going to take you with me on all business trips—or I'm staying home."

"I've not been able to sleep well either. I have been wearing one of your worn shirts to bed so that I can smell your cologne. It helps me pretend that you're with me, and it helps me to fall asleep. What time will you be home tomorrow?"

"I'm due to arrive at 3 pm and I'll have my arms around you by 5."

James had recently been chartering a private jet to use for his business trips. His financial advisor, Carolyn Speer, had informed him that he had become a very wealthy man, and that he could afford almost any purchase. He decided to fly privately to avoid the hassle of the crowds and the frequent flight delays of commercial airlines. He also preferred to be alone with his thoughts on a long flight—as opposed to listening to someone sitting next to him blabbering on about some social topic.

"Ha has arranged for a luncheon tomorrow with some of her friends, and I'm going to be the guest of honor. They want to help me plan for our wedding. I'm sure that I'll be home before you arrive, Dai Uy. I can't wait to feel your arms around me."

"Yes, I'm going to make love to you all through the night."

"Have a safe flight home, my love. I'll see you soon—good night."

"Good night, little one—sleep tight and I'll be there soon."

Brandon Foster drove Lan to the luncheon. He opened her door as she exited the car. He walked behind her to the entrance of the restaurant. As she proceeded to a table at the rear of the room, where Ha and her friends were seated, he scanned the room, checking out the other customers. He saw a table of eight young Vietnamese men, not far from Ha's table. They were drinking and toasting each other, while talking loudly in Vietnamese.

As Lan passed their table they stopped talking and stared at her. She was an amazingly beautiful woman. Their eyes followed her to Ha's table, and then they began murmuring among themselves—the only English word that was uttered was—Wow.

Brandon was satisfied that everyone in the room seemed harmless. He went back outside but stayed close to the entrance of the restaurant—in case Lan needed his help.

Lan was excited and laughing as she approached the table and she held out her hand to the women seated—to show off her ring. She was oblivious to the men who were ogling her.

The women stared at Lan's ring in awe. They congratulated her very loudly—with many oohs and ahhs. One woman exclaimed, "Oh my, Dai Uy is very generous. That ring must be worth thousands. How much did he pay for it?"

"It's not polite to ask," Ha scolded.

While listening to the women speak excitedly, and loudly to each other, Lan whispered to herself, "It's hard to believe that not too long ago the Communists were trying to kill me and my family. Now I'm getting ready to marry Dai Uy. I'm so fortunate that he has chosen me. Maybe our karma is good."

The restaurant was very noisy and busy with waiters delivering food and drinks. Busboys were cleaning off the tables to prepare for the next customers.

Suddenly, three gunmen, dressed in long black coats, entered the dining area from the kitchen. One of the gunmen moved quickly towards the entrance to the restaurant while the other two faced the table of eight Vietnamese men. The two gunmen were carrying Uzi Pro Pistols that had magazines holding 32 rounds. They fired at the table of eight and six of the young men died instantly. The other two victims writhed on the floor with multiple wounds.

The two shooters, calmy replaced their empty magazines. Once reloaded, they began spraying the room, targeting the customers hiding under tables or trying to escape.

When he heard the shooting, Brandon ran towards the restaurant and as he arrived at the entrance, the third gunman shot him twice in the chest. As he was falling, Brandon shot the gunman between the eyes. As he lay on the floor, Brandon realized that he was bleeding heavily from his wounds—he felt himself go into shock. He died seconds later.

The two remaining gunmen ran from the restaurant. One was seriously wounded and was bleeding from a wound to his left leg. They got into a waiting car and sped off.

When the first police units arrived at the restaurant, they were shocked to see the level of carnage. Tables had been over-turned and bodies were strewn all over. Blood was spattered everywhere—even on the ceiling. Many of the wounded were crying and screaming in pain.

The women at Ha's table were lying on the floor. Three of her friends were dead, and two were badly wounded. Ha called out to Lan. "Lan, are you okay?" she yelled in anguish.

"No, sister, I can't move. I've been shot."

"Hold on Lan, they are coming to help us. I can hear the policemen talking—please hold on," she cried.

Ha crawled to where Lan was lying on her back.

As Ha reached Lan, she could see that Lan was wounded in the chest and abdomen. She found a tablecloth and attempted to use it to stem the bleeding of Lan's wounds.

Lan began coughing up blood and her breathing was labored. As she closed her eyes and took her last breath she whispered, "I love you, Dai Uy—I'm sorry."

When James' plane landed and taxied to the terminal, he could see from the window, three men standing next to his limo. He did not see Brandon, but as the plane came closer, he recognized his two brothers and Victor.

When he exited the plane, he walked quickly towards the men.

"What's going on? Where's Brandon? Why are you here?"

"Calm down, Jim. We have very bad news—you need to sit down—let's get in the car," said William.

When they were seated, Victor began telling James about the tragic shootings of Lan, Brandon, and many others who were in the restaurant. He said that Ha had been wounded and was undergoing surgery at the hospital—she would survive.

"Jim, the shootings were between two Vietnamese gangs. Three gunmen came in through the kitchen and began shooting with machine pistols. They shot their rival gang members, and then continued to shoot innocent customers. They killed fifteen people, Jim. Brandon was killed by one of the gunmen as he came to their rescue. He was able to kill the gunman who shot him, before he died."

"Where's Lan?" asked James as he began to cry.

"She's at the morgue," replied Victor with tears running down his cheeks.

"Oh my God, what about the baby?"

"Jim, the baby couldn't be saved," cried Thomas.

"How is Ha doing?" asked James, sobbing.

"She was shot in the hip, Jim. She'll be okay. She's in surgery," said William.

"We need to contact Brandon's family. I've got his personal information in my office. We must take care of him and his family," declared James.

Victor drove the limousine to the hospital. James sobbed uncontrollably during the trip. By the time they had reached the hospital, he had regained his composure.

James walked up to the receptionist and asked to be directed to the surgical waiting room. As they entered the waiting room, Bui Quang Do stood up and put his arms around James. "I'm sorry, Jim. Those bastards killed many people. I don't know what to say."

"I went to the restaurant as soon as I learned about the shootings. I knew that was where Ha and the others were celebrating Lan. The police would not allow me to go inside the restaurant to find Ha, but I saw her being put into an ambulance. I asked the police about my sister-in-law, Lan. They told me she was one of the ones who didn't make it. The policeman said, that I should talk to the coroner. He was standing by his van. I talked to the coroner and told him that I'd like my sister-in-law taken to Grace Mortuary. He said that he knew where the mortuary was and he would make sure that Lan was taken there after they had completed their examination."

"How is Ha?" "Will she recover?" asked James.

"Yes, the bullet went through her hip, but it didn't hit any vital organs."

"Thank God. I'll contact you tomorrow to check on her. We've much to talk about my friend. I must go home to the children."

When the men were back in the limousine, James addressed his brothers and Victor. "Listen, guys. I need your help. I'd like you to be there when I tell the children about Lan. I don't think I can do it by myself."

We'll be there for you and the kids. Bill, Vic, and I were talking earlier, and we decided to have our wives and children there as well. In fact, some of the families are already at your house," said Thomas.

"Thank you, guys," said James.

The funeral service for Lan, began at St. Joseph Catholic Church in San Jose. James had ordered pink and white orchids to be placed throughout the church. He walked alone to her casket. It had been placed in front of the altar. When he stood before her, he whispered a prayer for her and their baby. She was beautiful, and looked like she was just sleeping. Her hands were folded over her womb as if they were protecting her unborn child. James placed his Captain's bars under her hands. He bent down and kissed her forehead. He whispered, "Your Dai Uy will always be with you—wait for me."

TWENTY-SEVEN
A PERSONAL DECISION

Two weeks after Lan's funeral, James arranged a trip to Maui with his children. He asked his former mother-in-law, Nancy Allison, who was a widow, to accompany her grandchildren and him. They stayed in a large house with five bedrooms and a panoramic view of the ocean—the house was secretly owned by James and the Vigilantes.

Nancy and the children had great fun, playing in the ocean, riding the Maui train, attending luaus in the evening, taking day trips to other islands, and just lying in the sun. James accompanied them to all the events, and he managed, successfully, to maintain a pleasant persona.

When they returned to Los Gatos, after three weeks in Maui, Nancy moved into James' guest house. She had made a commitment to him that she would assume the role of caregiver for her grandchildren.

James went to visit with Lan's sister, Ha. She was home convalescing from the wound to her hip that she had received from the shootings at the restaurant. She was happy to see him, and they sat down in her living room for some tea. She asked him how he and the children were doing. She was pleased to hear that they had just returned from a vacation. They engaged in small talk for a while and then they addressed the subject that was haunting James.

"Ha, I need your help. The only thing keeping me from going off the deep end is my responsibility to the children. I don't know what to do."

"Dai Uy, you must think about what Lan would want you to do. You did much more than save her from the Communists. You loved her and gave her hope and joy with her pregnancy. I never saw her happier than when you told her that you were excited about having the baby—and then you asked her to marry you. She would talk about that all the time. You were her salvation. She adored you, Dai Uy. She told me that you gave her a reason to live. She didn't want to live after losing her daughter, Hoa, and then the humiliation and pain of the beatings. She told me many times that she wanted to kill herself—it was only her religion that stopped her. You were only together for a short time, but the love that you had for each other, most people never experience. Lan would want you to continue to take care of the children and build a new life for yourself."

"Thank you, Ha. I'll try harder to adjust to life without Lan. I've been miserable, but I'll try to pull myself out of this depression. You've been a great help to me."

"Please stay in touch with me. I know you're working with Do, but I'd also like to see you, from time to time."

"I'll stay in touch. I'd like for you to visit the children when you can."

"I will, as soon as I'm able to leave my home."

"Thank you," said James as he left.

James continued the practice of a family home meeting every Tuesday evening. He became more involved with his children than ever before. He occasionally took on Lan's role in reading to them and acting out the characters in the books. He was a poor substitute for her when it came to mimicking the voices of the characters—but his children appreciated his efforts—he was there for them.

He took his children to school and picked them up every day unless he had to travel for business purposes. His new driver/bodyguard, William Fowler, was a Vietnam veteran, and had served in the military police.

When James had to travel, William would take the children to and from school.

After the death of his wife Georgia, James and his children would take flowers to her grave as well as to his parents' graves and recite a prayer. After Lan's death, they also took flowers to her grave and recited a prayer for her and the baby. They made this visit to the cemetery monthly. It was helpful for James in his healing process.

Two years after Lan's passing, James began to consider dating. Over the course of his travels, he had been introduced to several divorcees who were professional businesswomen— they were not known to each other.

When he determined that it was time to take a break from business and address his personal needs, he would contact one of them and arrange to meet. The date might consist of a dinner at a popular restaurant, a weekend trip to Carmel, San Francisco, Las Vegas, or a visit to a spa near Calistoga.

His dates could look forward to a wonderful time—it might be hours of engaging conversation, an expensive dinner with drinks, or a flight on a private jet to an undisclosed destination. It might also be a night or two at a luxury hotel.

James had made a personal vow that he would no longer seek a committed relationship. He avoided dating any woman who even, remotely, resembled either Georgia or Lan. None of the women that he dated would ever be introduced to his children.

With the loss of Lan, James' heart had turned to stone. He was lonely and felt a cold hatred overtaking him. He would never again allow anyone in—to know or love him.

He was always personable when interacting with strangers, but he had lost interest in getting to know any of them. He had withdrawn into himself.

He adored his children, and loved his close family members, but in many ways, he was a broken man. He knew that he had not had anything to do with the loss of the women that he had loved, but he had a nagging sense that their loss had something to do with his sins from the past. Maybe it had to do with the dark side of karma—caused by the many deaths that he had been responsible for in the war.

James' "blood was up" and he planned to aggressively wipe out the gangs and members of the drug cartels, as well as the corrupt politicians. This was a time for revenge. He would step up the attacks. He met with Do and the Vigilantes, who shared his outrage and determination. Do's wife, Ha, had been seriously wounded in the fatal attack that took Lan's life. Do was also seeking greater vengeance.

James contacted Sal Cuffaro and said, "Sal, I misplaced the contact information for your cousin. Please give it to me again. We're hiring veterans for our security company."

When he received the information from Sal, he called Ann Cuffaro Carlson and told her that his friends' company was hiring security personnel. It could be a good opportunity for her and her husband. Before Victor Davis had retired from the San Jose Police Department, he had founded a Personal Security Firm. James had helped fund the new company, and he requested that Victor provide two additional bodyguards to be assigned to his family, 24/7. James' driver, William Fowler, served as his personal bodyguard. Fowler had replaced Brandon Foster, who had been killed in a shoot-out.

Victor hired Ann Carlson, but her husband, Ron, decided to join an engineering company.

TWENTY-EIGHT
CRACK

A New York CBS poll said that drug abuse represented the most important problem facing America. It represented the most intense preoccupation by the American public of any issue in polling history.

At their quarterly meeting, James Greaney, told members of the Junto that it was his opinion that any politician that didn't aggressively fight against drug and human trafficking—killing our youth every day, was a traitor to the American people. He or she should be removed from their office, immediately.

He continued with, "Trafficking of illegal drugs and human trafficking often happen together. Criminals look to increase profits and market control through diversification. They use established trafficking routes for drugs, sex, and violence. Transporting women and children for sex is just another source of profit for these criminals. Traffickers don't care what product is sold—both sex and drugs are lucrative operations.

Drug cartels use trafficked women and children to smuggle drugs across our southern border—they are often referred to as 'mules.'

"These violent criminals see no difference between abusing a woman's body by forcing her to swallow bags of drugs or by forcing her to have sex with hundreds of men. Human traffickers use drugs as 'bait' to recruit people who already have a substance addiction. They force women and children into increased addiction by providing them with strong and potent drugs, as a means of control. Drug dealers and human traffickers should receive the death penalty, without exception," declared James.

Two of James' friends had lost teenage children to a drug overdose.

James continued, "The American Constitution was meant to protect all Americans, regardless of social status. Many in the State and Federal government have allowed the proliferation of drug and human trafficking entering our country—they are traitors."

Not all members of the Junto agreed with James' views on illegal drugs. Some members thought that his pronouncements were too harsh and too far right for their way of thinking.

One of James' neighbors had lost a son who had overdosed on crack cocaine in the dorm at his university. A high school friend's daughter overdosed on crack and meth and died in her bedroom in her parents' home. Her addiction was so out of control that she had resorted to stealing money and valuables from her parents to buy drugs.

James met with his friend Bui Quang Do, at Do's coffee shop, to discuss their strategy to move forward with their resources—and eliminate the drug dealers and politicians who had allowed illegal drugs to permeate society.

Do began, "There's a new problem with drugs in our city. Since killing some of those bastards a few years ago, who were dealing drugs to our kids, there's now a new drug called 'crack cocaine.' It's being sold everywhere. I understand that it's easy to find and is cheap to buy. We've got to do something about it."

"Let me talk to Victor and find out how the police departments are viewing the problem of crack. I've been concentrating on building my businesses, and investments. I'm not up to date on recent changes in the drug world."

"It's bad from what I'm being told and getting worse."

"Well, if we've got to go back and eliminate more scumbags, I'm all for it. We just need to decide on a strategy that will be the most effective."

The following week, James invited Victor to his home. He had asked him to bring an overview of the illegal drug trade in Santa Clara County, specifically crack cocaine use. He mentioned to Victor, while they were on the phone, that Do was really alarmed with the recent upsurge of this new type of cocaine, called crack, that can be smoked.

Victor began reading excerpts from an internal police report he had received that was being circulated throughout the department.

He read, **"Crack cocaine originates in Columbia and traffics through the Bahamas and Dominican Republic. Due to a** huge glut of cocaine powder, the price of cocaine dropped by as much as 80 percent.

"The drug dealers made a business decision to convert the powder to "crack," a solid smokeable form that could easily be sold in smaller quantities, to more people. It's cheap, easy to produce, ready to use, and highly profitable for dealers.

"Crack is prevalent in LA, Oakland, San Diego, Miami, Houston, New York and now in our local communities. Powder cocaine is sold at an average of 55% purity and crack is sold at 80% plus purity for the same price.

"The crack epidemic is worse in New York and Philadelphia, but it is heading out west, to local communities, very quickly. The worst affected are the Black and Hispanic communities. The death rate from crack use, in teenage Blacks, has more than doubled.

"The rate of fetal deaths in Black communities is climbing. Initial studies have found that mothers, dependent on cocaine, were having babies with a significantly lower birth weight. The babies had smaller heads, suffered seizures, had genital and urinary tract abnormalities, suffered poor mobility, had brain lesions, and exhibited moodiness and lower responsiveness.

"William Bennett, the federal drug "Czar," claimed that 375,000 crack babies had been born in the United States. That represented one out of every ten births.

"Ed Koch, the mayor of New York City, urged the death penalty for any drug dealer convicted of possessing at least a kilogram of either cocaine or heroin.

"President Ronald Reagan called for a nationwide crusade against drugs, a sustained, relentless effort to rid America of

this scourge."

"How big a problem is crack usage in Santa Clara County?" asked James.

"It was almost nothing just six months ago, but now it's used all over the county. It's very cheap, and the supply is huge," responded Victor.

"It looks like we've got to eliminate more of these drug dealers."

"Jim, I'm pulling the plug and turning in my shield in August. I've been a cop for twenty years and I've had it. I can't take any more of the bureaucratic bullshit that cops must put up with every day. So, I'll be ready to work with you guys full-time, on your missions. I already make more than twice as much income from our investments and my security company as I make in the police department."

"How will we be able to continue a source for intelligence gathering on crime if you aren't there?"

"It'll be easy for me to keep in touch with 'my guys' on the force. They'll give me the information that I request—and there will be no risk of exposure to the rest of the team."

"Well then buddy, welcome to the Vigilantes full-time. Get ready to kick some ass. Make sure you're able to get me as much detailed information as possible—and an updated list of the dealers. I'll be meeting with Do to develop our attack plan once we have enough information to work with," said James.

James Greaney and Carolyn Speer had agreed to meet each other, from time to time, in different locations of the world. They met at the St. Regis Hotel in Singapore as well as the Galleon Beach Hotel in the Cayman Islands. Their purpose for these meetings was to enjoy each other's company, as well as explore the sites in different locations. Carolyn would brief James on new business opportunities and investments in the evening. They had agreed to these private meetings, at least twice a year, until one of them met someone that they wanted to commit to.

While staying at the Hyatt in the Cayman Islands, Carolyn informed James about a famous investor and American businessman, Warren Buffett. Carolyn explained that her father, John Bailey, was very conservative and had been a long-term investor in Berkshire Hathaway stock.

In 1983, Berkshire Hathaway stock was trading at $1,029 per share and its path was on an upside spiral. Bailey's first purchase of Berkshire stock in 1979 was at $290 per share. He continued to buy more shares every year.

Carolyn said that Buffett was kind of a weird guy. He ate junk food almost every day and McDonald's burgers and fries were his favorite fast food. He took a $50,000 annual salary and lived in the same five-bedroom home in Omaha, Nebraska, that he had lived in since 1958. He had purchased it for $31,500.

Carolyn had a copy of Forbes magazine. Buffett had made the list of "Forbes 400" richest people in America. At the time the article was printed, Buffett's wealth was estimated at $250 million.

She said that Buffett explained his investment philosophy this way, "We have no formal program of acquisitions, but as a private investment partnership, we like to put our money into things with good value and good management."

When stock prices began to drop in 1973, Buffett became a buyer for the long term. By 1979, Berkshire continued buying stocks it regarded as valuable. Then it began to buy shares of ABC television network, among others.

James and Carolyn agreed to follow Buffett's investment program. They decided to purchase Berkshire Hathaway stock through the LLC that James had set up in Las Vegas.

Their first purchase was for 1,000 shares of stock at $1,030 per share.

"Since Buffett has dedicated his life to analyzing the stock market and corporate shares, let's let him do the hard work. We'll take the risk that he will be right most of the time," said James.

"At the same time, let's also purchase stocks, directly and personally, that Berkshire is buying and see how things compare for our personal gain," said Carolyn.

"I agree. This will be a good leverage buy program for us, and Buffett's strategies will keep us from taking major losses on stock purchasing," said James.

Carolyn made additional purchases of 1,000 shares in her name and another 1,000 shares in James's name through her brokerage firm.

"Okay. Let's confirm. We have agreed that you will make additional purchases, out of my personal account, of the same investments that you see Berkshire buying," said James.

"Yes. I will probably buy the same stocks for my personal account as well," replied Carolyn.

"Keep in mind that we'll continue to add the Silicon Valley

start-ups that we are funding, and helping find electronic components, to our stock portfolio as well. Some of these start-ups may turn into great investments. Let's get started on our path to becoming mega-millionaires," said James.

"Where are we going to meet in September, Jim?" asked Carolyn.

"How about Rome? I haven't been to the Colosseum and there are many sites that interest me. If you are interested, I will have my office make reservations," said James.

"Let's do it. I've never been to Italy," said Carolyn.

When James returned from his meeting with Carolyn, he met with Victor and his two brothers, William and Thomas.

"Carolyn and I have purchased 1,000 shares of Berkshire Hathaway at $1,030 per share through our LLC. The total cost was $1,030,000. We still have about $6 million in cash in Vegas," James informed the group.

He went on to explain that Carolyn and he were following Warren Buffett's investment strategy and that they believed it to be a conservative approach, as opposed to trying to understand a stock's value based on the opinion of a stockbroker or analyst.

He shared the background of Buffett and Berkshire Hathaway and showed them a copy of the Forbes magazine that Carolyn had given him.

"I want you to be aware that Carolyn and I each purchased an additional 1,000 shares of Berkshire out of our personal accounts. If anyone would like to do the same, give Carolyn a call and she will help you out," said James.

"Wow, $1,030 per share. I've never heard of a stock reaching such a high price," said William.

"This guy Buffett must be a genius," said Thomas.

"Well, he's kind of weird too," said James. He told them about some of Buffett's idiosyncrasies, such as his preference for junk food.

Later in the week, James met Bui Quang Do for dinner at Hue City restaurant in San Jose. After dinner, they moved into the bar for drinks. James informed Do about his decision to invest in Berkshire Hathaway.

Do was intrigued about the investment strategy and said, "I'll invest in it too, if you think it's the right thing to do, Jim."

"There are no guarantees Do, especially in the stock market, but I think that this Buffett character is someone we should watch. He's a conservative investor."

James gave Carolyn Speer's office number to Do and said, "Tell Carolyn that you and I are old war buddies and she'll take care of your investment needs."

TWENTY-NINE
LATINA

James Greaney met Mercedes Garcia-Romero at a party in Beverly Hills. Bill Tyson was the host of the party. Tyson was a movie producer and had been introduced to James by Salvador Cuffaro. Tyson had asked James to consider investing in a new movie that he was producing. The party had been organized to bring wealthy investors together, to listen to a financial proposal, from Tyson, about the proposed movie. Tyson had offered James the title of executive producer of the movie, if he would be willing to make a substantial investment.

James was standing next to the bar, when Mercedes approached him and said that she loved his blue eyes. James laughed at her comment and was immediately on the alert. He had been warned by Tyson and friends to be careful when attending Beverly Hills parties. "You have no idea what kind of kook is going to approach you—man or woman. So be careful," warned Tyson.

Mercedes was exceptionally beautiful. She had a great

smile and piercing brown eyes. She was Mexican and had been born in Morelia, Mexico. She told James that she was a tequila and beer exporter from Morelia. The United States was her largest customer base, and she was looking for investors who would help her expand her business.

Morelia was founded in 1545 and is the capital and largest city in the State of Michoacan. It is a beautiful city with magnificent architecture, a grand aqueduct, and historical plaza fountains. In the center of the city, is the Cathedral of the Divine Savior of Morelia.

Mercedes told James that she was aware that he was a very successful businessman, and that he was considering investing in Bill Tyson's new movie.

James responded by saying that, at this time, he was only considering an investment in the movie producing industry. He said that he wasn't quite sure if he liked the level of financial risk involved in moviemaking. He told her, "It's easy to say that the investment was a wise decision when a movie becomes a blockbuster. That's all after the fact. No one can guarantee going in, that a movie will be profitable unless you're talking about an animated movie made for children."

"I agree with you about the movie business, Senor. On the other hand, selling tequila and beer is a much better risk. Men and women, all over the world, love tequila and beer. May I provide you with a prospectus on my company? I'd love for you to consider investing with me."

"Yes, I'd like to consider your business. You may send your information to my office. Here's my business card. Now, let's discuss anything except business."

"Okay, James, thank you," Mercedes replied after receiving his card. "What would you like to talk about?"

"I don't know anyone here. Tell me about them. I'm curious as to who Tyson has invited. I recognize some actors and celebrities."

"Okay James, let me tell you about them. There are some people here though that I don't recognize."

James interrupted her. "Please call me, Jim."

"Most of the people here are looking to meet people like you. They want to meet rich and powerful people who they hope will help them in their careers."

"You mean, people like you," laughed James.

"Yes, people like me. I'm here to meet rich and powerful people like you," she smiled.

"I like that. At least you're honest."

Mercedes explained what she knew about many of the people at the party. It was interesting for James to hear how she described each person. He could tell that she was very intelligent and calculating. Her evaluation of the people that they were viewing was sometimes comical—and James laughed at her descriptions.

After two hours, he asked her if she would like to go to someplace else. He wanted to get away from the noisy chatter, and the shallow conversations of the guests. She told him that she knew a nightclub nearby where they could get some light food with their drinks—and plenty of privacy.

They continued their conversation at the nightclub over food and drinks. No one approached them except for their waitress. He learned that Mercedes was divorced and had two teenage daughters. She told him she knew that he was a widower and had children.

"It seems that you have an accurate scouting report on me," he joked.

"Yes, I wouldn't have left the party with you, If I hadn't known something about you."

"That's wise. You're very careful, aren't you?"

"Yes, it's a tough world. I must take care of myself—I don't have anyone to lookout for me."

"Would you consider leaving here now and going to my hotel—I'll call my driver."

"You're such a confident man, blue eyes. Yes, I'm ready to go with you."

When they were in James' hotel room, they kissed and groped each other, passionately. He began removing her clothes, and she began removing his. They were naked when they got into bed and immediately came together. They made love many times throughout the night. In the morning James ordered room service. They sat at a small table eating their breakfast while wearing white bathrobes that had been provided by the hotel. James scanned a local newspaper that had come with the room service delivery. As soon as he finished reading the paper, they began talking.

"You're a great lover, blue eyes—so powerful—the best."

"Oh, I bet you tell that to all the men that you capture."

"No, I don't waste my compliments. If a man is not so good, I say nothing," she replied with a serious expression.

"Well little woman, you were exceptional. You almost wore me out last night."

"I don't think so. You were strong and powerful every time."

"It's one of the reasons that I workout every day. I must be prepared to respond to beautiful Senoritas who have big appetites."

They continued to have sexual encounters for the next two months. James would fly to LA, and they would meet in a hotel. She would sometimes fly to San Jose to meet him at a hotel of his choice. He told her that he was not interested in investing in export businesses. She said that it was fine with her, as she would look for other investors. James found her to be a little mysterious, and he decided to hire an investigator. He wanted to find out more information about Mercedes and her tequila and beer business.

The investigator's report found that Mercedes had a cousin, Edwardo Romero, who lived in Morelia. He was known by the authorities to be the head of a medium-size drug cartel. His operations were expanding, and he was using Mercedes' tequila and beer business to transport cocaine, heroin, and other drugs into the United States. The report said that Mercedes had no experience in exporting or in the production of tequila and beer. Her company had been set up to be an exporter. Edwardo was funding her export business. He was using her company as a cover to smuggle drugs. The report also stated that she was divorced and raising two children. Her husband had been a drug addict and a domestic abuser. He had abandoned his family when his children were very young. Mercedes and her two teenage girls were living with her parents. Her parents were living in the United States, without the proper immigration documents.

James flew to LA and Mercedes met him at his hotel. They made love as soon as she arrived in his room. While they were resting in bed, James told her that he had something very serious to tell her.

"Mercedes, I want you and the girls to leave for Morelia tomorrow. I also recommend that your parents leave with you since they are not here legally. I've learned that Edwardo Romero is your cousin and that he's the leader of a drug cartel in Morelia. He's been importing drugs into the U.S. and has been using your company as a front for his drug business. He's going to be detained tonight at his mistresses' home. We also know that he owns the condo that she lives in with their child. She's some kind of wannabe actress. Edwardo isn't going to be allowed to leave the United States. The government has been monitoring him—sneaking into the U.S. to see his mistress and child. He's going to be arrested and he'll end up in Federal Prison. You must distance yourself from him immediately.

Mercedes had listened quietly to James' demand that she leave the United States at once. She was not the kind of person to panic. She began by asking, "Who are you, my blue eyes? Are you with the government? Why are you doing this?"

"It doesn't matter, my dear. Your cousin is a bad hombre, and he needs to be stopped."

"Would you let me warn him? We grew up together from nothing, Jim. Can't I just call him and tell him to leave?" she begged.

"No, I'm only concerned about protecting you and the

girls. If you warn him, the authorities might hold you responsible for interfering with the law. I don't want you to be detained here. You'll go to prison for drug trafficking like your cousin. You must leave right away."

"I've not been involved with drugs, Jim. You must believe me."

"I understand, but the authorities would not believe you. You've got to leave now. I'll give you cash. It will cover you for a few months—and then I'll send you more. I'll even set up a distributorship here to purchase your products so that you'll have an income. When you get to Morelia—I want you to call me. We'll stay in touch, and I can help you from here—but you must stay in Mexico."

"You must have been planning this for a long time."

"It hasn't been that long. I'm capable of acting quickly when it comes to protecting people I care about."

"Why are you doing this for me, blue eyes?"

"I care about you and your children—and I know that Edwardo has been using you."

"How long must I stay in Mexico? When can I come back to the United States?

"It'll be a very long time before you'll be allowed to return, if ever. Illegal drugs are killing many Americans. Our country is very upset. There's little sympathy for someone who is related to drug traffickers. Government officials won't believe someone is innocent if they get caught in between the drug traffickers and the government."

Mercedes, her two daughters, and her parents left Los Angeles on a flight to Guadalajara at 11:45 am the next day.

They were in a rush to catch the airplane. Mercedes could only take a few clothes and some cash that she had saved. James gave her a substantial amount of money and it helped calm her fear of having to leave with so little notice. Her daughters were crying and very upset. They did not want to leave their friends in LA. They both said that they hated Mexico.

After Mercedes reached her home in Morelia, she called James.

"Thank you, blue eyes, for helping us to leave LA. Please stay in touch with me. I want to return as soon as possible," she cried.

"I'm glad that you and your family are safely back in Morelia. Have patience and begin a new life."

"Adios blue eyes. Te amo," she said in a soft voice.

"Adios Mercedes. Te amo," he replied as he hung up.

While Mercedes and her family were boarding the airplane to Morelia, Edwardo Romero was already a dead man. No one from the American government was going to detain him. They were not aware that he was even in LA. It was James Greaney who had ordered his assassination.

Two of Bui Quang Do's hired hitmen burst into his condo and shot him with pistols that had silencers. Edwardo died instantly. His mistress and child were unharmed. She began screaming hysterically after the assassins had left her home.

After leaving the condo, the two assassins walked slowly towards a black Cadillac SUV. As they were entering the vehi-cle, they handed their weapons to a third man who was standing next to the vehicle. The man took the weapons away on his motorcycle. He had been assigned the responsibility of getting rid of all evidence pertaining to the hit. The two assassins were driven three hundred and fifty miles to their homes in San Jose.

THIRTY
BETRAYAL

Oliver "Ollie" Phillips had been a classmate of James Greaney in high school. He was married to Beatrice Eldridge who had graduated a year behind him in school. Beatrice's friends called her Bea. She was a gregarious and very pretty girl.

Ollie was 5'8" tall, slender, and athletic looking. He had played on the high school tennis team throughout his four years in high school.

He had graduated from Santa Clara University where he had studied business administration and accounting. His bachelor's degree was in accounting.

After college, he went to work for Bank of America in San Francisco—joining their commercial loan department.

He received his draft papers but was able to fail his physical by claiming a damaged knee, due to his tennis playing days. He took a letter from his doctor to the military examiners. It stated that he did not have much cartilage in his right knee. The examiners failed his exam and let him go free.

It was all a scam on Ollie's part. He had been playing tennis every day leading up to his induction appointment. He felt no guilt "beating the draft," under false pretenses.

Ollie had worked for B of A for five years when he had been recruited by a "Headhunter" to join a start-up company in Palo Alto. The Company was developing new software for databases, middleware software, and application software for hardware systems. He had been hired as their new CFO.

While attending college, Ollie had experimented with drugs. He also had become an addicted gambler. He borrowed money from his parents to cover his drug purchases and gambling debts.

When joining the business world, he had continued to use drugs and gamble. His wife Bea had no clue that he was trapped with these destructive addictions. The more money that Ollie made, the greater his gambling habit. It grew rapidly into huge losses.

Under great stress from his debtors, Ollie began embezzling money from his company accounts. He started with small amounts from a petty cash account—but it was not long before he was taking large amounts and finding it difficult to cover his stealing.

At one point he owed $300,000 to gamblers in Las Vegas. He was able to reduce his debt to them by $200,000 when he embezzled money from the company. It still left him with a debt of over $100,000.

Ollie's world started to crumble when his company's management decided to pursue another round of financing. They believed that it would be good timing to take advantage of the sales growth of their popular software. To qualify for another round of financing, his company needed an updated audit in order to justify the amount that they were pursuing.

Ollie panicked. He was wracking his brain trying to figure out how he was going to survive the audit. He concluded that he would not survive the scrutiny of the audit, so he would have to come up with a way out of his predicament.

The Bay Area and Santa Clara County news outlets were consumed with their reporting on the many deaths of drug dealers and politicians who were involved in drug abuse. Most of the public seemed to agree with the elimination of drug dealers and corrupt politicians but were countered by left-wing groups who were horrified by the killings. The left was advocating abolishing drug laws and making drugs free and available to everyone. Law enforcement at the local, state, and federal level were baffled by the killings.

Ollie remembered a speech given by James Greaney at one of their Junto meetings. Greaney had stated that he believed that drug dealers should get the death penalty. Not all Junto members agreed with his statement, but most did. Ollie also knew that James Greaney's background in the military, as a decorated combat officer, made him a perfect candidate for someone who would be capable of carrying out the killings.

Ollie had no evidence that Greaney was responsible for any of the attacks on drug dealers and politicians, but he had to take a chance that the FBI would listen to him. If he could be of value to the FBI, they might mitigate his problems with the IRS when the results of the company audit were revealed.

Ollie was worried and under great stress. He had snorted two lines of cocaine before he called the San Jose office of the FBI. He asked to speak with an agent. The receptionist asked him about the nature of his call. He said that it had something to do with the killings in the Bay Area. After a few minutes, Special Agent Robert Chappell came on the line and identified himself. Ollie gave him a brief explanation as to why he was contacting the FBI. He said that he had important information for them about who he felt certain was responsible for the killings.

Agent Chappell met with Ollie at his office in the software company. Ollie provided him with background on the American Junto and told him about the meeting where James Greaney had made comments that drug dealers should get the death penalty. He also told the Agent that Greaney was a combat veteran and was more than capable of eliminating people. Chappell took notes on his conversation with Ollie and said that he would get back to him after they had investigated the accusations against Greaney.

As soon as Agent Chappell left the software company and got into his car, he put in a call to Tony Siderine in Los Gatos. Siderine was Salvadore Cuffaro's right-hand man.

"Tony, I need to meet with you right away. Can we meet at Peet's Coffee?" I've got some interesting information for Sal."

When Chappell and Siderine met at Peet's, Chappell provided Siderine with the details of his meeting with Ollie.

"Tell Sal that I'll wait to hear from him before I do any paperwork on this new lead."

"Okay, we'll get back to you."

Special Agent Robert Chappell had been on Salvadore Cuffaro's payroll for two years. Chappell had become a drug addict, and when the drug supplier had been pressuring him to pay for the drugs he had consumed, Sal intervened. Sal was not in the drug business, but any illegal business in his territory came under his scrutiny. He had become aware of Chappell's dilemma and had offered to get him out of debt in exchange for a commitment, from Chappell, to protect Sal and his operations from FBI surveillance. Chappell readily agreed to Sal's proposal, and Sal got the protection from the FBI that he needed. Chappell also agreed to notify Sal when the FBI was investigating someone or when they were beginning a campaign against certain crime elements.

After meeting with Chappell, Tony Siderine, went to Sal's office to discuss the information that he had received from the FBI. "Our FED guy says that his source has named James Greaney as the guy behind the killings. I'm impressed, boss. Greaney looks like an accountant in an expensive suit. It's hard to believe that he's giving orders to kill."

"Don't get back to the FED until I've had time to check this out."

"Okay, boss. I'll wait for you to tell me what's next."

When Sal received the information that had come from Chappell, he immediately called James Greaney. They met in Los Gatos at Oak Meadow Park. Sal informed James about the information that Tony had received from the FBI.

"I don't care to know anything about the accusations. I just wanted to give you a heads up on what the FBI was told."

James listened carefully and did not respond to the accusations. He said, "Thank you, Sal. I appreciate the notice. I'll take care of this. You're a good friend. I owe you a big one."

"No problem, Jim. Just let me know when we can do that allocation business again."

"Will do. Have a good day, Sal," replied James as he got up to leave.

When Sal returned to his office he told Tony, "Tell our FED guy to lose the notes he took, blaming Greaney for the killings."

James was very disappointed with the news of Ollie's betrayal. He would never have thought that any member of the Junto would want to hurt him.

Two days after James had been informed of Ollie's betrayal, Oliver Phillips was abducted by two powerful men, as he left his house at 7 am. He was about to get into his car when the men dragged him to a car parked near his driveway. The men forced him into the rear seat of their car and subdued him with duct tape around his arms and plastic handcuffs on his wrists. They gagged him with a cloth rag that they taped over his mouth.

The assailants drove to the Los Gatos reservoir five miles out of town. They parked in a secluded area near the spillway of the dam. Ollie attempted to talk to his abductors, but the gag in his mouth only allowed him to moan and groan. He was terrified and guessed that they were mobsters from Las Vegas wanting the money that he owed them.

After an hour had gone by, a car drove into the area and parked near the car holding Ollie. James Greaney got out of the right rear door of the car. He walked towards the abductor's car. Ollie spotted James and his spirits rose. He was sandwiched between two big men in the back seat of the car.

James got into the front seat, passenger side. He turned towards the back and said, "Remove the gag." When his gag had been removed Ollie began crying.

He whimpered, "What's going on Jim? What are you going to do to me?"

"What did you tell the Feds about me, Ollie?" asked James, sternly.

"Nothing Jim. I didn't tell them anything, really!"

"Come on, Ollie. You must have told them something— you called them for a meeting."

"How did you know that I met with them?"

"It doesn't matter—I know what you did," replied James, calmly.

"Only one guy, Jim. I'm deep in debt and the mob wants their money. I told the Feds that the only guy that I knew of, capable of killing those drug dealers was you. I just wanted to get some help from the Feds to help me with the IRS. I know that you weren't the one responsible for the killings. I told them that you were a combat hero, and that you hated drug dealers. You even gave a speech to the Junto saying that drug dealers should get the death penalty, remember Jim?"

"Is that all that you told them about me?"

"Yes Jim. I'm deep in debt and I didn't know how to get out."

"Why didn't you come to me for money? You know that I've helped many of the Junto members when they needed money."

"I don't know, Jim. Maybe I was too embarrassed to ask you. The money is big. I still owe them $100,000. The IRS is going to go after me for the $200,000 that I embezzled from the company."

"Three hundred thousand dollars! You'd betray a lifelong friend for $300,000? On top of that, you told the FBI that I was the ringleader. How pathetic, Ollie. You know, I commanded young men in combat, some of them were still teenagers, who didn't hesitate to sacrifice their lives to save their buddies. You were willing to sacrifice a friend for money."

"I'm sorry, Jim. I know that you've been good to everybody. Please help me," pleaded Ollie.

"Ollie, we have been friends since our freshman year in high school. I'm deeply hurt that you would betray me for any amount of money. For old times' sake, I want you to rest assured that Bea and your children will be safe and taken care of. You don't have to worry."

"No, Jimmy, don't do this. Please give me a chance. I'll make it up to you, I promise," cried Ollie hysterically.

"Put the gag back," ordered James as he opened his door to exit the car.

The following morning, the Los Gatos Police Department was notified by a jogger, who had stopped to take a rest near a bench in Oak Meadow Park, that there was a dead man sitting on the bench.

Oliver Phillips was the dead man. He had been propped up on the bench with Caesar's Palace blackjack chips in his lap. He had been shot once in the back of his head.

A week following his death, the funeral for Ollie was held at the St. Edwards Episcopal Church on Union Avenue in San Jose. James and the members of the Junto attended the service.

James waited at the end of the line of mourners greeting Ollie's widow. When it was his turn to greet Beatrice, he conveyed his condolences and asked if he could be of any help to her and the children.

"Oh Jim. Ollie has left us broke. I have bills that I won't be able to pay off in a million years. I'm afraid that I'll lose the house. I don't know what to do, Jim. I need your help."

"I will help you and the children. We'll work things out, Bea," assured James.

"Thank God, Jim!" she cried.

"Don't worry. I'd like to meet with you next week. I'll bring my financial advisor. We'll work out a solution for your debt. In addition, I'll have some employment ideas for you. I want you to focus on the kids. They deserve your attention now—with the loss of their father."

"Thank you so much, Jim. I don't know how I'll ever be able to repay you for your kindness. I'll wait for your call."

James and his CPA, Pete Stoeland, met Beatrice at her home. They were there to address her financial predicament, due to Ollie's blowing their money on drugs and gambling. She was financially broke and had been left with a mountain of debt.

"Bea, do you remember Pete from high school? We're here to fix your money problems," said James.

"Yes, I remember Pete. We've never formally met, but aren't you married to Rosie, or was it, Robin?" she asked.

"I'm married to Rosie. My brother Art is married to Robin. Rosie and I were married after college. We have three kids, now," Pete replied.

"Bea, do you have a complete listing of your debt that I requested when we spoke on the phone?" asked James.

"Yes, here it is," she replied as she handed a paper to James.

He took the paper and handed it to Pete.

"Jim, did you know that the cops told my brother that they found casino chips in Ollie's lap?" asked Bea.

"Is that right? Sounds like something the Mob would do. Were you aware Ollie owed money to the Mob? They would not do something like that for some small amount of money."

"I don't know. I just know that we don't have any money. I don't know who or how many people Ollie owed money to," said Bea, as she began to cry.

James and Pete returned to Beatrice's home a week after receiving the listing of debt that Ollie had accrued.

"Bea, I have good news. Your entire debt will be paid off in the next two weeks. You'll not have a mortgage payment on your home. It will be free and clear. I have also set up an appointment for you with a company that needs help in their HR department. Are you interested?" asked James.

"Oh yes, I'm more than interested. I've got to go back to work. Thank God. I'll never be able to repay you."

"You owe me nothing. Ollie and I were very good friends for a very long time."

"God bless you. I'll never forget this. When the children are old enough, I'll tell them about you," said Bea, as James and Pete were leaving.

When they were in the car, driving away, Pete remarked, "I can't believe that you personally paid off that mountain of debt. I wish I could tell everyone I know. You're a great guy!"

"You promised me that you would keep quiet. There's no reason for anyone to know how deep in debt Ollie was—and that he left his family in such dire straits."

BOOK THREE

"Beware the fury of a patient man."
~John Dryden

THIRTY-ONE
DRUG WARS

The 1980s saw the beginning of "Drug Wars" between the United States Federal government, and multiple South American and Mexican drug cartels. With the surge of crack cocaine use and its distribution, there were gang wars fighting over the control of drugs.

Increasing crime and violence was seen in major cities throughout the Nation. Miami, Los Angeles, Atlanta, New York, Chicago, San Francisco, San Jose, Philadelphia, Baltimore, Houston, Detroit, Seattle, Dallas, Minneapolis, and Phoenix were experiencing a steep rise in crime.

James and Do met to review the police department's confidential internal affairs documents provided by Victor Lewis' contact. The documents highlighted FBI and law enforcement intelligence data on specific drug dealers who were known to be major sellers of crack cocaine to the public.

The names of several politicians in the county, believed to

be using and selling crack, were included. In addition, the documents provided the names and activities of Mexican gang leaders and members in San Jose, California.

"There is a major drug epidemic hitting the country," explained James.

"How can we address a problem of such magnitude?" asked Do.

"We can't handle the country's problems. We can only focus on Santa Clara County and do damage to the drug dealers here. We don't have the resources, at this time, to get involved anywhere other than this county. Let's focus and see how effective we can be."

"What punishment are we going to give the crack dealers? We can't be giving all of them speedballs. There are too many of them," said Do.

"You're right. The best method is to shoot 'em. We'll use silencers and just put a bullet in their heads. The police are overwhelmed with the drug problem and when caught, the local courts will just give the dealers light sentences or release them on bail."

"Let's just plan it. I'll use some of my guys and they'll do the job without risk to us."

"There are twenty-three names of Santa Clara County dealers and users on the list. Let's break them down and create an attack plan on each of them for your shooters. I'll take responsibility for the three politicians on the list," said James.

"Are you going to take out the politicians yourself?"

"Yes. I've got to take that step. I can't ask others to do all the dirty work and sit back and not be involved."

The FBI and local law enforcement documents provided by Victor's contact, included a summary of the history of drug trafficking origins.

In 1981, Miami was responsible for trafficking 70% of the country's cocaine, 70% of the country's marijuana, and 90% of the country's counterfeit quaaludes. Major traffickers, like the Falcon brothers and Sal Magluta, smuggled in around 2 billion dollars of cocaine from Columbia. Columbian drug lord, Griselda Blanco was a pioneer in cocaine trafficking and was responsible for more than 200 murders.

Miguel Angel Felix Gallardo, founded the first Mexican drug cartel, known as the Guadalajara Cartel. There was an alliance that included the Sinoloa, Juarez, Tijuana, and Sonora Cartels.

When law enforcement efforts became successful in South Florida and the Caribbean, the Columbian organizations formed partnerships with the Mexico-based traffickers to transport cocaine, by land, through Mexico into the United States.

Mexico had long been a major source of heroin and cannabis, and drug traffickers from Mexico had already established an infrastructure that was in place to serve the Columbia-based traffickers.

By the 1980s, the Mexican organizations were reliable transporters of Columbian cocaine. The Mexican gangs and the Columbian traffickers settled on a payment-in-product arrangement. Transporters from Mexico were given 35% to 50% of each cocaine shipment.

In June 1986, two popular athletes died of cocaine

overdose. A University of Maryland basketball player, Len Bias, overdosed on June 19th. He had been drafted by the NBA Boston Celtics. Don Rogers, a defensive back for the Cleveland Browns, overdosed on cocaine on June 27th.

THIRTY-TWO
A CONTROLLED RESPONSE

James Greaney invited his brothers, William, and Thomas, along with Victor to his home for a meeting.

His home office had been constructed with extensive sound-proofing. James wanted private meetings that would not be overheard by anyone.

James began the meeting by saying: "Please review the FBI and local police documents that were given to me. They provide a detailed list of crack dealers in Santa Clara County. I gave copies to Do and we are working on plans to terminate these crack heads."

"How are you and Do going to accomplish all of this? It looks like there are twenty names on this list," said William.

"There are twenty-three names. Do is going to use his shooters to take out twenty of them. I'm taking responsibility for the three politicians," said James.

"You're going to take out the three politicians? Are you saying that you're going to do it yourself?" asked Thomas.

"Yes. I'm going to do it. Look, things are out of control and everyday men, women, and children are dying from opioid overdoses. The crime rate is up because addicts must find ways to pay for their habit. They end up doing desperate things like killing or robbing people to get money for their daily fix.

It's too much for the police to handle and the courts don't support the police. The criminals are getting short sentences, or no sentences, and they are back on the street in no time. Politicians are not willing to support closing our borders, so the drug cartels are shipping carloads of drugs into America and poisoning our people. I'm going to ensure that the politicians on this list pay the ultimate price," said James.

"How sure are you, Victor, that the information given to you on these politicians is accurate? We don't want to be killing innocent people," said William.

"The information is accurate. They've been monitoring these people for a long time," said Victor.

"You know that old military axiom that we have often talked about? Sometimes it's better to wound an enemy instead of killing him. If you wound him, his buddies will try to get him help or carry him out of danger.

Therefore, you remove two to three more of the enemy from the battle. If you just wound a politician, you are going to fuck up their day big time. You get their families upset.

The police have to investigate and the media gets involved reporting about the personal habits of the politician. We can make it look like a war is going on. It will create fear that we can build on. Think about that, Jim," said Thomas.

"Tom's right. I've got a contact in the media, and I can feed him information and stories that he'll report. We can leak information about the politicians and what sleaze bags they are. We can control the narrative," said Victor.

"I like that idea. I don't have any qualms about killing a drug-pusher. But if you wound him, like Tom's recommending, we can send a message to a lot of people. Fear is what we want to accomplish. It makes people pay attention and avoid things. Fear will control them," said William.

"Trying to just wound someone is not easy. They could move the wrong way at the last second, and your bullet kills them. There are no guarantees. If you shoot them in the gut or the ass, you reduce the chance of killing them, as long as you don't hit an artery," said Victor.

"I'll take one of the politicians if we are planning to wound them. It'll get my adrenaline spiking again," said William.

"I'll take one of them too. You shouldn't have to take on all three of them yourself, Jim," said Thomas.

"Okay, by me. We need to do some planning for each of our targets. Victor, please re-confirm the information that you have on the three and make sure that they're the right targets for us. I'm going to meet with Do and discuss our strategy for wounding instead of killing," said James.

"I'll confirm with my sources," said Victor.

When James met with Do at his coffee shop, he informed him of the strategy of wounding instead of shooting to kill. Do thought it was an acceptable policy for his shooters. The exception would be the major crack sellers. Do said that if they determined that the target was a major dealer, they were going to eliminate them.

"I agree, let's make sure that your shooters know the difference. If they accidentally hit one of them and the dirt bag dies, it's okay with me," said James.

❧

The first week in August was very hot, with temperatures reaching into the high 90s. Five of the twenty cities in Santa Clara County, Gilroy, San Jose, Morgan Hill, Palo Alto and Campbell, experienced ten shootings. All the shooting victims were shot in the stomach. All ten victims survived, but most of them were severely injured and would need long-term care to recuperate.

Local police authorities did not consider the shootings unusual until the following week. Thirteen shootings took place, including three councilmen, representing the cities of San Jose, Cupertino, and Sunnyvale. All of the victims were shot in the stomach and all survived with the exception of a well-known crack dealer in San Jose. He was shot in the stomach and face and died from his wounds.

Do informed James that his shooters followed the plan of wounding their targets, except for Sonny Duran, who they knew to be a high-volume crack dealer.

"We couldn't let Duran get off with just wounding him. He's been pushing a lot of drugs on children and he's been hanging out around San Jose High School. He had to go, so we chose to terminate him," said Do.

"No problem. It was your call. Good job Do," said James.

❧

Victor had been feeding his contact at the San Jose

Chronicle, detailed information about each of the shooting victims. The newspaper published articles every day, highlighting the backgrounds of the wounded victims. The articles explained that the victims were chosen because they had been selling crack cocaine to children.

The three politicians, who were victims of the shootings, were Liberals in their early thirties. They were young, good-looking and were regarded by their party as up and coming operatives with promising, political futures ahead of them.

The San Jose police department contacted the local FBI office in San Jose and asked the Agents to meet with them regarding the shootings. The FBI soon realized that all of the victims, including the politicians, were on their list of known drug dealers.

All of the victims were shot with 22 caliber pistols. Many of them said that they did not hear a gunshot. Some said that the sound of the shots was muffled.

The FBI, Agent-in-Charge, reported that these shootings did not seem to be your typical gang war or conflict. These shooters are professionals. They are very calculating, leaving no clues as to their identity.

Fear ran rampant in the drug community. No one seemed to have any idea who the shooters were. It did seem to look as if there were many of them.

Most heavy cocaine users are paranoid. Many were panicking over the shootings. They were asking everyone that they met, "Am I on somebody's hit list? Is this a battle over territory with the cartels? Who are these shooters?"

THIRTY-THREE
A GLOBAL WAR BRINGS MORE DRUGS

The Berlin Wall, the prime symbol of the Cold War, fell in November of 1989, and Germany was reunited in 1990 after 45 years of separation. The Cold War was declared to be officially over with the fall of the Soviet Union on Christmas Day 1991.

On January 17, 1991, Operation Desert Storm began. On this day, Iraq attacked Israel with seven Scud missiles. A U.S. Patriot missile successfully intercepted the first Scud missile over Dhahran, Saudi Arabia.

On January 18, 1991, President George Herbert Walker Bush authorized the call-up of one million National Guardsmen and Reservists for active duty for up to two years.

The War was a short one, lasting only 43 days, from January 17 to February 28, 1991. The land campaign was famously known as the "100-Hour Ground War."

For the first time in history, U.S. Central Command commander, Army General Norman Schwarzkoof, partnered with a regional ally, Saudi Arabia's Prince Khaled bin Sultan, to co-command the allied forces.

On March 17, 1991, the Department of Defense (DOD), announced the first troop redeployment home of the 24th Infantry Division, Fort Stewart, Georgia.

James, William, and Thomas were discussing world events with Victor. Standing around the barbecue in Victor's backyard, they were in a serious discussion about the Gulf War that had ended with the return of the first troops in March of that year.

James was convinced that the Council of Foreign Relations (CFR) was responsible for the Gulf War. CFR members, and Oil Magnates, were lobbying to protect their controlling interests in the middle east oil supply.

The CFR is a United States nonprofit think tank specializing in U.S. foreign policy and international affairs. Its membership has included senior politicians, Secretaries of State, CIA Directors, bankers, lawyers, college professors and media leaders. The CFR runs the David Rockefeller Studies Program, which influences foreign policy.

William stated that the CFR was a global "shadow government" advising presidential administrations and the diplomatic community.

"The CFR is the root of all evil in the western world. They get us into losing nation-building wars, and we waste the precious lives of our soldiers and our nation's treasure. They prop up governments and people that don't appreciate, care for, or want our way of life," said William.

Thomas remarked that it was a major mistake for the U.S. military to be prevented from going further on to Bagdad and eliminating Saddam Hussain and his close followers. He said that "It won't be long before Saddam creates more trouble for his neighbors and he will have to be neutralized."

James was concerned with the widening of the global drug and human trafficking that had expanded due to the Gulf War.

As the Gulf War in Iraq came to a close, the Warlord period in Afghanistan was in its early stages. When the Soviet Army was forced to withdraw in 1989, a power vacuum was created. Various Mujahideen groups (guerilla fighters) started fighting against each other for power.

The Mujahideen relied on poppy cultivation to finance their military efforts. It was alleged, by the Soviets, that U.S. Central Intelligence Agency (CIA) agents were helping smuggle opium out of Afghanistan to Western Countries. They were financing the Afghan rebels who were penetrating the Soviet Union to weaken it through drug addiction.

Afghan farmers' share of the opium trade was distributed among thousands of families. Mujahideen leader, Gulbuddin Hekmatyar, the leading recipient of aid from the CIA and Pakistan, developed six heroin refineries in Koh-I-Sultan in southwestern Pakistan.

1994 saw the emergence of the Taliban in Afghanistan. By 1999, the Taliban was financing their military development with a huge crop, amounting to tons of opium.

The word Taliban in Pashto language means "Students." The Taliban refer to themselves as the Islamic Emirate of Afghanistan (IEA). It is an Islamist movement and military organization waging war in Afghanistan.

⌯

As the twenty-first century approached, James' chief investment manager, Carolyn Speer, advised him that his financial and real estate holdings had grown significantly, to a level that he was considered a multi-millionaire—at least on paper.

He had also guided the growth of the vigilantes' investments and their portfolio was valued at just under $50 million.

Bui Quang Do's personal investments grew substantially with the guidance of Carolyn Speer. She had recommended that he follow the same investment path that she had established for James and herself.

⌯

The late 1990s were a relatively peaceful time of prosperity. The 90s witnessed the OJ Simpson trial, the death of Princess Diana, the impeachment of Bill Clinton, the birth of Dolly the Sheep—the first mammal to be cloned from an adult cell, and the introduction of the Euro—the official currency of the European Union.

Orenthal James Simpson (OJ) was a former NFL running back, broadcaster, actor, advertising spokesman and convicted felon. He was accused of murdering his ex-wife, Nicole, and her friend, Ron Goldman.

Simpson was acquitted by a jury after a lengthy, and internationally publicized trial. After the verdict, the Associated

277

Press reported that Simpson had released a statement in which he claimed that he would try to find the "killer or killers." Now that he had his freedom, he could do so.

The families of the victims filed a civil suit against him, and the civil court awarded a $33.5 million judgement against him in 1997 for the victims' wrongful deaths.

Diana Frances Spencer (Princess Diana) was a member of the British Royal Family. She was the first wife of Charles, Prince of Wales—the heir apparent to the British throne. She was the mother of Prince William and Prince Harry.

Her activism and glamour made her an international icon, earning her enduring popularity that was exacerbated by her tumultuous private life. Diana and Charles were divorced on August 28, 1996.

A year later, on August 31, 1997, Diana died in a car crash in the Pont de l'Alma tunnel in Paris as her driver was fleeing the paparazzi. Her companion, Dodi Fayed, and the driver, Henri Paul, also died in the crash.

William Jefferson Clinton served as the 42nd President of the United States. Prior to his presidency he served as Governor of Arkansas and was a member of the Democratic Party.

Clinton was impeached on December 19, 1998 by the House of Representatives for perjury to a grand jury and obstruction of justice. The impeachment proceedings were based on allegations that Clinton had lied about and covered up his relationship with a 22-year-old White House employee.

The Senate acquitted Clinton of both charges. The vote in the Senate fell short of the constitutional two-thirds majority requirement to convict and remove an officeholder.

Clinton's law license was suspended for five years after he acknowledged to an Arkansas Circuit Court that he had engaged in conduct prejudicial to the administration of justice.

Dolly was a female domestic sheep. She was the first mammal cloned from an adult somatic cell, using the process of nuclear transfer. She was cloned by Keith Campbell, Ian Williams and colleagues at the Roslin Institute, part of the University of Edinburgh, Scotland, and the biotechnology company PPL Therapeutics, based in Edinburgh.

The cell used as a donor for the cloning of Dolly was taken from a mammary gland. The production of a healthy clone, therefore, proved that a cell taken from a specific part of the body could recreate a whole individual.

Ian Wilmut stated that "Dolly is derived from a mammary gland cell and we couldn't think of a more impressive pair of glands than Dolly Parton's."

Dolly, the sheep, died from a progressive lung disease five months before her seventh birthday and her death was not considered related to her being a clone.

The Euro was launched on January 1, 1999, as an "invisible currency," used only for accounting purposes in electronic payments.

Euro Cash replaced the banknotes and coins of 12 European nations (Austria, Belgium, Finland, France, Germany, Greece, Ireland, Italy, Luxembourg, Netherlands, Portugal, and Spain).

The Euro was the legal currency in the Euro Area, commonly referred to as the Eurozone, formed out of 17 of the 27 Member States of the European Union (EU).

The drug trade in illegal drugs began reaching epidemic proportions during the 1990s. By the end of the 20th century, it was estimated that profits from international drug trafficking were close to $10 trillion dollars annually.

The United States was the most lucrative market for international drug traffickers and tons of illegal drugs were smuggled into the country every day. Many of the drug couriers, paid to bring the drugs, were illegal immigrants.

"The United States is not winning the War on Drugs," declared James.

THIRTY-FOUR
A SURPRISE VISITOR

It was 9 am on a Tuesday morning, when a 13-year-old, Hispanic-looking girl rang the doorbell at James Greaney's home. She was average height and very thin. She was pretty with long brown hair and piercing blue eyes that immediately drew attention to her. She had a disheveled appearance and looked to be very tired. Her clothes were dirty, and it looked as if she had not bathed for some time.

The family cook and housekeeper, Margarita, answered the door. She spoke to the young girl in Spanish.

"Who are you?"

"My name is Marie Greaney Garcia and I've been sent here by my mother."

"What do you want?"

"I want to see Senor James Greaney. He's, my father."

Margarita was surprised by the young girl's request, and said that Senor Greaney was not home, but that he would return by 5 pm.

"Then I'll wait for him," declared Marie.

"Of course. Would you like something to drink? Are you hungry?"

"I'm very hungry. I haven't eaten since yesterday."

"Come to the kitchen with me. I'll fix you something."

After Margarita prepared eggs, tortillas, and milk for Marie, she went into James' study and phoned his office.

"I'm sorry to bother you Jefa, but you have a surprise visitor from Mexico waiting for you."

"Who is it?"

"She's a little girl who says that you're her father."

"Her father? How old is she? What does she look like?"

"She says that she's thirteen. She does have blue eyes like yours."

"Daughter from Mexico? How'd I do that? Are you sure Margarita?"

"I'm just telling you what she said, Jefa. I'd never tease you about something like this."

"Okay, I'll leave for home after I clean up my desk. I'm anxious to see my new daughter—I wouldn't want to keep her waiting too long," he laughed as he hung up the phone.

Marie's mother had paid her two cousins to smuggle Marie across the Mexican border into the United States. They crossed the border from the city of Tijuana, Mexico. The cousins had Mexican passports, but Marie had no legal documents in order to travel. They had traveled for three days, changing buses many times to get to Tijuana. It was almost 1,600 miles from Morelia to Tijuana. They stayed overnight in a cheap, dirty hotel. The next day they were smuggled across the border into San Diego, by a man who had charged them a thousand dollars. It took them over 20 hours to travel to Los Gatos from Tijuana.

When James arrived home, Margarita told him that his young visitor was waiting in the living room. He asked her to join them in case he needed a translator.

When James and Margarita entered the living room, Marie looked up and immediately recognized her father. Her mother had given her a picture of him years before that she had carried with her wherever she went. She began to cry.

James was moved by her behavior. He calmly asked, "What is your name?"

He and Margarita were surprised when Marie stood up and answered in English, "My name is Marie Greaney Garcia. My mother has sent me. She's very sick. I have a letter from her addressed to you."

Marie handed a large envelope to James.

"What is your mother's name?"

"Her name is Mercedes Garcia Romero."

"This is starting to make some sense," said James.

Mexican names often follow Spanish naming customs: [personal name] [father's paternal family name] [mother's paternal family name]

When James opened the large envelope, he found two smaller envelopes. One was a personal letter, and the other contained official government documents in Spanish.

The personal letter had been written in Spanish. James

asked Margarita to read and translate the letter out loud.

"Dear Blue Eyes, I have a big surprise for you. Two months after I returned to Morelia, I was shocked to learn that I was pregnant. I knew that the baby could only be yours. I was afraid to tell you, because we had gone through all those troubles with my cousin, the cartels, and U.S. Immigration. You were helping me with money and had set up that company to import my tequila and beer. I did not want you to think that I was trying to trick you by saying that I was having your child. Even though some of my family and friends wanted me to save face and have an abortion—I could never kill my baby. God would never have forgiven me.

When Marie was born, she looked just like you. She had brown, reddish hair and blue eyes. She had your nose. My mother accepted her, but the rest of my family wanted nothing to do with her. My father wouldn't speak with me and disowned me. My daughters told me that they were ashamed by Marie's birth. They said she was white and did not look like them. She had a different father, and they hated that I had had a child when I was not married.

Marie has never given me any trouble. She is very intelligent—I think she got that from you. She practices her religion every day. My older daughters are married now and live far away from me. They won't speak with me. I only have Marie now, but I had to send her to you. I'm very sick and can't take care of her anymore. My doctor has diagnosed me with pancreatic cancer. He says that I don't have too long to live. Remember when we were in Pebble Beach and that real estate lady told you that I was very beautiful and exotic looking? I'm no longer beautiful. This cancer has ravaged my looks. I would never allow you to see how I look now.

I am sending Marie to you, because I know that you are an honorable man. I know that you would never reject your daughter. Please welcome her into your family. I have sent you documents of her birth. They are in Spanish, and I know that you will honor them. When she was born, I registered her birth certificate with your name as the father—it is the truth.

I am sorry that you are learning about Marie this way—I was planning to keep her a secret—I never wanted to burden you.

Please love her—like I always will.

May God bless you, Blue Eyes,

Mercedes

By the time Margarita had finished reading the letter she was sobbing. James' eyes were filled with tears and as he stood, he beckoned Marie to come to him. He put his arms around her and kissed her forehead.

He said, "I'm very happy to welcome you to the Greaney family. This is your home now, my beautiful daughter."

The three of them stood together in the middle of the room, crying, and hugging each other.

"Margarita, all this crying is making me hungry. When is dinner? James asked, laughing.

"Dinner will be ready in one hour, Jefa. Marie needs to take a shower and I have some of your daughters' old clothes for her to wear."

James gave Marie another hug and a kiss and said, "Great,

I'm going to my study to call my daughters and son to give them the good news. I'm also going to have a glass of Macallan to toast my good fortune."

James made a call to Mercedes' home in Morelia. He wanted to thank her for sending their daughter to him. The woman who answered said that Mercedes was sleeping, and that she was too ill to speak on the phone.

Marie had mixed feelings. She was thinking about her mother's letter while she was showering. It was sad for her to hear her mother admit that she was dying. She was surprised to learn that her mother and father had been doing business together, and that he had been sending her money to help her family survive. She was excited that her father, who she had only known from his picture, had immediately accepted her as his daughter. He seemed to be so happy and was now calling his other children to tell them about her. No one in her mother's family had ever hugged and kissed her or welcomed her as a member of their family.

After Mercedes' cousins, who had escorted Marie to James's home, had been well-fed and showered, they enjoyed a good night's sleep in comfortable beds. The next day, James had them driven to the San Francisco airport to take a direct flight to Morelia. He paid for their travel and gave them spending money. They had been amazed to see the mansion where Marie would now be living. It was clear to them that her father was a wealthy and powerful man who had treated them with generosity and respect. They were both envious of Marie's good fortune.

The following weekend, James' daughters, Elizabeth and

Georgia, visited to meet Marie. Marie was nervous while waiting to meet her older sisters. She was afraid that they might reject her—like her mother's older daughters had done. As soon as Elizabeth and Georgia entered the house they walked directly to Marie and threw their arms around her, kissing her on both cheeks.

Georgia said, "I always wanted a younger sister to play with when I was growing up."

"You're so cute," said Elizabeth.

Their warm greetings stunned Marie. She had never been treated so well.

James came from his study and said, "I see you've met Marie. What do you think?"

"We love her already," said Georgia.

"We're going to take her to lunch and shopping, before you have a chance to begin indoctrinating her," declared Elizabeth.

"Good, make sure that you buy her lots of outfits, including workout clothes and shoes."

"Dad, we grew up with your programs. We know what she needs. Don't waste your time making suggestions," said Georgia.

"Is Bill Fowler driving you?"

"Yes, we called him yesterday. He's agreed to provide us security this weekend and take us wherever we want to go," said Elizabeth.

"There will be other security personnel observing you as well."

"Thanks Dad, we knew that you would have us well

protected," said Elizabeth.

"Marie, you're in good hands with my girls. Enjoy yourself today," said James as he hugged her and returned to his study.

"Thank you, father," replied Marie.

"You can call him Dad," whispered Georgia.

Elizabeth and Geogia were athletic looking, pretty, blonde women. They took Marie to a large shopping mall in San Jose. When they arrived at the mall, they stopped at a restaurant for lunch. While eating they explained to Marie about their father and some of his peculiar ways. Marie was very shy at first, but soon loosened up as she began to feel comfortable with her sisters. It was hard for her to believe that they had accepted her so quickly as one of the family.

Marie began to talk about her childhood and how she had been shunned by her sisters in Mexico—they had never accepted her as a member of their family.

"Sometimes they would beat me up when my mom was not around. They made fun of my blue eyes and said that my father was evil."

She told them that she had carried a picture of James with her since learning that he was her father. She pulled the picture from her purse to show her sisters. It was faded and worn. "I used to dream about him, and my mother told me that he was handsome and that he was a good man."

Marie continued to say that she was extremely happy that he had accepted her as his daughter—and that he was so kind.

Elizabeth explained, "Our father is a great man. He's very disciplined. He'll expect you to be disciplined as well. Get ready to learn about the American Constitution. You'll learn more from Dad than from any of your teachers. You'll have Tuesday night home meetings with him, and you'll discuss history and world events. You'll have a daily workout schedule to follow. After a while you'll be in better physical condition than any of your friends. We'll be buying you workout clothes and shoes. You'll take Karate and Taekwondo lessons. You'll learn how to protect yourself using a sap."

"Don't misunderstand what Liz is saying. Dad will always be very protective of you, but he also wants you to be independent. Liz and I think that we've figured him out—it's one of his ways of showing his love for us," said Georgia.

"Let me tell you a funny story about the time Georgia had to protect herself with her sap," said Elizabeth. "There had recently been some carjackings and assaults on women. Georgia was in the Safeway parking lot loading groceries into her car when a man suddenly rushed at her making weird sounds. She immediately pulled her sap from her purse and hit him twice on the head, knocking him down and out. It turned out that the man was frustrated because he had noticed that one of his tires was flat. He also had locked himself out of his car with the key still in the ignition. He just wanted Georgia to help him call a towing service."

"When he regained conscientiousness, he said he was okay," said Georgia. He even apologized for rushing at me and scaring me. I told him that I was sorry that I had hit him, but that I had been trained to defend myself. I helped him contact a towing service, and we went our separate ways."

"I hope someday that I can be as brave as you," said Marie.

"When I told Dad about the incident, he said that he was very proud of me," said Georgia.

"I asked Dad what he would have done if the man had died," said Elizabeth. Dad said, "Well it would have been the man's misfortune."

"You'll soon meet our little big brother, Vincent. He's a war hero, and he's just like our father. You'll get to know him and love him. He'll love you too," said Elizabeth.

Three months after Marie's arrival in Los Gatos, James was notified that Mercedes had passed away. One of James' attorneys had contacted Senator Thompson's office and obtained a passport for Marie on a rush basis. Senator Thompson had been on James' payroll for many years and would respond quickly to any request from James Greaney. James and Marie flew by private jet to Morelia to visit her mother's grave site. They were accompanied by five armed bodyguards provided by Victor's security firm, and they spent three days in Morelia before returning home. Sadly, Mercedes' mother had been the only relative in Mexico willing to meet with Marie. Marie was happy to leave Mexico and return to California where she was making a new life for herself with her father.

THIRTY-FIVE
THE POSSE

James Greaney met L. Franklin Slye in Dallas, Texas while on a business trip to meet with bankers. James had been in Texas years before when he was considering relocating his many companies. Lan's tragic death had curtailed his plans to make the move at that time. He had slipped into a depression which had lasted for months. Now, years later, he was finally able to revive his interest in Texas and travel to Dallas to meet with Jerry Pate. Pate had been a college roommate of Jim Bob Chandler, the former Chief of Staff to the Texas Governor. Chandler had recommended, years ago, that James meet with Jerry Pate. Pate was a Vice-President of Wells Fargo Bank in Dallas. James was looking to expand his investment operations, and Texas had been encouraging companies to relocate from all over the nation. Texas was looking to lure companies with its low tax base and state programs that favored the growth of private-owned business.

James' major business accounts were with Wells Fargo

Bank in San Jose. The Vice President of the San Jose branch was Dave Bishop. He was a close friend and golfing buddy. Bishop favored James' business interest in Texas and told him that he would be happy to help facilitate a move. Bishop offered to send a letter of introduction to whomever James wanted to meet with in Dallas. The letter would praise James' business acumen and it included a flattering description of his military service.

Jerry Pate and James Greaney got off to a good start. They liked each other immediately. Pate was short in stature, tan, with a pudgy body. He wore his hair in a crew cut that had been popular in the 1950s. Pate was impressed with Bishop's recommendation letter and asked James about his military service. Pate had also served in the Army during the Vietnam War, but had been stationed in Germany throughout his time in service. He was curious about James' war record and his many decorations. James was respectful in responding to Pate's questions but would only discuss amusing experiences that occurred during his time in the military. He refrained from discussing any battlefield experiences. Towards the end of their meeting, which lasted for an hour and forty-five minutes, Pate said, "I have someone special that I would like you to meet. How long y'all staying in Dallas?"

"Well, I had planned to spend a few days here and would like to see some of the local communities. If I'm going to relocate, I'd like to see the area and check out some of the housing developments. Maybe a few small ranches too. I might consider buying one. I'd also like the opportunity to talk with some locals," said James.

"I want you to meet my good friend, Len Slye. We grew up together in Tulsa. He's been a very successful businessman in Dallas. Slye's a Nam Vet like you; a Captain in the 101ˢᵗ. You fellas should get along really well. He'd be better bout advising you bout the business climate then me," said Pate.

"Please set it up, and let me know when and where to meet," said James.

Pate made reservations for their lunch meeting at the Lonesome Dove restaurant in downtown Dallas. He reserved a small, private dining room in the back of the restaurant. Pate introduced James to L. Franklin Slye. Slye was 52-years-old, 6'2" tall, lean, and muscular. He had a ruddy complexion from outside exposure due to horseback riding and golf. He was wearing sunglasses, a cowboy hat, boots, and jeans belted with a large fancy buckle.

James was wearing a black pin-striped suit, white shirt with no tie, and black loafers.

It was a lunch meeting for the three of them. Pate motioned to Molly, a middle-aged, stout waitress.

"What'll you boys have?" she asked.

"Yes, let's have some drinks before orderin'. I'll have a Balcones, and how bout you fellas?" asked Pate.

"I'll have the same, and make it two fingers," said Slye.

"I'll have a vodka Gibson up with three onions," said James.

"We have Smirnoff in the house," said Molly. "Do you have Stolichnaya or Ketel One?" asked James.

"What's Stolichnaya?" asked Molly.

"It's a vodka made in Russia," said James.

"This is Texas honey. We don't sell Commie drinks hea," she said as she wrinkled her nose. "I'll ask about this Ketel One."

"I would prefer Ketel One, if you have it," said James.

Molly handed them lunch menus as she left to order their drinks.

"Interesting lady," said James.

"Yeah. She's a good ole girl. You don't want to cross her. She's been working here for 20-years or more," said Pate.

When Molly returned with their drink orders, she told James that the only vodka they had was Smirnoff. "I went ahead and ordered you a Gibson with Smirnoff," she said.

"Thank you, Molly. I'm sure it will taste just fine," said James.

"Yer welcome, sir."

"So, L. Franklin, cheers," toasted James.

"Call me Len."

"Okay Len, I understand that you served with the 101st."

"Yep, I commanded a company in Nam. Jerry here says that you had quite a war record in Nam."

"I spent over a year there. Where were you located?"

"We were in the A Shau Valley for my two tours."

"I know that there was a lot of fighting in the A Shau. We heard a lot about it. Were you close to Hamburger Hill?"

"No, that was a major fuckup. 'Dumbshit' higher had those boys climbing that hill a number of times and for no strategic reason. They got chewed up. Totally unnecessary. When they got to the top of the hill, there wasn't any advantage worth the slaughter that they endured. After all of that, they abandoned the hill in a few of hours. That's why I left the Army when I did. Too many 'dumbshits' in charge and high-ranking staff that never got their boots dirty. They were making decisions that cost too many lives," said Slye.

"I left the Army for similar reasons. I commanded a team with the Popular Forces and I learned that the upper-ranks in MACV-Saigon were inflating the body count. We were taking and re-taking the same territory a number of times, after we had captured and controlled it. I had many 'dumbshits' in my command too. They never visited the front lines, but thought they could make strategic decisions on fighting the enemy, twenty miles in the rear," said James.

Molly returned to their table and asked, "Have you boys had a chance to look at the menu? If not, do it now so as I can get your orders in before the main dining room starts orderin'. A large group has come in and you will want to get your order in before they start."

"We'll look at them now Molly. Shouldn't take long," said Pate.

"Okay. I'm goin to stay ritch hea and take your orders now. What'll you go for Jerry?"

"I'm gonna have that 16oz-prime, and I'd like it blood red, with a Caesar. Can I have a plain ole baked potato? I don't want any of that puree stuff," said Pate.

"Anything for you, sweetheart," said Molly.

"You go ahead and make your order, James," said Slye.

"Call me Jim, Len. Okay Molly. I'll take the 16oz also. Do you have a medium end-cut?"

"Yea, I'll getchya one," said Molly.

"I'll take a butter lettuce salad with oil and vinegar," said James.

"G'mme the stuffed tenderloin medium and a bowl of chili," said Slye.

"Well, here's to the men we served with and God Bless the dead ones," toasted Slye.

They each responded with Amen, before they took a drink.

During lunch, Slye gave James an overview of the Dallas area and included the best neighborhoods for him to consider. He also mentioned the business climate. They finished lunch and Pate paid the tab. Slye and James had agreed to get together in two weeks, when James planned to return to Dallas.

"Plan to stay awhile next trip," said Slye.

"I sure will," replied James.

As James was getting into the car, he chuckled to himself. "Am I already starting to speak with a drawl?"

As Pate was driving James to his hotel he said, "I can tell that Len likes you, and I can tell he respects your background in the military. You know, we're real patriotic hea in Texas. We're not like the rest of the country. Len will be open to doing business with you—if that's your plan."

"I like him too and I like what I heard at lunch. I'd like to move some of my business here. California is overwhelmed with this crazy shit, left-wing agenda, and high taxes. It costs a fortune to hire people for mid-level jobs and they aren't grateful to have a job. It's business un-friendly out there."

"I hope we can fill the gap for ya."

"I hope so too."

When James returned to California he met with his top advisors.

"I want to move all of our company's headquarters to Texas. We can operate in California, but I want to change our tax base to Texas. I want to change the employee culture of our businesses as well. I want to have employees who appreciate a good job. They are business-friendly in Texas. We can also have more privacy and we can take advantage of their incentives to move there."

"Which businesses are you considering?" asked Pete Stoeland.

"All of them, as soon as possible. I'll need your help on that Pete. Many of you will not have to relocate. Look, we have this huge investment in computer systems. Many of my top executives should be able to live anywhere in the country and still do their job. I know that there will be some exceptions, but we will make it work."

James returned to Dallas two weeks later and asked Jerry Pate for Len's contact information. Pate provided James with Slye's private phone number. James called Slye and asked him to meet at his hotel. He reserved a room for the meeting.

Pate and Slye arrived together. As they sat down in the meeting room, James asked, "Len, Jerry, what would you like to drink? I'm having coffee."

Slye and Pate both answered together, "I'll go for coffee, too."

"We have a thermos over there at the bar. Go on over and

fix what you want."

When they had fixed their coffees, the three men sat down at a small table in the room.

James opened the discussion with, "Gentlemen, I'd like to come to the point and provide you with an overview as to why I want to relocate my operations to Texas."

Slye and Pate nodded in the affirmative.

James continued, "California has gone from being the richest State in the Union, and a haven for new business, high tech, and tax friendly, to becoming a welfare state.

California has one of the highest poverty rates in the country now. Drug use is out of control and thousands of homeless veterans are living on the streets. Everyone is burdened with environmental politics. It is a one-party State—a Democrat State. The cost of living is sky high. I can't hire reliable people at a reasonable rate anymore. Most workers can't afford to live near my companies. They have to commute, sometimes two hours one way to work. Four hours, sitting in a car every day, doesn't make for a happy employee. I have had to organize shuttle-services for many employees.

The State's political base is left of Mao Zedong, and they are coming after big business with draconian social policies and rising taxes. That's why I want to move my businesses to Texas."

"It sure makes sense to us. We'll help you in any way we can," said Slye.

"Yeah. You've got to get out of that state, before it gets worse," said Pate.

The three men took a break for lunch. When they returned, James began another discussion that focused on the threat of the drug epidemic raging across the country.

"Texas has the same neighbor that California has been struggling with—Mexico. Mexico is now totally controlled by the Drug Cartels. The Cartels are operating as a 'shadow government.' They are in control of every department of the Mexican government, including the President. The Cartels also control the provinces and the local communities.

"The Mexican government claims that they are dismantling the cartels and stopping the drug trafficking, but it's not true. The cartels are in control of everything. The Mexicans have been providing 'lip-service' to the Americans in order to receive financial help, and at the same time, prevent American interference in their domestic affairs."

Pablo Escobar, from Columbia, was the main exporter of cocaine and he collaborated with a network of criminal organizations worldwide.

He began distributing powder cocaine, and organized the initial smuggling routes from Peru, Bolivia, and Ecuador through Columbia. The eventual destination was the escalating demand for cocaine in the United States. Escobar changed his distribution model and allowed other organizations to be responsible for trafficking the cocaine into the United States.

His Medellin Cartel would manufacture cocaine, and Miguel Angel Felix Gallardo would oversee distribution from Guadalajara, Mexico. Gallardo would traffic large cocaine shipments by land into the United States.

Gallardo was imprisoned for life in 1989, for the murder

of an American Drug Enforcement Administration (DEA), Enrique "Kiki" Camarena. Camarena and his sister, Myrna, had joined the DEA together, in 1973. Camarena had been tortured, including having his skull pierced with a drill. His body was wrapped in plastic and dumped in a hole on a ranch in the small town of La Angostura, Michoacan. Camarena was 37-years old and the father of three sons.

While incarcerated, Gallardo remained one of Mexico's major drug traffickers. He maintained control of his organization by mobile phone from his prison cell. He ordered his lawyer to organize a meeting of Mexico's top drug dealers at a house in Acapulco. The lawyer divided Gallardo's distribution network, and designated territories for each of the drug dealers. The Ciudad Juarez route went to the Carrillo Fuentes family. The Sonora route went to Miguel Quintero. The Pacific Coast territory became the responsibility of Joaquin Loera and the newly formed Sinaloa Cartel. Since the meeting in Acapulco, the drug dealers have expanded their operations, controlling the entire country of Mexico, by forming numerous drug cartels.

Pablo Escobar, the notorious "King of Cocaine," was killed in Medelin, Columbia by Columbian special forces who were aided by American DEA. The Cali Cartel took over the cocaine market after his death.

Power struggles, involving murder and vicious violence between cartels have been heating up throughout Mexico.

Cardinal Juan Posadas and six others were killed in the parking lot of the Guadalajara Airport. The government claimed the killings were due to disputes between rival cartels.

Attorney Jesus Pedrote has proclaimed that the assassination of Cardinal Posadas involved people of the "inner circle" of Carlos Salinas de Gortari, President of Mexico. Cardinal Posadas had been threatened for complaining about the drug cartels in Jalisco.

The cartels had murdered the Tijuana Municipal Police Chief, Jose Federico Benitz Lopez. The following year they killed the Director of the La Mesa State penitentiary, Jorge Castillo. He had cracked down on guns and drugs in the prison.

In 1996, the cartels were responsible for killing the Tijuana District Chief of the federal narcotics agency and three federal agents who served as his bodyguards. They murdered the Baja Director of the Federal Judicial Police and a State Judicial Police Agent who had provided evidence on what he said were ties between Judicial Police and the Arellano Felix drug cartel.

In 1997, the cartels killed a respected state prosecutor. He had been investigating the assassination of Jose Lopez, a Tijuana Police Chief. They wounded the editor of, Zeta, the Tijuana news weekly and killed his bodyguard.

In Ensenada, disputes between two cartels erupted into the massacre of 18 people, including women and children. The killers used AK-47s to shoot the victims.

⁓

"This Mexican drug war has now spread to cities in the United States. We must develop a plan to stop this violence. The U.S. government seems to be 'asleep at the wheel,' and local authorities are outgunned," said James.

"Sonavabitch, those 'Beaners' have no respect for human

life. They're killing our youth with their drug shit, and no one is stopping them. We should declare our own war on them," exclaimed Slye.

"How can we help, and what can we do?" asked Pate.

"A few years ago, we had a drug problem in our county. It was endangering the families of some of my friends. Some of us took it into our own hands to get rid of some drug dealers.

We started by going as far as to "brand" some of the bad guys, who were hurting children, by cutting off their thumbs. When that wasn't enough, we injected some of the dealers with 'speedballs.' That sent them to their maker almost immediately."

"Really, what are "speedballs?" asked Pate.

"They are a drug cocktail of cocaine and heroin. John Belushi died from an overdose—a 'speedball,'" said James.

"That sounds like a good solution to me," said Slye.

"For a while, drug activity slowed down significantly, but I understand that it's back and on the rise in the San Jose and adjacent areas."

James went on to explain, in greater detail, to Slye and Pate, the activities of the vigilantes. When he finished, they asked to take a break.

"Wow," said Pate to Slye. "I really like this guy. He's like one of our good old boys—a real professional. We should include him in our program."

"I'm thinking the same thing. We shud partner with guys like him. Do you feel comfortable opening our 'kimono' to him about what we've got goin on?" asked Slye.

"I do, he's doing a high level of business and I think he's

looking for people like us to join with him and his people against the same shit we're seein goin on here," said Pate.

When Slye and Pate returned to the meeting, they told James that they had a special program that they had been conducting in Texas and other nearby States. They indicated that they wanted to reveal their program to him at dinner that evening.

"I think that you'll like what you hea, tonight. Let's take a break now and resume the discussions at dinna," said Slye.

"We'll pick you up hea at six," said Pate.

Pate and Syle arrived at James' hotel at 6 pm. Pate drove them to a family-owned, Italian restaurant called Campisi's. The restaurant was founded after World War II, and it maintained an old-style atmosphere with booths and pictures of Italy on the walls.

The maître d, Johnny, recognized Pate and Syle and immediately began a conversation with them about the weather and the Dallas Cowboys.

"Your regular booth is ready," said Johnny.

When the waiter came to take orders, James asked for spaghetti and meatballs with a glass of house chianti. Pate and Slye each ordered their favorite small pizza and beer.

While they were waiting for their dinners, and after receiving their drink orders, Slye began explaining the program that they had referenced earlier in the day.

"We have simila opinions about the condition of Ameerica today. What I'm goin to tell ya is very confidential. If you decide not to go further with us, we hope you'll honor our confidential agreement," said Slye.

"You have my word of honor, as a former Army Officer, that I'll not divulge any information that you share with me. Tonight's discussion will go no further, without your okay, whether we agree to work together or not," said James.

"Good enough for me. Well, we've got an informal group hea that we call the Posse. We're not formed like a corporation or club, or any thin like that," said Slye.

"Our people down hea don't always do business with contracts. In fact, handshakes are just as legal and binding as far as we're concerned," said Pate.

"Our members are reel wealthy and they control lot's a businesses, politicians and things in Texas, Oklahoma, Kansas, Arkansas, and Louisiana," said Slye.

"We also own a lot of property in other states," said Pate.

"Our leading members are combat veterans or they've served in the military at a high level. It's our one common thing. We're all Patriots and we love Ameerica and our Flag. We don't like what we see happenin in Ameerica and we're doin somethin about it," said Slye.

"This sounds good so far. Please explain more," said James.

Slye continued, "We all respect the poleece hea, but they don't get any support from these wimpy politicians. Sum of these fuckin judges let criminals out of jail or give them breaks on sentencing. To put it bluntly, we're takin the law inta our own hands," said Slye.

"Can you get control over the politicians here?" asked James.

"In some cases, yeah. We own a numba of them in local

towns where we have business or property. The inna cities are the problem and at the State level too.

"So, what are some of your solutions?" asked James.

"We have connections with security organizations hea and in other states. These are reel professionals who've served with the Seals, Delta Force, and Rangers.

"We decided to take soma these assholes out, using the teams that we've hired," said Pate.

"We go by the motto, 'Kill the head and the body will fall every time.' We go afta the leaders in the problem areas. Doesn't matter to us whether it's a gang leader, a corrupt politician, or a crooked cop, we've been eliminating them down hea," said Slye.

"I've got to say one thing about politicians. If a corrupt politician is one of ours, we use him until he's no longer of value to us," said Pate.

"We've been doing the same in our area in California. Up until now we have focused on Santa Clara County. It's the center of high technology and probably one of the richest counties in America. It sounds to me like we've been headed in the same direction. We should plan to collaborate in our efforts to blanket more of the country," said James.

"We are of the same mind. If we work together, we might change the country for the good," said Slye.

THIRTY-SIX
THE ART OF PERSUASION

James Greaney and L. Franklin Slye concluded a hand-shake agreement, whereby their two secret organizations, the Vigilantes and the Posse would collaborate. Nothing about their agreement would ever be in writing.

James had shared the details of the Vigilantes' attack plans and methods with Slye during his last visit to Dallas. Slye liked the plans and told James that the Posse would adopt the same, or similar methods in attacking their targets. The plans called for them to use methods of persuasion to change the policies and practices of their political targets. If their methods of persuasion failed, they would eliminate the target.

They agreed to inform each other about the results of their attack missions for the purpose of curtailing the left-wing crime wave raging across America. James recommended they use a fictitious organization online to communicate and send each other updates of their activities. Slye recommended they use the name Heartland. Slye said his favorite country and western singer, George Strait, recorded a song called Heartland, and he gave James a copy of the lyrics.

"I love the lyrics and they define what we've been saying about our commitment to America," said James.

When communicating online, both parties would send their messages, in coded language, to a secure website, addressing their messages to, "Notes from the Heartland."

The Vigilantes would operate in the West and the Posse would continue their missions in the East. Their plans called for them to come together at some point in the future and "blanket" the entire country with their combined operations.

"We must target areas in the country where local and state governments have been suppressed and controlled, for decades, by one political party. Where one party has control of the media and, therefore, the message. Where one party decides what's truth and censor speech, while silencing the opposition. Where one party has been harassing people who hold a different point of view," explained James.

James had explained to members of the Posse that the Vigilantes had decided, long ago, that they must do something significant to stop the crime wave raging throughout the nation.

"We couldn't continue to sit on the sidelines and watch our country being driven into the ground by these socialist/communists. We decided to take a page out of the Viet Cong's playbook—they were the first shadow government that I was aware of. Many of our veterans fought against the Viet Cong who were able to take control of villages and hamlets by assassinating the leaders of the local government."

"What level of concern do you have about federal agencies

and law enforcement finding out who is responsible for the killings?" asked Franklin Slye.

"Of course, we must be careful and disciplined in how we carry out these eliminations. Do you realize that according to FBI statistics, only 50% of the homicides in America are ever solved? We're highly skilled professionals—we're not the incompetent mafia or street thugs. We'll be able to conduct our program without being exposed or without bringing undue attention to ourselves."

The Vigilantes developed an attack plan that was comprehensive. It focused on individuals in power who were aiding the criminals and fueling the out-of-control crime wave. Many of the individuals that they targeted were district attorneys, city mayors, state and local politicians, and political party officials who had been "aiding and abetting" the unrest and criminal behavior. They would begin by targeting cities that had been controlled by left-wing progressive politicians for decades. California was the prime choice to begin their attacks. District Attorneys and other politicians in the counties of Santa Clara, Alameda, and San Mateo were the first targets that they had chosen to implement their plan.

James and William Greaney had researched and developed a very intricate program for interrogating captives. Their combat experiences in Vietnam had convinced them that traditional methods of torture were ineffective. Harsh methods of torture were only acceptable when there was very little time to respond to the enemy. They believed that almost everyone in America eats too much. They decided that they would base their program on deprivation and fear. Depriving their captives of food and water would be one of their most effective methods of persuasion.

At the same time, using silence to create fear of the unknown, or fear of what was going to happen next, was another method of interrogation that they believed to be very effective.

Only a small percentage of the American population maintains a healthy diet. Obesity increases the risk of dying prematurely. One in five children and one in five adults in America are obese. Obese and unhealthy people are the most vulnerable to any demands—when deprived of food and water.

It takes about 24 hours, without eating, for a person's body to change how it produces energy. During the first 24 hours without food, as their glucose storage is depleted, a person's body will begin to convert glycogen from their liver and muscles into glucose.

A person might only survive a few days without water. Dehydration happens quickly, causing extreme thirst, fatigue, organ failure and death. A person might go from feeling thirsty on the first day to having organ failure on the third.

The Vigilante's program was to keep their captives on the edge of starvation and dehydration while being interrogated.

It was late in the evening, around 10:30, and District Attorney Jorge Gasson, of Santa Clara County, was leaving his mistress' apartment. As he stepped away from the door, he was abducted by three men wearing ski masks. Gasson's bodyguard was not with him. He did not want anyone around when he spent time with his mistress. He had been resorting to excessive measures in order to protect his privacy—from his family, his staff, the press, and his political enemies.

Gasson had recently been featured in the nation's media. He was a controversial DA who had implemented unpopular policies of no-cash-bail, reducing drug possession from a felony to a misdemeanor, and investigating police officers. Gasson had been favoring criminals and ignoring the rights of victims.

The three men worked quickly to subdue Gasson. They were very strong and two grabbed his arms while the other one placed duct tape over his mouth. One of the men calmly whispered in his ear not to resist, and he would not be hurt. Gasson decided to comply with their demands and chose to remain as calm as he could. They forced him into a white van, directing him into the rear compartment.

The van did not have any windows in the back and it was impossible for Gasson to see where they were taking him. One of the powerful men put handcuffs on Gasson's wrists while another duct taped his ankles together. It seemed to him that in just a few minutes, after leaving his mistress, he was under his captors' complete control.

The van traveled, for what seemed to Gasson, like thirty minutes when it stopped. A masked man put a blindfold over Gasson's eyes.

The man, who had whispered to him earlier, removed the tape around his ankles and told him to walk quietly with the three of them. He heard a door open and was guided into a room. One of the masked men removed his blindfold and told him to sit on the bed. He also removed the duct tape over Gasson's mouth. The masked man removed one handcuff and secured his wrist around the iron bedpost, limiting Gasson's movement. He calmly warned Gasson to remain quiet.

Gasson was left alone in the room. He was not afraid yet. He figured that his captors were holding him in an attempt to ransom him for some large amount of money.

It seemed like an eternity, but had only been twelve hours, when a masked man entered the room. He placed a bottle of water on the end table next to Gasson, who was sitting on the bed. Gasson asked to go to the bathroom and the masked man uncuffed him from the bed. He motioned him towards the toilet and stood several feet away while Gasson relived himself. When he finished, the masked man directed him back to the bed and fastened the handcuff to the bedpost. As the masked man left the room, he ignored Gasson's question as to why he had been abducted. The masked man closed the door behind him without saying a word.

Exactly twelve hours later, a masked man entered the room and placed a bottle of water, a small hamburger, and some potato fries on the end table next to the bed.

The second day following Gasson's abduction, a masked man entered the room and placed a blindfold over his eyes. The masked man sat down in a chair and proceeded to inform Gasson about their demands.

"You are an incompetent, left-wing bastard who has not followed the law with your anti-cop policies. You've been harassing cops with your false accusations, and trumped-up investigations. Your policies are allowing criminals to stay active in the community and commit more crimes. You have refused to do anything about the rampant drug epidemic and the pitiful conditions of the drug addicted homeless, who are spreading disease and filth in the streets.

If we allow you to return to your home and job, you will change your policies to mirror the law and cut out your communist programs," said the masked man.

"I've done the best job that I can do, when faced with the realities of societies' problems with the poor and the underprivileged. I'm not going to change my policies for any right-wing terrorists," replied Gasson.

"Consider what is happening to you now as a grace period, where you get to decide to keep your life or end it," said the masked man.

The masked man stood up and removed Gasson's blindfold. He did not say another word as he left the room.

Exactly twenty-four hours later, a masked man entered the room and placed a bottle of water and a small Subway sandwich on the end table, next to the bed.

The lack of food and the silence of his captivity was beginning to get to Gasson. He felt weak and his mind was imagining all kinds of threats to his life. He kept asking himself if he could negotiate with these people and be freed. Should he lie to them and tell them what they wanted to hear? Would they kill him even if he gave into them? Will they soon be asking for money?

These hours of silence and boredom were torture for him. He needed to be set free.

Exactly twenty-four hours later, a masked man entered the room and placed a bottle of water and two tacos from Taco Bell on the end table next to the bed. He did not speak to Gasson and left the room.

The only time that the captors deviated from their planned routine was when Gasson cried out to use the toilet. A masked man did not utter a word when he helped Gasson. Silence and deprivation were the key elements of the interrogation program.

It was now four days after Gasson's abduction. A masked man entered the room and placed a bottle of water and a McDonald's Big Mac on the end table, next to the bed. The masked man left the room without saying a word.

On day five of Gasson's abduction, he was ready to agree to anything in order to be set free. He was very weak from not having enough food and he felt the silence during his captivity was killing him. He was hallucinating and seeing people who were not there. His abductors gauged that Gasson was ready to agree to their demands.

Jorge Gasson was dropped off at 5 am, wearing a blindfold, near the emergency entrance to a hospital. While being interrogated, he had agreed to all the demands of his abductors. After hearing his captor's vehicle drive away, he removed the blindfold, and walked slowly into the hospital to ask for medical attention.

While Gasson was enduring his captivity, the District Attorneys in San Mateo, and Alameda had also been kidnapped. They were undergoing the same deprivation and confinement that had convinced Gasson to cooperate with his captors.

❧

As agreed during all three of the kidnappings, the District Attorneys had 30 days to implement the new policies that followed the law of the land. Not complying, would jeopardize their existence.

Jorge Gasson and the District Attorney in Alameda soon made significant changes to their policies within the 30 day-deadline. The District Attorney of San Mateo County, Hilary Waters, made no effort to comply with the demands of her abductors when she returned to her office. The abductors waited an additional 30 days to see if she would implement the appropriate changes to her policies. She received an anonymous call reminding her of her commitment to change her policies. When no effort on her part was apparent, she was assassinated while on her way to her office, by an assailant using a pistol with a silencer. Her bodyguard had no chance to respond, and the assailant disappeared into the crowd.

The three District Attorneys had been interviewed by the FBI when they had been released by their captors. They were not able to provide the FBI with any helpful information about their kidnappers, other than they were masked and very disciplined in the way they conducted themselves.

They had only seen masked men and one had spoken to them in a very low and calm voice. They had all experienced the same routine and treatment.

They had all received the same policy demand and the threat to their lives if they did not comply. They were each given a bottle of water every day with a small amount of junk food. The most difficult treatment to endure though, was the long periods of silence and boredom. The deprivation of food and water was also extremely difficult for them.

When Hilary Waters was assassinated, fear and outcry

spread throughout Northern California. The news media spread the story of her demise nationally, and all news outlets across the country spent the next week retelling the details of her murder. The District Attorney's in Santa Clara and Alameda, learning about her demise, understood that their captors had been serious. They now feared for their safety as well. They did not realize that Waters had defied her captors by ignoring and not complying with their demands. Their fear dissipated, somewhat, when the FBI explained to them that Waters had refused to go along with her captor's demands. She paid the ultimate price for her defiance.

When the Vigilantes launched their attack plan on the three DAs in California, James posted a message on the secure website. His first comment was, "The Eagles have Flown." Slye knew immediately that it was the agreed upon code words for the Vigilantes' attack on the politicians.

After he had read the message on the website, Slye called Jerry Pate and ordered, "Go ahead with that new fishing trip," and hung up. They were code words for Pate to give the go ahead to launch the Posse's attack plan on politicians in Houston, Chicago, and Atlanta.

The attacks on the politicians ignited an explosion in the media across the nation. Newspapers, TV news programs, and talk shows were dominated by the discussions of the attacks 24/7.

Fear of the unknown dominated all discussions. Were there going to be more attacks?

Many politicians ran to the media outlets and demanded

to be interviewed. They wanted to express their outrage over the attacks. Democratic politicians were accusing right-wing groups for the attacks and starting a race war. Republican politicians accused left-wing groups and other progressives of sponsoring turmoil and lawlessness.

James Greaney was pleased to see the hysteria and chaos playing out in the media outlets. It was the exact response that he and Slye had hoped to create.

With all the fear and accusations dominating the airwaves, the progressives who oversaw state and local governments, were traumatized. They were afraid to institute, or carry out, their communist-influenced programs that were doing so much damage to the general public. They felt confused and impotent. Their leadership had crumbled, and no one seemed to know what the next step should be.

James knew that creating fear in the minds of his enemies was his most powerful and effective strategy. He could neutralize them, or manipulate their movements to his advantage. The Posse was a powerful ally and together they would destroy the influence, and effectiveness, of the left-wing progressives for a long time to come.

The Vigilantes and the Posse had many more targets to pursue. Turmoil, chaos, and fear would continue to spread throughout the country—and it all worked to their advantage.

THIRTY-SEVEN
WINE COUNTRY

James Greaney had read an article about the Paris Wine Tasting contest that took place in 1976. It was known as "The Judgement in Paris." The contest reported that Napa Valley wineries had won a blind-tasting contest, over some of the most prestigious wineries in France. The judges of the contest were all Frenchmen. The article highlighted the fact that Napa Valley wine production had emerged to be the highest quality in the world. The Napa wineries were producing quality wines at the same level or better than French winemakers.

James was particularly interested in the quality of wine since he had recently decided to quit drinking vodka or any strong alcoholic beverage. He made an exception for an occasional shot of his favorite McCallan whisky. He rarely drank beer, and he disliked the sugary taste of soft drinks. He had decided to change to drinking wine, and he wanted to educate himself about the possible health benefits of the various varietals.

His many businesses located in Silicon Valley and Texas had become very successful over the last ten years and he now possessed a large amount of income that his accountant was advising him to diversify within his investment portfolio. His accountant had mentioned that he might want to investigate the possibility of acquiring winery and vineyard land to help spend some of his discretionary income and generate substantial tax write offs.

James did a background search of three real estate firms in Napa. They were Levinson Realtors, Michele Franks Real Estate Group, and Stubbs & Jenkins Realtors. He placed calls to the three firms leaving a detailed message saying that he was interested in acquiring a winery. He requested a call back from each firm. Only one individual returned his call. She was Judith Jenkins from Stubbs & Jenkins.

When Judith returned his call, he explained his interest in acquiring a winery and vineyard land. He asked whether she knew if there were any available for sale.

Judith sounded bubbly on the phone, and it was clear that she was excited that he had called her office. She told him that she and her partner had founded their firm the previous year. She said, "Mr. Greaney, I know that there are two wineries up for sale, but I'll do a thorough search and send you what I'm able to find."

"That will be very helpful, Judith."

He gave her his contact information and said, "I'll look forward to your response. Hopefully, you'll get back to me soon."

"Yes, of course, Mr. Greaney. I'll be getting back to you

very soon."

"Just call me, Jim."

"And you may call me, Judy."

Later that same day, Judith faxed information to James on three wineries that were listed for sale. She also included information about an additional two wineries that she believed might soon be for sale due to their declining business.

James was impressed with her quick response and professional manner. The other real estate firms had not returned his call. He decided that he was going to commit to working with Judith and her partner.

Two weeks later, James phoned Judith and informed her that he would be taking a three-week working vacation in the Napa Valley.

"Judy, I'll be staying at a hotel in Calistoga. I'd like you to set up visits to the wineries that are listed for sale and others that you think might be good acquisitions. I would also appreciate it if you would provide me with a tour of the entire Napa Valley. My driver will take us wherever you direct him to go."

"I'd love to do that, Jim. Just let me know your arrival time and I'll block out my schedule to accommodate you. If you don't mind me asking, why are you staying in Calistoga?"

"I'm a very private person. I like to stay away from crowded areas when I'm taking a vacation. Privacy is very important to me."

"I understand. You'll have a lot of privacy there."

"I'll send you, my itinerary. Let's plan it from there."

"Okay, Jim. I'm anxious to meet you."

Judith was an attractive woman who looked younger than her years. She was 5'3" tall with long blonde hair. She wore it pulled back in a ponytail, which accentuated her high cheekbones and large green eyes. She had an engaging, friendly smile and people enjoyed being in her company. She was a widow with three daughters who were married and living with their families in Napa.

She had married at a young age. Her husband had been physically and emotionally abusive to her and her daughters. They divorced after eight years. She had remained a single mother for ten years, taking care of her children and undergoing therapy. She had finally met a nice man and decided to give marriage another try. Unfortunately, she was now a widow. She hid her pain and troubles well. She was gregarious when meeting new people, and it helped her real estate business grow. She was wary of men due to the extensive abuse that she had received from her first husband. In fact, Judith did not like or trust most men that she met.

After James had arrived in Calistoga and checked into his hotel, he called Judith. James' driver/bodyguard was assigned to a room next door to his. Two other members of James' security personnel, who had traveled in a separate car, checked into the hotel as well. They would monitor James' travels and be ready to provide instant protection if needed.

"I'd like to meet you for dinner in Napa, tonight. Are you available?"

"Yes, but that's quite a drive from Calistoga. Are you sure?"

"It's no problem. How bout you choose the restaurant and I'll meet you there?"

"What kind of food do you like?"

"Tonight, I'd like a good steak. I'm usually a steak and potatoes man," he laughed.

"Then let's meet in downtown Napa at Cole's Steakhouse. Does 7 pm work for you?"

"That'll be great, see you at 7."

Judith was carrying a briefcase full of documents when she arrived for dinner. She had detailed information on wineries and vineyard land that she wanted to discuss with James. She had categorized them in order of best to least opportunity.

James was very impressed that she was so organized and that she had spent the time analyzing the best opportunities for him. They soon chose a winery as their number one target to acquire.

The following morning, they visited the prospective targets and decided by late afternoon that a winery in North Napa was the one that they wanted to purchase. It had a large home on the property, a wine barn that had been used for public wine tasting, and a processing plant that specialized in producing cabernet wine.

Three days later, they had concluded the purchase of the winery and ten acres of vineyard that surrounded the property.

"Judy, I'm very impressed with your professionalism and business acumen. Would you consider living in the home at the winery and managing my wine business? I will pay you well and you can continue with your real estate sales. You could even use part of the wine barn as an office for your real estate business. What do you think?"

"Well, Jim, I have a home that I've lived in for over twenty-five years. What would I do with that?"

"Whatever you decide. Keep it, sell it, or rent it out. It's your decision. I wouldn't want you to do anything until you were comfortable with our business relationship. You know, I plan to retire here within the next ten years—that's how committed I am to this area."

"Let me think about it. I don't have to give you an answer now, do I?"

"Take your time—you need to feel comfortable with your decision. I hired the wine maker Joe Giacomo, who the previous owner had employed. In the future, we can decide whether to keep him on or replace him with someone who better fits our requirement."

The following week, Judith notified James that she had accepted his offer of employment. James had decided that the home at the winery needed considerable renovation. He told Judith to handle the remodel. "I trust your judgement. Just get it done." James and Judith agreed that she would live in her own home until renovations were completed at the winery.

James and Judith traveled throughout the Napa Valley. They took balloon rides to view the valley from above. They rode the wine train from Napa to St Helena and had lunch on the train. They hiked many of the trails that wound through the valley. They could not go bike riding because she had never learned to ride a bike, but she took him to her health club for daily workouts.

James was drawn to Judith. He had not been this attracted

to a woman since Lan. She seemed to have all the qualities that he admired most in a woman. He felt that she could be an excellent companion for him. The past two weeks had given him a glimpse of what retirement would look like with Judith in his life. They became lovers, and she told him that she really cared for him.

"I really care for you too, but I think that you need a man who will come home to you every night. That's not me. I don't live a normal life like most men, and I'm often traveling. I'm involved with activities that I can't share or explain to you."

"Jim, you said that you eventually want to retire here. I've been single for a long time and I'm happy with my life as it is. For now, I'll manage your wine business. Let's leave it at that and see what the future brings."

"That's the kind of response that I appreciate and one of the things that I admire about you. You never know, maybe I'll retire to Napa sooner, rather than later, just to be with you."

Judith invited James to her grandson's birthday party. She wanted to use the opportunity to introduce him to her daughters and their families.

He declined, saying, "I think it's too soon for me to meet your family. "Maybe on my next trip to Napa, you could set something up for me to meet them."

"I understand. How about meeting my best friend for a casual lunch?"

"Okay, why don't you set it up for next Friday. I'm planning to return to Los Gatos then, and we could have lunch before I leave."

"Good, I know just the place. You'll be coming from Calistoga and my favorite restaurant is on the way in Rutherford. It's the Rutherford Grill."

"Set it up and I'll be there. I look forward to meeting your friend."

Dianne Neece was Judith's best friend. They had been friends for over twenty years, and she was also a widow. Her husband had died in a freeway car crash four years before. She was originally from Oklahoma and had a slight southern drawl. She was attractive and stood just over 5' tall. People loved to be around her. She was quickwitted, and fond of telling bawdy jokes.

The lunch reservation at the Rutherford Grill was for 12 pm. Judith and her friend Dianne came together in Judith's car. They sat at a table on the patio to wait for James to arrive. They both ordered iced tea.

As they waited, Dianne said, "Okay, let's get to the good stuff. What's he like in bed?"

"He's strong and virile."

"What do you mean by virile?"

"You know, he's very strong, and he has a strong sex drive."

"Really? A strong sex drive, huh? What do you mean?"

"Well, he moved me around in bed like I was a rag doll, although he was gentle."

"Rag doll, I like the sound of that. I'd go for being a rag doll."

"Did he do anything kinky?"

"No, but we did make love in different positions, and he was always careful with me."

"Different positions huh, what do you mean different positions? I think that I could go for different positions. When are the two of you getting together again, if you know what I mean?"

"Not for a while. He's leaving for Los Gatos this afternoon."

"You've got to keep me informed. Your sex life is more interesting than Young and Restless."

It was close to noon when Dianne spotted a tall man at the entrance to the restaurant. He had gray hair and was wearing a black suit.

"Is that him? I want one of him."

"Yes, it is. Let's go meet him."

The two women met James as he was talking with the restaurant hostess.

"Jim, I'd like you to meet Dianne," said Judy.

"I'm happy to meet you, Dianne. Judy has told me that you're her best friend."

Dianne stared up at James' face and at first did not know what to say. Finally, she said "It's nice meeting you Jim, I'm Dianne Neece."

They enjoyed a pleasant lunch as they talked about their families, friends, and social issues of the day. At 1:30, James announced that he had to leave. He said, "I'm paying for the meal, but the two of you should stay. There's no reason for you to rush."

When he stood up, he kissed Judith and shook hands with Dianne.

As James walked toward the exit, two men in black suits

emerged from the waiting area. They quietly exchanged words with him. They then escorted James as he left the restaurant.

"Wow, you really found yourself quite a man. Were those two guys his bodyguards? Why does he have bodyguards? Is he with the government? Could he be with the mob?"

"Yes, he always has bodyguards nearby. There are others that follow his car. Dianne, I don't know the answer. I just don't know."

"Why does he wear suits?

"He always wears a black or gray suit and a tie. When we traveled around Napa Valley, he wore a black sport coat and a white shirt. When I took him to my gym, he changed into workout clothes. Other than those two exceptions he wore suits."

"Well, you've seen him naked. What did he look like then?"

"He's in good shape and muscular."

"Is he well endowed?"

"Use your imagination, Dianne."

When James returned to Los Gatos, he had a message waiting for him from an old Army buddy, John Mullins. Mullins had left his contact information with his phone message. When Mullins answered his phone James asked, "Are you still as black as Michael Jordan?"

"Yes, you racist capitalist, none of my blackness has rubbed off since I last saw you."

John Mullins had served at MACV headquarters in Vietnam. He had served as an intelligence officer. His duty responsibilities were to brief James and other Advisory Team Leaders about the troop movements of North Vietnamese and Viet Cong units.

"It's great to hear from you, how did you know how to reach me?"

"I read an article in a magazine about your rise to fame and fortune in Silicon Valley. It was so flattering that it had to have been written by one of your employees—you probably dictated it to him."

"No, believe it or not, I was uncomfortable about the interview. I don't like to share personal information. What have you been up to?"

"I've got a small law practice in Oakland with two associates. I take on any cases that clients bring to me. I can't afford to be choosey. Just trying to keep my head above water."

"You know, I might have a lot of business for you. I hope you know what you're doing. I wouldn't want you to fix a parking ticket for me and then I'd be sentenced to three months in jail."

"You might get 30 days, but I'd come visit you every day. What do you have in mind?"

"Not to hurt your feelings, but I don't trust most lawyers. I have many businesses that require legal consulting and I'd like to have someone to advise me who I can trust. Plus, I have a special project for veterans, and you might be just the one to fit the bill."

"What's the program that you have in mind for veterans?"

"There are many veterans that are getting screwed by the VA. They're not even aware of the benefits and services available to them. The VA has been neglecting them, and some veterans have even died waiting for medical treatment. I want to go after the VA with a legal approach. I've been contributing a lot of money to a legal defense fund that my lawyers have set up for veterans. You would be the perfect man to manage the fund."

"I'm interested. Would I be able to operate from my office in Oakland?"

"Sure, we can use some of my funding to make your office a center of operations on behalf of veterans. You'll be able to hire a larger staff."

"You're amazing, Captain. I take back all the negative things that I used to say about you. When could we meet up and start this new operation?"

"John, your call was perfect timing for me. I would always rather be lucky than good. I've been looking for the right person to hire and you call me out of the blue. It's great karma. How bout we meet at my offices in Los Gatos next Wednesday?"

"Will I need a special passport to visit Los Gatos? I hear that everyone there is Lilly-white."

"Don't worry, I'll tell everyone that you're Jordan's cousin. That'll be your passport. He's considered a superhero, here."

"See you soon, Captain."

THIRTY-EIGHT
THE PROTÉGÉ

It was Sunday, July 4, 1999. James Greaney's family was celebrating Independence Day. It was an annual event because it was James' favorite holiday. His family would celebrate other holidays and birthdays at their own homes or in different locations. The 4th of July was the only holiday that attendance was mandatory at his home.

Elizabeth and Georgia arrived at 7 am to join Marie in helping Margarita prepare meals to be served throughout the day and evening. They also shared clean-up duties after each meal. Elizabeth and Georgia's husbands would arrive with their children just before noon. James' son, Vincent, and his girlfriend, Sandra Johnston, arrived just before lunch as did Marie's two high school girlfriends, Jeanie Burger and Nancy Bush. Throughout the day James and his family would entertain the young children by including them in competitive outdoor games.

When the family and guests sat down for dinner at 7 pm,

James started with prayers in remembrance of those family members who had passed. He then offered toasts to the United States of America and to the combat veterans who had made it possible for everyone to enjoy their liberty and freedom.

James had always encouraged discussions of social and world-wide topics during mealtimes. Everyone at his table was expected to participate. The younger children ate their dinner at a separate table. He began the discussion by reminding everyone that in January 1999, the U.S. Coast Guard had intercepted a ship with 9,500lbs. of cocaine aboard. It was headed for Houston, Texas, and was the largest drug bust in history.

Elizabeth mentioned the impeachment of President Bill Clinton. She informed everyone, "That low-life, son-of-a-bitch was acquitted by the Senate in February. He has mistreated women throughout his career—yet Democratic women vote for him in droves. They make me sick."

"That's because the Democratic Party is made up of angry women and weak men," responded Elizabeth's husband, Jeff.

Georgia was next, and she asked, "Can you believe it? The government of Columbia announced that it included the estimated value of the country's illegal drug crops, exceeding a half billion dollars, in its gross national product. How can we fight the illegal drug trade when a third-world nation has been including illegal drug sales in their government financial reporting?"

"It demonstrates that the U.S. government has been irresponsible in not holding nation's leaders accountable regarding the drug trade. These countries are the origin of illegal drug production. Both political parties are responsible for the drug epidemic that America has been suffering," said James.

Marie brought up the announcement that George W. Bush was seeking the Republican nomination for President. "Does anyone care about Bush junior running for President?"

"No, he'll probably be as weak as his old man. He'll just be another do-nothing, good old boy," said Don, Georgia's husband.

Vincent asked his father, "Pop, what's your opinion of Y2k? Is it going to be a problem for everyone?"

"I don't think so, son. All this foolish hysteria is not called for. Experts in the computer industry have already solved the transition of the computer networks to the new century. There are always a lot of 'wackos' out there trying to 'gin up' fears of catastrophic breakdown once the clock strikes the year 2000. It's all hype in my opinion. Nothing unusual is going to happen."

James and his driver/bodyguard, William Fowler, had purchased fireworks from a vendor in San Jose that would be safe for the children to enjoy on the lawn, as soon as the sun began to set. At 9:30 pm, the family gathered on the second-story balcony of the home, overlooking the Santa Clara Valley. From this vantage point, they could view the many locations that were setting off fireworks that were bursting simultaneously in the sky.

At 10:40 pm, the fireworks demonstrations were over. The family standing on the balcony began saying their goodbyes. Elizabeth and Georgia left with their husbands and children.

Marie and her two friends went to her room. Tonight, the three were going to have a slumber party. Vincent and Sandra were staying the night, and they were walking to their room when James asked Vincent to join him for a nightcap in his study.

Vincent was tall, handsome, and closely resembled his father. He was blonde, muscular, and had stayed in excellent physical condition. He had been an exceptional athlete in high school and college. He graduated from San Jose State University with a BA in Business. He had always planned to join his father in business, but not before serving in the military. From the time he was a child, he had wanted to grow up to be an Army Ranger, like his father. He was sworn into the Army as a second lieutenant after having completed ROTC. He was soon able to obtain his wish of being an Army Ranger. After two overseas tours where he had been decorated for heroism in combat, he was discharged from the Army. He joined his father's business. James assigned him to oversee the family's investments in farmland and ranchland, located in Idaho and Utah.

James and Vincent sat down in leather lounges in James' study. James poured them each a glass of his favorite McCallan whiskey. He also picked out two cigars from his humidor and gave one to Vincent. He enjoyed a Churchill cigar with his whiskey. James opened their conversation with, "Vince, I'm very proud of you and your military service. Most young men your age who come from wealthy families, avoid any risk taking, let alone two tours of combat. Hopefully, your experiences have not left you with too many scars."

"No Pop, I might have some memories that I'd like to

forget, but for the most part, I'm doing fine."

"How do you like overseeing our farm and ranch operations?"

"I enjoy working at the ranch in Idaho, and the Utah location is also a good challenge for me. I like working outdoors and our workers have taught me a lot about ranching."

"As you learn more about our real estate operations, I'll be adding more responsibility to your plate."

"Elizabeth told me that you recently purchased a winery and vineyards in Napa. What are your plans there?"

"Over the past two years, I've been slowly moving our business interests out of California. This state has become business 'unfriendly' with harmful corporate regulations and higher taxes. Eventually, the only type of investments that I'll keep in California will be wineries and vineyards. I've been studying the wine industry since they had that contest between French wineries and Napa wines. It's an industry that continues to grow. I want to purchase as much vineyard land as possible before the price per acre becomes too prohibitive."

"How did you decide to get into the wine business?"

"As I mentioned, I was researching the wine industry because of that wine contest between France and Napa. Napa wineries kicked Frances' ass in the contest. I contacted some real estate companies, and I met a lady who convinced me that the wine production business would be a good investment. She helped me purchase a small winery that produces cabernet as well as a few acres of land. I also hired her to manage our wine business in Napa Valley. I plan to buy additional wineries and land to expand our business there."

"That's very interesting, Pop. I never imagined that you'd be in the wine business. It does make sense though, since you own a lot of ranchland and farmland. You always told my sisters and me that owning land was a safer investment than the stock market or high tech."

"When you feel you're ready, I'll add our wine business properties to your responsibilities. I'll introduce you to our Wine Director, Judith Jenkins. She'll be happy to teach you the wine business and it'll be a great challenge for you. It'll also keep you working outdoors. I don't want to push you too fast, but I'm hopeful that you'll want to take over more management of our properties as time goes by."

"I'm all in, Pop. I want to be involved in everything that you want me to do. I've been waiting for the right time to bring up something that I'm sure is very sensitive to you. I want to be involved in what you and my uncles have been doing."

"What does that mean? What about your uncles and me?"

"Pop, let me tell you a story and you'll understand where I'm coming from. When I was little, I always wanted to grow up to be an Army Ranger and fight in combat like you did. And I succeeded in doing just that. I spent a lot of time alone as a little kid, and I would play Army Ranger most of the time. I would hide in places in the house and pretend that I was on a mission behind enemy lines. One of my favorite hiding places was over there, under your large oak desk. You know, it has a large empty space behind the drawers. I would hide there for hours—sometimes I would fall asleep there. Sometimes I would be hiding there when you were having meetings with visitors. The only person who knew that I hid there was Lan.

She always treated me specially. One time she went looking for me when I was playing Army Ranger. I had fallen asleep under the desk, and she must have heard me snoring. She told me to come out and took me to the kitchen for milk and cookies. I made her promise never to tell anyone about my secret hiding place—and she never did. She never told you, did she?"

"No."

"After she died, I would hide under the desk and pretend that she would be coming to get me—but then I knew that she couldn't—she was gone forever."

"Do you remember much about Lan?"

"Oh yes, I was hoping that she would become my mother. She would stay up late with me when I couldn't sleep and when I was sick. She would sit with me for hours, and we'd talk about things that were occurring in the world. I think that she felt sorry for me. I didn't have many kids my age to play with like my sisters did. I don't remember my real mom, like Liz and Georgia do. I was too young when she died to remember anything about her."

"Lan was a wonderful woman. I loved her very much and think about her every day. She'll always be with me."

"I loved her too, Pop. I still miss her."

"Someday I'll tell you more about her. She was very brave, and she suffered terrible treatment from the Communists."

"I'd like to hear more about her."

"Please go on Vince and tell me what you have in mind."

"Sometimes when I heard that my uncles were coming to visit you, I would hide under the desk and listen to your conversations. I have always considered Victor Lewis to be my uncle too. After listening to a few of your meetings I began to understand what you were doing. I remember Uncle Bill saying, 'The only good drug dealer is a dead drug dealer.' And then I heard Uncle Tom say, 'And corrupt politicians should pay the ultimate price for betraying the peoples' trust.'"

"Your Uncles—they always had a way with words," laughed James.

"I heard you mention the term vigilante several times, and I asked Lan what it meant. She didn't know, so we looked it up in the dictionary. I remember her explaining that a vigilante was a person who upheld the law when the authorities had failed to do their job. Then there came a time when it seemed that everyone on TV and in the newspapers were talking about the killings of drug dealers and even politicians who were using drugs. I put two and two together and I came to realize that you and my uncles were responsible for eliminating those bad people. You were doing it because the judicial system and law enforcement had failed the people. I wanted to be one of you guys. I knew that I was too young to even talk to you about it. You know, growing up I never had an interest in your wealth— I just wanted to be powerful like you are. Do you remember that quote from Henry Kissinger? 'Power is the ultimate aphrodisiac.' Now, with my military training and combat experience, I have accomplished what you and my uncles had accomplished when you went to war. I want to join you. I can be an asset."

"So, you think that we're the good guys. Do you think that we're saving society?"

"No, but I think that you're putting quite a dent in the

criminal world. You've been doing a lot of damage to them."

"It's an uphill battle, son. Sometimes I don't know if we can do enough to protect society."

"Society is really screwed up now. I know that what you've been doing is the right path to follow. After all, the government has trained men like us to be killers and they've sent us to all parts of the world to help people in distress and fight their wars. Yet, the government's policies at home have been harming the poor and underprivileged people. Government officials and federal agencies are so corrupt that they fail to support law enforcement. They haven't been protecting the people and our minority populations suffer the most from neglect. Career politicians have been getting rich by taking advantage of their positions in awarding government contracts to their friends. For years, many of them have been trading on the stock market using inside information that they've acquired by participating on certain congressional committees. I know that you and my uncles have been working to help the disadvantaged people who have no one to represent them."

"Have you mentioned this to anyone?"

"No, I haven't said anything to anybody and I won't. I just wanted to discuss it with you."

"I think that you're kinda imagining things, son. I'm not clear about what you're trying to get at. Give me a minute while I freshen our drinks."

James walked slowly to the liquor cabinet and refilled their drinks. He had an expression of concern on his face.

"Pop, I know that this is a very serious subject to be discussing with you. You never have to worry about me. I've done a lot of dangerous things in my life, and I know how to handle myself."

"Are you sure that you're not dreaming this up?"

"I'm positive and especially now that I see the look on your face and your reaction to my comments. I know that you and my uncles are vigilantes. And that you're the main man, Pop. **You're the Vigilante.**"

James' concerned expression relaxed, and he began to smile.

"Vincent, I can't say that I'm disappointed that you have figured things out. In fact, I'm pleased. You have grown up to be like your uncles and me. You're a Patriot like us who have pledged an oath to the Constitution. The oath we took wasn't just for when we were serving in the military—it was for life. We are a rare breed of men who love our country and respect the Constitution. We are different from most men. We believe in God, Country, Honor, and Duty. The Left laughs at us for believing in what we do. There's a great quote from the Godfather film, 'Crime and Politics—they're the same thing.' The quote is accurate in that it describes the condition our country's in today. Corrupt government officials and politicians who do not support the Constitution and law enforcement, have by their actions or lack of action, declared war on the rest of the country. It's true, today in government, crime and politics are the same. We've pledged to win this war using tactics that the government spent millions in training us to do. We see our role as protecting the American people from criminals and corrupt policies that have been destroying the social fabric of our nation. We know that a large part of the government has been controlled by left-wing socialists who have been dragging us down and toward a communist state."

"I totally agree with you, Pop. That's why I want to join you. I want to fight these bastards who have been destroying our country."

"You know Vince, this isn't going to be over anytime soon. We're going to be waging war against corruption for many years to come. For me, it's a lifetime mission and I won't live long enough to see the conclusion. You're going to have to take over at some point in time."

"You might be surprised, Pop. If we continue to build our organization, we could realize tremendous results sooner rather than later."

"What about this young woman that you're with tonight, Sandra? She seems to be very nice. Are you serious about her?"

"Yes, I'm very serious. We've decided to get married next year."

"I welcome you to join us, son, but you must understand that you're making a lifetime commitment to the Vigilantes. Once in—there's no turning back. You can't allow Sandra to know about us—even after you're married."

"I understand. She'll know nothing from me. I'm with you, Pop, for the rest of my life."

"Good, I'll set up a meeting with your uncles. They'll be pleased that you'll be joining us. Tomorrow, I'll tell you about our partners in Texas. I've also been considering asking your cousin Ken to join us, but that will happen sometime in the future."

"Ken will be a great choice as well. He had a lot of experience in combat, and he's an expert in telecommunications."

They both stood and raised their glasses. James offered a toast, "May God Bless America, and here's to the success of the Vigilantes in the new century."

The Vigilantes, led by James Greaney, continued to attack the political systems in the American West that were favoring and supporting the left-wing elements in society. They collaborated their efforts with the Posse who were conducting missions against corrupt politicians and organizations in their area.

At their meeting in Texas, James had explained his views to the leaders of the Posse: "The Democratic and Republican parties are corrupt and incompetent. They're only interested in their own power base, and they fight with each other at the expense of the American people. Equal justice in America is impossible for most people today. We must take extraordinary measures. There will be times when we must go above the law in order to save the law of the land—the Constitution of the United States."

The Vigilantes and Posse were guided by the premise that five or fewer people controlled the decision-making in most government and corporate organizations. By eliminating a few key people, the corrupt system would become crippled and inoperable. Their combined efforts to eliminate corruption in America brought the attention of federal, state, and local law enforcement. Law enforcement agencies, at all levels, were frustrated and confused because they could not identify the source of the attacks.

In time, the Vigilantes and Posse were able to build networks that "blanketed" the entire country. They were feared by the leaders of the political parties and left-wing politicians. Their exploits were becoming legendary in the poor and rural communities. Their popularity was growing rapidly, and they were supported by most of the American people.

They had become a very powerful, "Shadow Government."

EPILOGUE
ELEANOR RIGBY

James Greaney was a creature of habit. Every Wednesday and Friday morning at 9 am, his driver/bodyguard, William Fowler, dropped him off at Peet's Coffee shop on Blossom Hill Road in Los Gatos. Fowler would park his car and observe James from a distance.

Two bodyguards from Victor's security firm had arrived at the coffee shop at 8:30 am to provide protection for James. Ray Jordan was dressed in casual clothes. He sat at a table drinking coffee and reading a newspaper. His gun was in a holster that was strapped to his right calf. The other guard was Ann Carlson, and her table was ten feet away. She was dressed in a business suit and her pistol was in her briefcase under the table. She had purchased a coffee and a slice of pumpkin bread. She was reading a biography of Jacqueline Onassis.

James' decaf vanilla latte was usually prepared and waiting for him. He would pay for his coffee and then take a seat at a table outside the shop. He would be wearing either a black or grey suit with a tie. On sunny days he would be wearing sun-glasses. He enjoyed watching people and being alone with his thoughts as he drank his coffee. It was usually an hour of peace and quiet without interruptions.

It was a Friday morning when an attractive elderly woman approached him and said, "Mr. Greaney, may I speak with you for a moment?"

James stood up to greet her and replied, "Of course, how may I help you? Please take a seat." When she sat down at his table, he asked her if she would like tea or coffee. She declined saying that she had already had her morning tea at home. She looked to be distraught.

The observing bodyguards were immediately on the alert when the woman approached James' table. They were trained to know that an assassin could come in all shapes and sizes. They began to relax as they watched James invite her to sit down and saw that they were talking amicably.

The woman began, "Mr. Greaney, my name is Eleanor Rigby. I'm eighty-four-years-old. A real estate development company has been harassing me about selling my home. They want me to sell it to them so that they can tear it down and build condominiums. My husband, John and I were schoolteachers, and we paid $17,000 for our home in 1955. This company is offering me over $1,000,000 if I'll sell it to them right away. I don't want to leave. I've lived there for over 45 years. My husband and I raised our three daughters there. Two years ago, my husband had a heart attack and died while working in our garden."

"How are they harassing you, Mrs. Rigby?"

"They've been throwing stones on my roof and at the side of my house in the middle of the night. They've kept me awake all night. I can only get to sleep during the day. Last week someone killed one of my cats and left it on my doorstep."

"Have you contacted the police?"

"Yes, they've been to my home three times. They told me that there is nothing they can do. I even complained at a Town Council Meeting. They treated me like I was a crazy old lady."

"Mrs. Rigby, please write down your name and address. Also, please give me the name of the development company."

Mrs. Rigby took pen and paper from her purse. She wrote down the information that James had requested and handed the paper to him. When he read the information, he smiled. "Eleanor Rigby, huh? I bet you were teased about that after the Beatles' song came out."

"Oh yes, I was fifty-years-old when that song was played on the radio. My husband and my girls would sing it to me. I got kinda sick of it—but it was funny. Some of my students asked me about it. One student asked if the song was written about me, she laughed. My maiden-name is McKenzie. My ancestors are from Edinburgh, Scotland."

"My ancestors are from Tralee, Ireland. It's good to remember our heritage, is it not?"

"Yes, it is Mr. Greaney. As the saying goes, 'You're never lonely if you have good memories to revisit.'"

"Well, Mrs. Rigby."

"You may call me Eleanor, Mr. Greaney."

"And you may call me Jim. I'll investigate this issue that

you have with the development company. I've never heard of them, but I'll make sure that the harassment stops, immediately. Enjoy your day today and don't worry any more about them." He handed her a business card and said, "This is my office phone number. Feel free to call me any time that you feel threatened."

"Thank you, Mr. Greaney, I mean, Jim. You're a real gentleman," she said as she stood up to leave.

James stood and they shook hands goodbye.

Two weeks later, William Fowler knocked on Mrs. Rigby's door. When she opened the door, he introduced himself and said that he worked for James Greaney. He was there to check on her well-being. She invited him in and asked if he would like a cup of tea.

"No thank you ma'am," he replied.

"Well sir, how may I help you?"

"Mr. Greaney wants to know if everything is okay and how you're doing? Has there been any more harassment?"

"I'm doing just fine, sir. After I met with Mr. Greaney, the harassment stopped. In fact, last week I was able to sleep through the night, every night, without interruption. My health is starting to improve, and I don't worry anymore about anyone trying to harm me."

"That's great to hear. So, no one has bothered you since you spoke to Mr. Greaney?"

"Yes, and no one has come here to try and buy my house, either. The rock throwing stopped two weeks ago."

"Great, Mr. Greaney will be happy to hear that you're doing well. Is there anything else that I may help you with—or do for you?”

“Nothing now. Mr. Greaney is such a good man, and he's so handsome. You know Mr. Fowler, my girlfriends and I play bridge twice a week and we've been talking. We believe that we know who Mr. Greaney really is but we're keeping it a secret.”

“Is that right, Mrs. Rigby?”

“Yes, please tell him that I'm very grateful for all that he has done. I've told all my friends about his interceding for me. They were very impressed.”

“I'll tell him. He'll be pleased. Goodbye, Mrs. Rigby.”

ACKNOWLEDGMENTS

A very special thank you to Judith Jankiewicz and Karen Chandler for their encouragement, insight, and careful editing.

ADDENDUM

1970s

Two major events controlled the attention of the American public in the 1970s: the Vietnam War and the Watergate scandal. Both events dominated the front pages of every newspaper in the country for a good part of the early 70s. American troops left Vietnam in 1973 and the last Americans were airlifted off the roof of the American Embassy in April 1975, as Saigon fell to the Communists.

The Watergate scandal ended with the resignation of President Richard Nixon in August 1974. The American public was stunned by the revelations revealed in the investigations. The American people had lost faith in their government leaders.

In May 1970, President Nixon had authorized the American military invasion of Cambodia. College campuses erupted into demonstrations against the government's policies. The Ohio State National Guard was called to Kent State and Guardsmen fired on protestors, killing four students.

At the Olympic Games in Munich, Germany, in 1972, terrorists killed nine Israeli athletes. Five terrorists were killed in the firefight.

In 1973, the Supreme Court made abortion legal in the United States with its Roe vs Wade decision.

Skylab, America's first space station, was launched.

Vice-President Agnew resigned in disgrace.

In 1976, the Tangshan earthquake killed more than 240,000 people in China.

The first Ebola Virus outbreaks took place in Sudan and Zaire.

Apple Computers was founded.

The Muppet Show premiered on American TV.

In 1976—"The Era of Stagnation"—a term expressed by Mikhail Gorbachev was considered by several economists to be the worst financial failure in the Soviet Union.

In 1977, Elvis Presley was found dead in his home in Memphis, Tennessee.

"Star Wars" premiered.

In 1978, the first test-tubed baby was born.

In March of 1979, Three Mile Island, Pennsylvania, was the site of the worst nuclear accident in United States history.

In May 1979, Margaret Thatcher became the first female Prime Minister in British history.

John Wayne died from stomach cancer on June 11, 1979.

In July 1979, Sony introduced the Walkman. It allowed everyone to take their favorite music everywhere.

The decade ended with 52 American hostages being held in Iran. The hostages had been retained on November 4, 1979.

1980s

During the 1980s, many Americans embraced a new conservatism in social, economic, and political life. President Ronald Reagan was the driving force behind new conservatism. The decade saw the rise of the "Yuppie" and a focus on materialism and consumerism.

There was an explosion of blockbuster movies and the emergence of cable networks that introduced music videos.

At the beginning of the decade, the Cold War was ongoing between the United States and the Soviet Union. Many arms control advocates lobbied for a "nuclear freeze" among nations.

The 1980s witnessed the practice of sex-selective abortion in China and India using new ultrasound technology to selectively abort baby girls.

Human immunodeficiency virus (HIV) and acquired immunodeficiency syndrome (AIDS), were recognized in the 1980s and went on to kill an estimated 39 million people. It had been determined that HIV virus, though a bloodborne illness, could be transmitted through the transfer of genital secretions during sexual activity.

Global Warming became a new term in the scientific and political communities.

Television became commonplace in the Third World, with TV sales in China and India increasing by tenfold.

Mount St Helens erupted in Washington State on May 18, 1980, killing 57 people.

In 1980, Pac-Man was introduced to the arcades, and became the most popular video game of all time.

On January 20, 1981, Iran released the American-held hostages. They were released minutes after Ronald Reagan had been sworn-in as the 40th President of the United States.

In 1981, the **IBM PC** became the dominant computer for professional users. Commodore created the most popular home computers of both 8-bit and 16-bit.

The Compact Disc (CD) was released in October 1982.

In 1984, Apple Computers introduced the first MacIntosh Computer—replacing its Apple II and Lisa models. The MacIntosh introduced the first commercially successful personal computer to use a graphical user interface and mouse. These features became standards during the middle of the decade.

During the decade, Microsoft released the operating systems **MS-DOS**, Windows 1.0, and Windows 2.0. (1987).

In January 1986, Challenger (STS-51-L) suffered a tragic loss, and seven astronauts were killed. One of the astronauts was a schoolteacher, Christie McAuliffe. The loss of the spacecraft was due to a faulty O-ring on the right solid rocket booster.

"Black Monday" highlighted the stock market crash on October 19, 1987. The Dow Jones industrial Average fell by more than 22% causing interruption in world financial markets.

American Space flights resumed with the launch of Discovery in 1988.

By 1989, Nintendo Entertainment claimed to have 90% of the United States market.

Under the leadership of Deng Xiaoping, China embarked on new reforms in the late 1980s. They opened the nation's economy to the Western World and allowed capitalist corporations to begin operating in domestic China.

1990s

The decade of the 1990s has been referred to as the decade of peace and prosperity.

1990

East and West Germany were reunited after 45 years of separation.

Nelson Mandela was freed from prison in South Africa, and he became the leader of the African National Congress.

One of the most complete T. Rex fossils was found in South Dakota—it was named Sue.

Margaret Thatcher resigned as Prime Minister of the United Kingdom.

Lech Walesa became the first President of Poland.

The Hubble Telescope was launched into space.

1991

Operation Desert Storm began and ended quickly after Iraq invaded Kuwait. Allied forces, led by the United States military, destroyed the Iraq Army within six weeks (January 17 to February 28).

The 24-hour news cycle became popular with the coverage of the Gulf War.

The Internet became available for unrestricted commercial use.

Freddie Mercury, the lead singer of the band Queen, died from AIDS.

On Christmas Day, the Soviet Union collapsed, officially

ending the Cold War.

Boris Yeltsin became the first elected President of Russia.

"Otzi," was the natural mummy of a man who had lived between 3350 and 3150 BC. He was found at the border between Austria and Italy.

1992

The European Union was formed when the Maastricht Treaty was signed.

After the boom of the U.S. stock market in 1992, Alan Greenspan coined the phrase "irrational exuberance."

The beginning of the genocide in Bosnia.

Euro Disney was opened in France.

Hurricane Iniki, hit the island of Kauai in the Hawaiian Islands, making it the costliest hurricane on record in the eastern Pacific.

Czechoslovakia separated into the Czech Republic and Slovakia.

NAFTA (North American Free Trade Agreement) was signed into law.

New York's World Trade Center was bombed.

The compound of the Branch Davidians was raided by the ATF. Six cult members and four ATF agents were killed.

The Hubble Telescope was repaired in space by a crew on the Space Shuttle Endeavor.

1993

Intel introduced the Pentium Microprocessor.

The United States and Russia signed the START II Treaty.

Genocide and Civil War took place in Rwanda with an

estimated 500,000 people killed.

The Battle of Mogadishu: The U.S. Army conducts 'Operation Gothic Serpent' in the city of Mogadishu.

1994

Nelson Mandela was elected President of South Africa.

The Channel Tunnel was opened between England and France.

Major League Baseball canceled its season when the Players Association went on strike.

The 1994 World Cup was held in the United States—Brazil won the title.

1995

The American Space Shuttle Atlantis, docked with the Russian Mir Space Station.

A federal building in Oklahoma City was bombed by domestic terrorists, killing 168 people.

Prime Minister of Israel, Yitzhak Rabin, was assassinated by an Israeli extremist.

The World Trade Organization (WTO) was created.

The online auction website, eBay, was founded.

The Java Programming Language was released.

A sarin gas attack took place in a Tokyo subway.

1996

The Internet search engine "Ask Jeeves" was created.

"Mad Cow" disease broke out in Britain.

Prince Charles and Princess Diana were divorced.

The "Unabomber" was arrested.

The Summer Olympics were held in Atlanta, Georgia. The Centennial Olympic Park was bombed. Richard Jewell discovered the bomb and was falsely accused of the bombing. Eric Rudolph was eventually found guilty of setting off the bomb.

Bill Clinton was reelected President.

1997

Scotland created its own Parliament.

The first Harry Potter book was published by J. K. Rowling.

Scientists at the Roslin Institute introduced "Dolly," the first successfully cloned sheep.

The United Kingdom returned Hong Kong to China after 156 years.

The Hale-Bopp comet made its closest approach to Earth.

Britain's Princess Diana died in a car crash in Paris.

1998

The search engine "Google" was founded.

Apple Computer launched the iMac computer.

Ireland and England signed the Belfast Agreement.

Hurricane Mitch devastated Central America.

India and Pakistan tested their nuclear weapons.

President Bill Clinton was impeached.

Viagra became popular in the United States.

1999

Napster, the file-sharing service, was founded.

The Dow Jones closed above 11,000 for the first time.

President Clinton faced an impeachment trial.

The Euro was introduced as the European currency.

Control of the Panama Canal was returned to Panama.

The World feared the Y2K bug, as the millennium turned.

ABOUT THE AUTHOR

James Peifer is a retired business owner from Silicon Valley. He was an Army Captain and a combat veteran of the Vietnam War. He lives in Napa, California.